"From the very fir:
more information a
Scott Fitkin transports you into 1949 with his spot-on
vocabulary of the time. Add to that, descriptions so clear
and precise, you'll swear you can see the events happening
right before your eyes. Bravo Mr. Fitkin for giving us this
slice-of-life depiction of Hell's Kitchen and a bygone era."

—RICHARD FUTCH
Casting Director for *Army Wives*

"The time, 1948. The Place, New York City. Philip
Marlowe revisited by Private Eye Jamie Foley Dugan in
the sparse, concise style of the time."

—B. DITTER, Author

"…a sleazy private investigator/former cop whose wise
guy persona obscures the brutally honest character who
you'll want to spend more time with from Page 1. Fitkin's
straightforward style exposes opinions and judgments
not everyone dares to share anymore, and his ever-sharp
descriptions of 1949 New York society and working
class are delivered candidly by PI Dugan like secrets
between friends. As the revelations and suspicions roll out
conversationally and under his breath, so will the details
flow about the PI's own scars, cars, and views of the
streets, the interiors of the brownstones, whether mansions
or cheap flats; and Scott Fitkin makes us skid right onto
the scenes behind Dugan."

—SUSAN HARTMAN
Executive Administrator, College of Charleston, SC

THE
WRONG GUY

— A Jamie Dugan Mystery —

SCOTT N. FITKIN

LUMINARE PRESS
WWW.LUMINAREPRESS.COM

The Wrong Guy
A Jamie Dugan Mystery
© 2017 Scott N. Fitkin

Printed in the United States of America

Cover Design: Claire Last

Luminare Press
438 Charnelton St., Suite 101
Eugene, OR 97401
www.luminarepress.com

LCCN: 2017937100

ISBN: : 978-1-944733-20-9

With deep appreciation and gratitude,
I am dedicating this book to my chief
editor and critic: Kay.
Thank you for all you have given in the
birth of this story.

To my friends that have had to put up
with request after request to read sam-
ples of the manuscript and provide their
insights, thank you.
I know of no other words to let you
know how appreciative I am.

THE SET-UP

C lay Morgan and I were having a beer at Maxie's Tavern, a gin-joint on 43rd Street. Times are tough and jobs are not backlogged in my in-basket, so I make my office at Maxie's, at least until things improve.

Maxie is a real peach of a guy I bailed out of a jam a few years back. I've known him for quite a while now and he puts up with me, not necessarily because I'm broke. E. Maxie Norris is a Scotsman whose last name means "wet nurse." He lets me use a back booth for my business. It is quiet and kind of private, and the inviting smell of stale beer and frying meat is an added bonus. I also give out Maxie's business phone number for those who need to call me. After all, it's my office, at least until Maxie boots me out.

Most of my business is detecting, finding wayward husbands and missing wives, usually in the arms of some lover. You know, very private affairs. Yeah, I'm a private detective. It sounds glamorous, but it's not. It's more about climbing fire escapes to get a better pic or dumpster diving after midnight to grab a possible clue.

It's unfortunate that those of us in this line of work have poor reputations, about one step removed from used car salesmen or a jackleg lawyer, probably because of what we are hired to do. It's not really our fault you let your spouse run around with whomever they please. You should consider taking better care of your relationships; it would be a lot cheaper for you and save wear and tear on my suits.

However, some of my business is miss-detecting—horses, mainly. Yeah, I play the ponies, although not very successfully. My therapist says that it's not really an addiction; it's my

1

cover for other problems I have, and there are lots of those. And that is one reason I don't pay him any more visits. That and he's not cheap. Deep in my heart, I've known there is no addiction here, anyway; it's more like eating hot dogs when you go to the ballgame. Just natural. I eat a lot of hotdogs. Screw the other problems.

Clay was an out-of-work reporter looking for a job at another rag. He had come to New York from some city in South Carolina a few years back and landed a job at a morning newspaper. He had a column on what it was like to be a New Yorker from a Southerner's point of view. Yeah, I know. It was a real barnburner, but it attracted the locals. They loved it. He had been laid off for about a month now, so I figured he wanted to tap me for a few bucks. Unfortunately, there was none to be had. I used to have the cash, but now my bookie had it. Oh, yeah, and an IOU for an additional grand. Let's see, that was about $4,000 down the toilet on a nag that couldn't find the rail coming out of the first turn. And the worst part? I had just been paid up front for a job and never was able to deliver the goods. It made an easy case gone bad, really bad.

Clay was a handsome lug in his early 30s with longish blond hair that always looked like he needed a haircut. We're about the same age, but my black hair and broken nose make people believe we should be archenemies. Not that I'm ugly, mind you. I just look the role of a tough guy and pretty women shy away from guys like me. That is, unless they need my help.

Clay believed himself to be a dapper man; he was prone to the latest fineries and liked to dandy about with the ladies. The only drawback to his wardrobe was his shoes. He never seemed to get around to cleaning them up, you know, putting a little polish on them. He had a Southern drawl that could stretch out a word for two minutes and a charm that attracted more problems than he could solve. He also smelled like a gigolo, all perfumed up with the latest aftershave. Yeah, a real dandy, but a real friend.

We had been friends for several years now. We met about six months after he arrived in New York City. It was like throwing a mouse in with a boa constrictor; only this boa just watched him go from one troubled encounter to another. He reminded me of a wind-up toy. Twist the key, and Clay would run around in circles looking for trouble, or trouble would search him out. The day we met, the mouse was on the other foot. He was enjoying watching me dangling from trouble's door, but soon after, he was up to his dandy lapels in some misadventure.

It was a weekday, a day when normal people should be at work, not sitting in a tavern having drinks. Clay had asked me why my arm was in a sling and where the cuts and bruises on my face and hands had come from. I told him it was a long story, hoping he would let sleeping dogs lie, but he pressed me for more information, just as a good reporter probably would, until I finally relented.

Clay called to Maxie and ordered another round for us. "C'mon, James, give. What happened?" he asked, quieter. He had this thing about calling me James when it wasn't my name. It was Jamie, and Jamie wasn't short for James, at least not for me. My Ma wanted no nicknames for her son, so I was baptized Jamie Foley Dugan. Later, she told me that the family had a history of pirates on her side, the Foley side, but my father came from a long line of honest, upright, Irish cops, if there ever was such a thing.

"It was a typical April night, no moon, plenty of wind,

and a twist of rain thrown in to make you real uncomfortable. You remember last Wednesday, don't ya?"

Clay nodded and I continued. "It'd been a long four days. I had tracked down the floozy that was sleeping with my latest client's husband and taken some wonderful pics of the two of them in the act sometime around noon."

Clay nodded enthusiastically while I drank the foam off my latest beer, some of which stuck to my upper lip. The sweet smell tickled my nose.

"Well, I stayed around across the street from the apartment for a while then walked a couple of blocks to a deli to get a Reuben. When I got back around three PM, the husband's car was nowhere to be seen. So I waited 'til about five-thirty to see if he would re-appear. When he didn't, I headed back toward QuickPic over on 49th and 8th to develop my steamers so I could give my client the pictures and my report. I needed the cash. When I left my stakeout, the rain went from a mist to a drizzle, and it just got worse.

"The couple that own the QuickPic did a few quick jobs for me, and I needed two shiny mattes to deliver. In just under two hours, I was on my way to the client's brownstone with my mattes and the address of the mystery woman my client's husband was with, but no name."

Clay looked across the table at me with increasing interest. I was beginning to believe he wanted to take my story and sell it, probably as fiction for the afternoon press.

"The weather was weird, though; the clouds were moving fast and low across the street, almost just above the awnings, making the street lights seem wispy, almost ghost-like. It didn't help that all the buildings looked gray because of the weather and all. It wasn't a calm night, either. Gusts of wind were picking up between the buildings and rattling the windows of my Jag. The wind whistled through the cracks between my car windows and the molding. That and the rain. The wipers on my Jag were still thin. I hadn't replaced them yet, due to the lack of funds, so I was poking along about twenty-five, listening to the scraping wiper blades, watching them dig a trench into my windshield. With all the sound effects and low clouds, the city felt haunted, as if it was Halloween in April

"I had made up my mind not to go down West Side Highway to try my luck cutting across town and going down Second, trying to find this broad's—sorry, my client's—brownstone in Chelsea. I was banking on the fact that the FDR and Hudson River would be mired in fog traffic and the city streets would be easier to navigate. I was right until I started to get near the upper 30s. The weather was so bad that the traffic coming off the Queens Midtown was snarling the intersections for a four-block radius. I stopped for every light and even a small fire in the upper 20s. The rain must have knocked the fire down, but that didn't stop fire fighters from littering the streets with their trucks. It must have taken me twenty minutes to find my way around all those damn trucks and meat wagons.

"I should have known it was going to be a tough drive. This whole week had been an up-hill fight. After the better part of an hour, I arrived at the address, but New York's finest were all over the place, blue lights flashing and O'Malley in the street, directing traffic."

"You mean you were working for old lady Rumsfeld?" Clay asked.

"Yeah, you got it." I didn't notice it then, but he had this look of dread on his face.

"Her demise has been splashed across all the rags! And

you had to run into Sergeant O'Malley." Clay began grinning from ear to ear, just hearing the sergeant's name. "He really has it in for you, you know that?"

I nodded and waited for more humor from the other side of the booth. "That's an official news bulletin?" I asked.

"Well, that doesn't explain the arm and scratches. What happened? Were you trying to get your fee from an irate husband who didn't appreciate your photography?" He smiled and chuckled.

"Do you want to hear this or sit there and make fun of me?"

Clay held up both palms and beckoned me to continue.

"If only it had been as easy as telling her she was right, that her husband was sleeping with another woman," I said, taking my arm out of the sling and stretching it, feeling the aches and pains from the previous few days. "But Mrs. R. wasn't in any shape to see me when I arrived."

WEDNESDAY

I circled the brownstone, trying to figure out what happened and see if my client was involved. On the second pass, I pulled up next to Sergeant Seamus O'Malley, rolled down my window, and asked him what gives.

"Move along, PI. This doesn't concern you."

"It does if it involves my client," I responded.

"Okay, I'll bite. Who's your client?"

"The Rumsfeld woman."

O'Malley's face lit up, and he said, "Park your car over there." He pointed to a spot reserved for loading and unloading, not too far from the city morgue's meat wagon.

"Isn't that better used by city officials, Sarge?" I responded. "I know you guys need all the room you can get, and I don't want to get a ticket."

"Park," O'Malley said. At forty-five, he had the bulbous mug of a cartoon flatfoot and stood about five-foot-seven or -eight inches tall. He was enough over weight that his blue NYPD uniform was a size small in the stomach and his gold buttons strained beyond the edge of his blue NYPD duty uniform. His biceps were as thick as a weight lifter's, but I figured it was more blubber than muscle. He was clean-shaven, but he let his sideburns grow into muttonchops that extended to his jaw line. With reddish hair and bushy eyebrows, he looked comedic when riled, a state I inspired every chance I got.

After maneuvering the Jag into the space, I got out and made sure it was locked. You never knew when a wealthy neighbor in this part of town might take a shine to my wheels and go for a joy ride. I pushed my fedora back on my head and sauntered toward O'Malley, scanning the area for hints as to what was happening. A pair of white coats from the coroner's office wheeled a gurney toward the morgue van near my car. The wind ruffled the white sheet draped over the body as the gurney bumped along the sidewalk and road.

O'Malley approached me with a big, lecherous smile. "So, another typical evening, Dugan? Out taking pictures, huh?"

"How'd ya guess?"

"Cause that's about the extent of your line of work these days, Mr. Private Dick."

"Oh, yeah? What's it to you?"

"We might want to see those photos."

"Don't think so," I said. "Client, PI privilege."

Feeling the wind tug at my hat, I lowered the fedora on my head. I had stashed the pics in the trunk. I kept an envelope in the spare tire boot for precious cargo like photos and such. In my line of work, you never know who might want what when.

"Why don't you be a good PI and give me the keys to your car so we can find those pictures, huh? That way we won't have to scar up your paint job or something worse." Sarcasm dripped from his tongue.

"Screw you," I said, staring defiantly at the sergeant.

"Suit yourself." O'Malley turned and yelled at another flat foot. "Hey, Joey. Probable cause. Tear that white Jag apart until you find me some photos."

The sergeant and I have never gotten along, even when we were on the force together, but it was a mystery why he went to extremes to make my life miserable. This wasn't the first case on which we had clashed, and the way things were going, it wouldn't be the last.

My face paled as Joey and another of New York's finest headed toward my car. Joey had a crowbar and an evil grin on his face. That didn't bother me as much as the bruiser who went with him. He had hands the size of Staten Island, narrow, beady little eyes, and he walked as if he could take Atlas in a wrestling match. I didn't know if Joey was going to pop all the hinges off my car with the bar or if Mr. Muscle was going to pick it up and shake it until all the screws came loose.

"Wait a minute here. That's my car," I stammered to O'Malley, who was holding my arm to keep me from dashing to save my precious Jag.

"You got that figured out already, huh? Smart guy." The sergeant was all brawn and no manners. He could've used some lessons from a good girl's finishing school.

"I know this lawyer that—" I said, pulling against Sarge's restraining arm.

Joey jimmied the door open with the crowbar and inspected the interior.

"Hey, you, get out of my car!" I yanked out of O'Malley's grip and ran to the Jag.

King Kong grabbed me and flung me to the ground. "Hold on, little fella. This ain't gonna take long."

"Isn't. Isn't going to take long. And oh, yes, it will." I wheeled around with my elbow and caught him in the groin as I stood up; the monster crumbled to the concrete in a heap with a lot of "oohs" and "aahs," grabbing at his private parts, if you catch my drift.

As I reached for Joey, O'Malley grabbed me from behind and twisted my arm until I heard something pop in my shoulder. O'Malley threw me down again. This time, he cuffed me. I was lying in a puddle of rainwater, mud, and automotive oil. I didn't want to watch the rape of my Jag, so I lay there, staring at my fedora. It was top down, marinating in the puddle with me. Man, I loved that hat.

9

"Continue," said the sergeant.

O'Malley helped me sit up and we watched Joey go through the cockpit of my car and release the trunk latch from the passenger side glove compartment. They seemed to know where to go, as if they had done this before. *Damn. I need a better hiding place.*

"Aha. What do we have here?" O'Malley smiled one of those little, self-satisfied grins. "Let's take these to the lieutenant." He waved the envelope of photos in my face.

"Twelve-year-old," I muttered in O'Malley's direction. "Please tell me Dingle isn't on this case."

O'Malley smiled. "Uppie, uppie," he said as the gorilla hoisted me off the ground. O'Malley mushed my wet hat on my head and the water ran down the side of my face and back of my neck, as I looked back toward the brownstone steps.

"No hard feelings," I said to the large cop, "but is there really a need for you to carry me?" I smiled up at the ape cradling me in his bulbous arms.

It took a few seconds for my comment to register. When it finally did, I found myself back on the ground, lying on my side. "At least you could uncuff me now that King Kong is vertical," I said.

O'Malley leaned over and took off the cuff. "You be a good little boy, and we will get along just fine. Now march." O'Malley lifted me to my feet and shoved me in the direction of the Rumsfelds' front door.

It was a handsome, three-story brownstone with five steps up to the oak-stained front door. From where I stood, it looked more like a boutique hotel than a house, and the

Rumsfelds owned the whole building. I had never been in the place, which I guess wasn't much of a surprise since I didn't run in their circle. I was looking forward to seeing how the better half lived, although I hadn't dressed for the visit. The door was wide open and a blue jacket stood by it to keep it propped that way, I guess to allow the chilly wind to blow in and dampen some of the heat the Rumsfelds were paying for. He nodded at O'Malley, gave me a once over, and shook his head as we walked in.

I turned to the doorstop and said quietly, "Close the door. You're creating a draft." I pulled the lapels of my coat up to keep the wet goo on my neck from getting any colder.

The entry hall was wood paneled with high ceilings. Fancy sconces provided light. A black table sat tucked against the wall to the left of the entry with a dark red vase-like lamp resting on top. The lamp was off. A set of keys was laid out on the table and a center drawer was partially open. I took a glance to see what was in the drawer for a clue as to why it was open. There were all sorts of loose keys in the drawer, like a discard pile.

Just beyond the table was a staircase with a shiny, carved wood railing that had to have cost a pretty penny. There were several doors off the wide hall on the right. All in all, it gave me a sterile feeling. There were no family pictures on the walls or tables, and except for an abstract of the New York skyline, there were no paintings, either. It looked like one of those show houses, all stripped down and ready to be sold.

The first door led into a drawing room where Lieutenant Matt Dingle stood with his arms crossed, giving a solid profile of a cop in deep thought. Dingle was a slight man of average height and clean-shaven. He wore a dark suit and a white shirt, as was his custom. A wide, dull tie, slightly loosened, dangled from his neck. The throat button of his shirt was undone. Dingle and I go back to when we were detectives and partners on the force. Eh, sort of partners. Matt has always been a straight shooter—never taken a bribe, always turned in the evidence. What I'd call a good cop. His modus operandi was methodical, ploddingly slow, most times. It usually turned out better in the long run, but I was more of a sprinter. There are just some things you can't wait for, and I usually ended up taking things into my own hands. Until recently, we remained pretty good pals, but our work styles got in the way of our friendship, like two cooks on the same pot of stew—one waiting for all the ingredients to gel while the other is adding seasoning, tasting, then adding more, all the while stirring. Yeah, oil and water. After all, it's 1949, and a guy's got to make a living, even when he's no longer on the force.

The lieutenant was listening to another plain-clothed detective as the city coroner finished up. I watched the detective and Dingle carry on. Every once in a while, Dingle nodded. I only wished I were standing a little closer. At the end of what seemed to be a complete run-down of the situation, the detective turned to Dingle, answered a quesion or two and then left, passing right by me on the way out to the front door.

"Lieutenant, look who I found driving around the block. He had these with him." Sergeant O'Malley gave the envelope to Dingle. "He was nice enough to pass them on to us."

"Right," I said.

"Hey, if it's not Jamie Dugan," Dingle said. "What did you get mixed up in this time?" There was a tired tone in his voice. "You goin' for a new look? Early hand-me-down?" He looked me over more closely and added, "You out tending the garden tonight or working on your car? Both at the same time?" He smiled, clearly enjoying himself.

"Just a little play time before I popped in on your police social here. What's going on, Lieutenant?" I asked.

About five feet from where Dingle stood a pool of blood soaked into the wooden floors of the drawing room. The rug had been pulled aside, and I could see where the blood had soaked through the pile. There was a drawer-less desk in the far corner; it looked like a fancy European one, an antique. A lamp was knocked over on one side of the desk, its glass base broken into a few larger pieces. There were a number of smaller glass shards on the floor, just waiting to be stepped on. Two comfortable looking chairs were in front of the desk, looking like someone had moved them; sure enough, there were scrape marks etched into the wood flooring. On the far wall was a large bookcase. It took up the whole wall and was filled with books and knick-knacks. Along the wall next to the door was a bar that looked like genuine mahogany. Nice touch for a residence, I thought. Two glasses sat on the bar beside a decanter reclining on its side. The smell of liquor commanded the room; the bar top was soaked in the stuff. It was scotch, expensive scotch, the kind I can't afford anymore.

"The missus got herself stabbed," Matt said. "The back door's locked and bolted, as was the front. O'Malley and his crew haven't come up with the weapon yet. We'll have to wait for the coroner's report, but it looks like a knife."

I looked around the room. Blood spatter everywhere. The bar. The books. The walls. It looked like someone's throat must have been slit during the struggle.

"You got time of death?"

"Not just yet, but our guess is around six PM, give or take an hour or so. I guess you saw the coroner Doctor Potts?"

Dingle said it more as a statement than a question as he nodded in the direction of the medical examiner. "He gave us a window for time of death, between three and seven PM."

"Big window," I said, checking my watch; it was almost eight-twenty. "Just happened, then?"

Dingle nodded as he looked over my photos.

"Mind if I look around while you enjoy my pretty pictures?" I asked. "I think time has run out on my client privileges anyway."

"I got a question for you first." Dingle gave me a serious look. "Where were these two love birds holed up?" He waved an incriminating photo of them in my face.

"Nice photos, huh?" I said. "They were really going at it until the dame dragged him away from the window. Too bad."

"Quite the angle, there, Dugan. Did you have to climb a tree to take these?"

"Naw, fire escape. The building across the street had a real nice one—easy access and a platform I could relax on." I took another look at the photos and added, "Some telephoto lens, huh?"

"Enough," Dingle said. "The address. Give."

"Oh, well, if you must know. Upper East Side, 78th Street, apartment 2A. There's an address in the envelope, in case anybody gets lost and needs to ask for directions." I smiled my best smile.

I looked around the room one more time as Dingle checked for the address before sending his troops out. "I suppose you've canvassed the neighborhood as well? You guys must have been here for some time now."

"We did an initial canvas covering the neighbors and anyone across the street."

"Nothing, I take it."

Dingle seemed a bit preoccupied with something; normally he didn't share information with me, especially at the onset of a new case.

"Huh?" He came back to Earth. "Naw, not yet, but we've just started."

"How about that look-see?" I asked.

"I don't mind. Help yourself. We're just about through our prelim here, but be careful and don't touch anything."

"Is the mister at home? I'd hate to run into him after bringing home the incriminating evidence," I said.

"Nope, he hasn't shown yet, but we expect him within the hour. He's been detained by his work. I had to send him an escort," Dingle responded with a note of exasperation. "You would think with his wife's murder, he would drop everything and come a-running."

"Well then, how'd you find out about the murder?" I asked.

Dingle pulled up from looking at the mattes and scratched his head as he looked into my eyes. "Huh? Oh, a friend of the deceased had come over for a drink before they were suppose to head for dinner, or so she said."

"She found Mrs. Rumsfeld dead with the doors locked and the windows about a half a story above the street?" It was like old times as I continued to dig. My body gave a shiver as I stood there without a hat on my head, water seeping through my clothes. I brought my arms around my chest folding my hands into my armpits in an attempt to keep what little heat I had retained within my clothing.

"Suspicious little mind you have," Dingle said to me. "Thinking that all was well and that Mrs. Rumsfeld was home because of the lights still on, this friend became alarmed when she didn't answer the front door after ringing the door bell and knocking for several minutes." Matt's gaze wandered back around the room making me wonder if I had his full attention. He had stopped his story and let other thoughts in.

"Well this "friend", using quotes around the word friend trying to make it obvious he had not come forward with a name, "couldn't peek in through the solid door or windows unless she brought a ladder…"

Matt interrupted me, "I know, I know. She called us as a concerned citizen and we came over and discovered the body. Why the concern, Dugan? Your job is over here."

"Not really. Who was she?" I asked trying to keep Dingle focused on giving up more information.

"Who?" He looked back over at me.

"The concerned citizen." I answered.

Mrs. Mum…why should I tell you. Go wander around but I repeat don't touch anything. Got it?" Matt Dingle looked at me sternly. I had his full attention.

I took one last look around the drawing room then moved down the hall with O'Malley following me like a dog trailing the local butcher. We entered the dining room and I noticed two windows on the far side of the room draped with heavy maroon curtains. I pointed to the window with its curtains drawn shut. "Looks like we found your point of exit. You might want to look outside under the window for foot prints and, if you're really lucky, the knife."

O'Malley blanched as he stared at the slight movement the fabric was making against the storm's gusting wind. "Joey!" he yelled. "Get your carcass in here."

I heard footsteps coming down the hall. "You know, the color of your paling skin looks kinda sexy against your blues," I told O'Malley, playfully batting my eyelashes.

"Shut up," O'Malley said. He walked toward the curtain

and pulled it open. O'Malley turned to Joey and said. "Get a guy outside this window and you check it from the inside." O'Malley jabbed a finger toward the open curtain exposing the slight opening in the window. "See if you can find the weapon or any other clues, like foot prints, and let's finger-print the window." O'Malley's voice got sarcastic. He twitched a few times as his muscles bunched in anger. "Now get!"

"Now you're thinkin," I said to the sergeant. "Maybe even some blood residue, what with all the blood sprayed around the den, ya think, Sarge?"

Joey turned and mumbled something to the big gorilla I encountered in the street and proceeded toward the window. I walked out of the room and into the kitchen. After a cursory scan, I checked the knife stand on the counter to see if any knives were missing. Nothing. Then I opened a few kitchen doors until I found more knives. There was a carving set with a missing blade, and it, the blade, was big. There was also a set of smaller knives, but both were still there. A paring knife with a three and a half-inch blade, and another dull-looking knife, about the same size, for what I figured had to be some kind of cheese or other delicacy that would be forever out of my price range. I figured the knife used was probably the miss-ing carving knife. It had to be a big blade, and I doubted the smaller instruments would be choice weapons. That should make it easier for the police to find. After all, it looked like a ten-inch blade or more.

"Clever, really clever," I said aloud.

O'Malley was standing just outside the kitchen. "What'd you say, Dugan?"

I ignored the sergeant and headed to the second floor. I heard O'Malley's hooves clomping up the stairs, behind me; he was either a heavy breather or extremely out of shape. I selected the latter. "You should go on a diet," I said just loud enough he could hear me.

On the second floor, there were two bedrooms, with no door for a bath or toilet from the hall. What else would you have on the second floor but bedrooms and baths? I assumed each bedroom had its own bath; sort of like being in a hotel suite. There was a staircase leading to the third floor.

"What's up there?" I asked.

Catching his breath, O'Malley replied, "Guest rooms that ain't been slept in for a long time. We checked them pretty good, and they're clean."

"Right. Like the dining room."

The first bedroom I came to was at the back of the house. "This must be his room," I murmured. The bedroom was pretty big, about the size of my whole apartment. There was a four-poster double bed against the wall to my right with a pair of windows straight across from me. Heavy green curtains obscured the view to the outside. A desk with a leather writing top and lone inkwell sat between the windows. A windowless bathroom, containing the usual toilet, sink, and tub, were to the left, the very back of the house. If there had been windows in the bathroom, they would have overlooked a back alley. Just up the wall from the bed stood a large dresser with hairbrush, bottle of cologne, and a tray that held cuff links and tie tacks. Rounding out the room was a wardrobe. Inside the wardrobe was men's clothing, neatly arranged by jackets and pants. A few pairs of polished shoes were at the base of the wardrobe. The bed had not been slept in; there wasn't even an indentation of a butt from someone sitting on it.

I walked over and sprayed the cologne that was on the dresser, King's Men. Of course, it was all wrapped up in gold, as if it was still for sale. I went through the desk but found nothing of interest except a piece of paper with some numbers and a title, *Estimated Rent Collections,* which I casually slipped into my coat pocket as O'Malley wandered back toward the hall.

I moved to the other bedroom and found pretty much the same arrangement, just in reverse. Instead of a small writing desk, there was a dressing table with lots of women's toiletries and a pen and ink blotter scattered about the top. That was a strange thing to see on a woman's dressing table. I went through the drawers to see if I could connect the pen to something else, anything else. Nothing.

This room also had a large closet, something the other bedroom lacked. In the bathroom, there were some men's toiletries in the medicine cabinet, but not *King's Men,* rather *Alfred Dunhill.* I recognized the brand from heavy advertising over its release six to eight months ago. I sprayed it in the air and took a small whiff.

"Hey," O'Malley shouted. "You can't do that."

"You mean this?" And I sprayed the mister one more time, drinking in the scent. It was strangely familiar.

I moved to the closet, opened the doors wide, and peered in. One side of the closet held neatly arranged women's frocks, lots of them, sorted by style. On the other side were empty hangers. It looked like someone, in a rush to leave, grabbed an armful of clothes. A few hangers were strewn about the closet floor, too. Maybe they fell in the excitement. I caught a glimpse of something in the back corner and reached in to find a pair of well-used and poorly maintained oxfords.

"Hey, what d'you have there?" O'Malley asked.

"Size nines," I replied. "Missed these, too?"

"Let me have those," demanded O'Malley, wrenching them from my hands. The sergeant's attitude was beginning to grate on my nerves. This wasn't the first time tonight he'd rubbed me the wrong way.

There was something oddly familiar about all this—first the *Dunhill* and now the well-worn shoes. My interest was piqued.

"Let's go see how the dear lieutenant is doing, shall we?" I said.

O'Malley led the way back down stairs to find Dingle. I didn't follow, at least not right away. At the end of the hallway on the second floor was another staircase. I had almost missed it due to a well-camouflaged door. My feet carried me down the second set of stairs into a mudroom at the back of the house. One door from the mudroom led into the kitchen and the other door to the outside and the back alley. I checked the doorknob to the outside and the door was locked. Surprise, surprise.

I went through the kitchen and down the hall to the den, where I joined O'Malley and Dingle. Matt was standing in the hall talking with one of the blue jackets, but I couldn't hear a word they were saying. Dingle dismissed the cop before I got close enough to eavesdrop.

"We found these," O'Malley said, holding up the shoes, "in the lady's closet!"

Dingle's eyebrows arched. "Looks like you were watching the wrong person," he said.

I took off my fedora and rubbed my scalp. "Yeah, I think it was a two-way street. What is good for the goose…"

"What else did you find?" Dingle asked me.

"These people really know how to live right. Separate bedrooms, bathrooms, closets. Not much intimacy here, was there? Did you find any footprints, size nines, outside this brownstone?" I asked.

"Yeah, how'd you know that?" Dingle replied.

I nodded at the shoes in O'Malley's hands.

Dingle shook his head and continued. "We found the knife, too, thrown into the bushes. Looks like our guy climbed out the window, tossed the knife, and made off down the side of the building to the back alley."

"Kitchen knife?" I asked.

"Yup, just like the one missing from the drawer," Dingle said. "O'Malley saw you poking around in the kitchen drawers." The sergeant smiled as if he had made some great discovery.

"Maybe I should follow him around then?" I asked.

"Hey…" O'Malley said as Dingle put up his hand restraining the sergeant.

"Did he jump out the window?" It was a half-spoken question. "That's not a bad drop. Five steps up to the front door, add a couple more feet for the window. I wonder if…" I trailed off.

"Huh? What was that, Dugan?" Dingle looked at me curiously.

"Oh, sorry. You sure it was the kitchen knife, maybe the carving knife?"

Dingle nodded. "Yup. Just like the one that's missing. I'll get the coroner to verify it was the murder weapon, don't worry." He shook his head and continued. "He landed partly in the flower bed, where Joey found the footprints. Looks like he attempted to climb down the trellis, but it snapped under his weight."

"Now all you need to do is find a guy with a slight limp who wears size nine shoes and Alfred Dunhill cologne and might have to go on a diet," I said. "Of course it could just be a weak trellis…"

"Huh? Where did the limp and Dunhill come in?" Dingle gave me a puzzled look.

"The limp is from when the trellis broke, and the Dunhill is from the toiletries upstairs. Maybe you better send O'Malley back up there to go over the place."

"I don't know how I coulda missed that, Lieutenant," O'Malley said quietly. He stepped away from me, as if I was some kind of plague-carrying parasite.

"Another recommendation, Lieutenant. Spread your canvassing to the building at the back of the house. If the killer left that way, he or she may have caught someone's eye. Besides, with all that blood, the garments probably got discarded somewhere, maybe in a trash can back there."

Dingle nodded, then turned to O'Malley and told him to begin the search, house-to-house and garbage can-to-garbage can. You gotta love the way these guys are dedicated. I know I do.

"Well, listen, I wish I could stay and chat, but I'm kinda tired and need to head home. I'd like to try to get some stains out of my clothes, or do I just send you the dry cleaning bill, Sergeant?" I turned to O'Malley as I finished my question, but he was gone. "The man must like his garbage cans," I said to no one in particular.

"Go on, get out of here," Dingle said. "If you learn anything, don't be a hero. Gimme a call."

"Just like the old days, huh? Let me know if you need any more help." And I headed for the door. I stopped a few feet away from where Matt Dingle stood and turned back to him. "You never did tell me who reported the suspicions... sorry, the concern," I corrected myself.

Dingle just smiled at me, "You can read about it in tomorrow's paper just like the rest of the world."

I left the room and stopped once more at the table in the front entrance and checked the keys lying on the table. A door key to the front door and some other kind of key, a skeleton key. Huh? Old lock? Then I noticed that one of the two drawers was open; the one I checked when I first entered. The other was closed, so I pulled on the drawer knob. It didn't budge. I tried the skeleton key in a keyhole below the knob and presto, the drawer slid open. Inside was nothing, nada, zip. I scratched my head feeling the oily moist residue from the earlier encounter with O'Malley and crew. Once again I felt a cold shiver race through my body telling me to head home. About that time, one of the cops standing guard at the home's entrance peered around the corner at me.

"You got a problem there, PI?" he asked.

"Naw, just leaving," I replied and walked into the night.

THE STORM HAD BLOWN ITSELF OUT BY THE TIME I REACHED the Jag, which now carried scrapes and dings from Joey's crowbar. It broke my heart. It was the one thing in life that made me feel good, really good, especially since it once belonged to Rocky DeNato. Notice the past tense.

It was the kind of car that made women stop whatever they were doing and stare. Men pretended to ignore it, but still snuck glimpses when they thought no one was looking. I once read somewhere that "Americans don't buy automobiles. They buy dreams of sex, speed, power, and wealth." And my Jag is exactly that. We were entering another age of automobile mass production, now that we could take a break from churning out weapons to fight the Huns and Nips. Mass production led to cheaper looking and less reliable cars. Crap, in other words. None of the modern autos looked as sharp as my Jag.

It was pearl white from bumper to bumper, and without leather straps to hold its bonnet in place; just a smooth piece of metal. Its white wall tires matched the body. The interior was red leather, and boy, did it smell like a new car. The steering wheel was wrapped in leather and located on the right side, which made for awkward driving in rush-hour traffic, or any kind of traffic, for that matter. The doors opened back to front, which meant you had to be extra careful getting out if you parked on the wrong side of the street. And the engine, wow, it purred like a big cat ready to leap down your throat, sort of like a…Jaguar.

The very first time I got into my "new" car, there was a cross hanging from the rear view mirror by a chain of rosary beads. I guess DeNato was concerned for his soul in the afterlife. I pulled the plug on that and jammed the cross and beads in the glove compartment. There was a camel hair overcoat in the back seat. I guessed he didn't want it, so I kept it. I never wore the thing. It just looked nice, and I figured it was part of my winnings. I had such fond memories of Rocky. Someday I'll bury the bum.

I drove my Jag over to my apartment; it's in Hell's Kitchen. The most common version of how this part of the city got its name traces back to a story of Dutch Fred "The Cop," a veteran policeman, who with his rookie partner was watchin' a riot on West 39th Street, not too far from Tenth Avenue. Apparently, the rookie remarked, "This place is hell itself," to which Dutch replied, "Hell's a mild climate. This is hell's kitchen." That was back in the late 1800s. It's not much different today, in 1949.

In the 1920s, Hell's Kitchen was the location for smaller "start-up" gangs. The many warehouses in the district were ideal breweries for the rumrunners who controlled the illicit liquor. The earlier gangs gradually transformed into organized crime entities around the same time Owney Madden became one of the most powerful mobsters in New York. It helped me keep focused.

Being that I like sports so much, I tried to find a flat close to Madison Square Garden off 8th Avenue. Well, I found one, all right, not quite as close as I wanted or nice, but it became home for me. It was a three-story brown tenement that had been converted from a house of ill repute into an apartment building. There was always a business doomed to fail operating out of the ground floor. Now it was a dry cleaner. Last month it was a liquor store, and two months before that it was a knife and gun shop. The protection rackets never seemed to work for these shops.

I lived on the second floor, as did three other tenants. The stairwell was the only way up to or down from the second or third floor, unless you used the fire escape. Unfortunately, I didn't have access to the fire escape. Instead, my window opened to a view of the building next door, about four feet away. In this part of town, it would be nice to have an armed guard at the front door, but the way the super figures it, the tenants were lucky to have keys to lock a common front door, a door that would have no trouble holding back a seven-year-old intruder.

I arrived in my apartment around midnight. I cleaned out my pockets and saw the piece of paper with all the numbers and "Rent Collections" scribbled at the top. I stuck it on my night table after a closer look. It made little sense to me in my current state, so I let it sit there. It looked like rental incomes, just as the title said. I couldn't tell if the numbers were meant to be that insignificant or needed some additional zeros.

Estimated Rent Collections
BB TP AB CT T
1. (215) 100 125 50 35
2. (125)
3. (100)
4. (75) find the breakeven point
5. (15) and trends
6. 25
7. 50
8. 75
9. 127
10. 225
11. 280
12. 300T 652

I stripped off my soiled suit and shirt, throwing them in a pile near the door. They might have to go to the cleaners now. The underwear, well, I might be able to get an additional day out of them, but not the socks. I took a whiff. No, definitely not the socks.

It's not like living in New York is all that glamorous. Don't get me wrong, I love living here, but things can be expensive. Take my apartment, for example; it's kind of small, with minimal amenities. I guess I should feel lucky there are walls, although they absorb about as much sound as a wet towel. The good news is I can tell if there is a fight next door. The bad news is my neighbors moved out a month or so ago to avoid the roach infestation. The super has his solution, though. He sets off bug bombs in the hallways, forcing the roaches to scatter to the individual apartments.

My flat is one room with a sofa that pulls out into a double bed. I have a bathroom with a sink the size of a glass of water, and a shower. Well, I think it was meant to be a shower. There's evidence there used to be a kitchenette, but now there are just burn marks on the wall and ceiling where the stove used to be. I eat out a lot.

After a quick shower, I wrapped my shoulder and used a makeshift sling to hold the painful pieces in a less painful place. There is nothing like a sling to get sympathy and easy access into offices. I looked into the mirror to shave and saw a face that had been through a long and grueling day. There were cuts over my eyebrow and one down my left cheekbone. My dark grey eyes looked back at me over a crooked nose that had been broken several times. I smiled at the rugged face, thinking how well I use it to intimidate and reassure. From my perspective, it was a handsome mug, but beauty is always in the eyes of the beholder. Now in my thirties, I look good for my age. No big girth, nice build, and decent muscle tone. Yup, I look good.

However, O'Malley's thugs had really done a number on me. I couldn't help wondering what I did to the guy to get him so upset with me. Maybe Dingle had an answer. O'Malley and I worked together once or twice while I was on the force, and I figured we got along just swell. I guess I was wrong. Now it's just a love/hate relationship and I just love to hate the guy.

My hands and one wrist were scraped like—the scuff marks on my face. I poured hydrogen peroxide on my open wounds, lathered up some soap, and took a razor to my face, removing the stubble. I have found that shaving in the morning is no good; it just creates more blood, and I hate the sight of blood first thing in the morning.

Moving back into my bedroom/living room/dining room, I opened the sleeper sofa for a well-earned night's sleep, but I could tell it was going to come at a price. Staring at the ceiling with reflections of the neons from across the street, I couldn't get a few things out of my mind concerning my client's demise. While the ideas were floating around, I jotted down a few questions.

Scuffed shoes, why left behind? Planted?

What was the pen and ink blotter on the dressing table used for?

I got the separate bedrooms; it was obvious this was a relationship in ashes. At least, that was the way it appeared, or was made to appear. I wonder.

Infidelity:

Was the infidelity one sided, or did both parties have lovers?

What role did Mr. Rumsfeld's playing around have in his wife's death?

What was the real issue between Mr. and Mrs. Rumsfeld?

What is the significance of the rental numbers?

What was in the hallway drawer, the one that was now empty?

Who was the "friend" that called in the cops? That I guess I'll have to wait until tomorrow to find out. Was she just a friend or was there more to it?

Those weren't all the questions spinning round in my head, but it was a start. A guy has to focus.

Finally, sleep.

———◆———

DOWNTOWN, SEAMUS O'MALLEY STEPPED THROUGH THE darkened foyer of an office building located south of Tribeca, near Battery Park. He was on his way to a bank of elevators ready to take passengers soaring to spectacular views of the harbor. It was a nighttime view he had rarely seen, and one he actually preferred not to take in. The city's nightlife had moved uptown by now. The lobby was next to vacant; his footsteps echoed off the walls. He was glad he had stripped off his duty uniform, put on his suit, and repacked his police revolver in his shoulder holster for the trip. He didn't feel quite so dirty in a suit, but he couldn't wash away all the filth, no matter how hard he tried.

The twenty-eight-story ride was made in silence until the bell sounded as he arrived at his floor and the doors silently slid open. Seamus advanced into a glass-enclosed anteroom, where he was met by two strongly armed men. He handed over his police revolver to one while the other patted him down, checking for other weapons in his pockets or on his person. The one holding the revolver nodded, and Seamus walked toward a glass door that opened into a hallway paneled in expensive-looking foreign wood. He had no idea what kind. It just looked expensive. He turned right down the long corridor, his footsteps muffled by the rich pile of an oriental runner leading to a set of double doors at the end of the hall. There was a scent of furniture polish, as if someone had just wiped down the walls. Another large man stood in front of the door. This one was armed with what looked like a double-barreled shotgun. Seamus nodded at the man and opened the doors into the palatial office space.

There was a small outer office that was open to the grand inner office, which enjoyed a spectacular vista of the city's harbor. A large desk in the far corner was the focal point of the room, allowing the occupant a view of passing ships and the northern shore of New Jersey on the Hudson River. The best seat in the house. Once again, the carpet was deep and luscious, masking footsteps and reducing noise in the room.

Seamus steadily plodded toward the desk, as if on his way to the gallows. He dreaded these encounters and wondered why and how he had gotten involved in this. It seemed like a bad dream now—a dream he wished would end, freeing him. O'Malley stopped about five feet from the desk.

The sergeant tried to squash his dread by contemplating the monetary cost of the office and what it took to get here—the body count it took to get here. He didn't bother to gaze out the window and enjoy the scenery. He did that early on in this "relationship," and he had been sternly admonished for his lack of focus and appreciation for why he had been summoned to the office. No, he thought, focus on the desk, and just wait. Finally, he was rewarded by a soft baritone voice from the other side of the desk.

"I heard you were called in on a crime scene tonight, Sergeant. Some sort of murder. Who was it again? A Mrs. Rumsfeld?"

It was a pleasant voice, like a radio announcer, but with a foreign accent, one Seamus couldn't quite place. It was like an Irish accent with Scottish overtones. *Maybe this is what Australians sound like?*

O'Malley nodded.

"Jamie Dugan showed up and embarrassed you by finding the exit route the killer used, leading your men to the murder weapon and clues as to who might have killed Mrs. Rumsfeld." The sergeant nodded again.

"But not before you and Dugan had a slight run in." O'Malley passed on nodding to this statement. Rather, he just stood there, staring at the center of the desk.

"Seamus, Seamus, Seamus. I don't understand you. There's no need to rough up the man. Now you've allowed your personal life to become involved in our work, and I don't like

30

it." The voice got louder and much harder. "I don't want you acting like an imp. You need to act more godly and less like a man seeking compensation." O'Malley, still quiet, folded his hands in front of his crotch, as if protecting himself, and continued to stare at the desk.

"It is more beneficial to treat your fellow man with respect. I don't care if you love or hate this Dugan fellow. You can't go out of your way to bring attention to yourself. Do you understand? Can you comprehend this? You're a constable! A police officer, for the love of Mike!" The speaker corrected himself. "Do your job on a more professional level!"

O'Malley just nodded.

Wham! A fist came down hard on the wooden desktop as the agitated voice boomed, "A lack of vocal response means nothing to me. Damn you! Do you hear me or not? Are we understanding each other here?"

"Yes, sir," O'Malley said in a quiet, docile voice that he almost didn't recognize as his own. He looked into the speaker's eyes and noticed the clerical collar once again. Puzzlement raced through his mind. Why was a man of the cloth sitting across the table from him? *Was it a costume to throw him off?* He never could figure out who did what in this office. This was the third time he had been summoned, and he hoped it would be the last.

"If I want his soul returned to his maker or his body recovered from some minor mishap, I'll take care of it. You are a valuable asset—one I don't want risking your position for a wanton display of...of God knows what. If you kill him, Dugan's ex-partner will hunt you down, throw you in jail, and have you put away for a long, long time. Then I lose my Gabriel, my protector and avenging angel. For what? For some petty murder that has no purpose except to soothe your sense of vengeance? And if you hurt the man, Dugan may turn his interest to you and expose you for the Judas they will believe you are. Either way, we both lose, and we don't want to do that now, do we?"

O'Malley looked into his tormentor's eyes. "No, sir," he said, his voice barely a whisper.

"You did a good job on that crime scene, just like I asked you to. Granted, Dugan was a surprise and an unexpected addition." There was a lull in the conversation, as if the next idea was being reconsidered. "I am going to have need of your services again, Sergeant. I have a client that needs protection, and I don't like disappointing my customers. Comprende? This job should be right up your alley."

O'Malley stared at the figure across the desk, wondering who was in need of protection and from what? He caught himself and muttered, "Yes, sir, I understand."

O'Malley heard the desk drawer quietly slide open and then close again. His eyes got larger as he clenched his fists in anticipation of the worst, but tensions eased as he watched the man snip the end of a large cigar and use a silver lighter to ignite the tobacco leaves. Blue smoke rose from the cigar and from the mouth and nostrils of the man across the desk. A slight smile crossed his lips, as if he enjoyed Seamus's nervousness.

"When I need your assistance, I will have Erskin contact you and provide you with appropriate instructions. In the meantime, see if you can discourage your friend Mr. Dugan. Try verbal persuasion this time, but let him know he needs to move on to other ventures. For his own good, that is."

"Yes, sir," O'Malley said. He watched an envelope slide across the desk towards him.

"Put this away for a rainy day, Sergeant."

O'Malley gathered the envelope and put it in his coat pocket.

"That's all, Sergeant. Good night, and may the good Lord look over you."

A man who had been standing in the outer office escorted Seamus to the hallway. O'Malley trudged down the hall, head down and sober. At the elevators, he received his weapon back then took the ride back down. Out in the New York air and away from the office, he opened the envelope and counted the cash—$25,000. He let out a low whistle and stuffed the envelope into his inside coat pocket. He gave it a few pats then walked another block before hailing a cab.

As the cabbie drove away, O'Malley couldn't help but think how important this case must be. One thing was for sure—O'Malley's benefactor knew a lot more about this case than the NYPD. He knew enough about the NYPD to make O'Malley nervous. And that fact kept nagging at the police sergeant. Who was this priest and how did he know so much? O'Malley would have to watch his step if he wanted to keep in front of this tidal wave. Maybe even dig around a little and learn the identity of the man behind the collar.

THURSDAY

At seven AM, my alarm went off. I didn't remember setting it. Matter of fact, for months now, I have tried to fix that damn clock so it never rings, but it just goes off every morning at seven anyway. I hate to admit it, but I'm getting used to it.

Time to rise and shine, I thought. Maxie would be opening in a little while, and there were no breakfast foods at the tavern. Maybe I should talk to him about opening early for breads and coffee and call it a breakfast bar? Naw, it would never catch on.

I had just enough time to get up, get dressed, and head out for a cup of joe and a Danish before the doors opened for me to check into my office. The way I felt after being dragged through the streets by O'Malley and his goons, it would take me at least until lunch before I recovered. That's a lot of coffee.

I pulled the Jag in front of Maxie's just after he opened.

"Hey, Maxie. How ya doing?" I shouted as I entered the bar.

"God. Where the hell you been?" he responded. He was standing in front of the bar counter with a broom in his hands. His white apron was wrapped around his waist, covering his dark pants from the knees up. Along with a white shirt, Maxie sported a green, blue, and orange tartan bow tie. His salt and pepper mustache drooped around his lips and matched the bushy eyebrows that merged over the bridge of his nose. A full head of more salt than pepper hair that he never combed sat on top of his head, rebelling against its mistreatment. He was handsome, with a long face and sparkling blue eyes that dared you not to be friendly. He had that trusting look that reminded me of a father confessor,

34

and with his Scottish accent, most women were enraptured by him. Today, like most mornings, he appeared fresh off a nap with that "bed head" look.

Maxie was a big Scotsman, standing about six-foot-one. He has put on a little extra weight each of the fifteen years he's lived in the States. He told me once that he had come from Edinburgh after a stop in Ireland for a few years. He had taken a steamer about ten years after graduating from the local university in Scotland with a law degree and then practiced law with a lesser-known firm in Ireland for nine of those ten years, earning a name for himself and amassing a tidy sum before seeking greener pastures here. After naturalization, Maxie passed the New York bar and tried to set up shop in the Big Apple, but he ran into problems with some financier and his attorney over a property deal seven or eight years earlier. Some thugs beat him up pretty bad and threatened to start a bonfire in his one-man law office while they trashed it. I was on the force then, still a tad wet behind the ears, just trying to stay alive. We were called in, Matt and me. One thing led to another, and Dingle and I caught up with the thugs. I did a little tap dancing of my own on the creeps until Dingle dragged me off one of them. We did manage to get the names of the financial firm and the jackleg lawyer with a little leaning on the right people who preferred not to spend any time in the slammer. The financier made restitution and paid off Maxie handsomely for his trouble, and the judge let him off with a warning. Not what Matt, Maxie, and I were looking for or expecting. So Maxie found this bar and bought it. It was in terrible shape, but he didn't care. The real estate market was soft back then—residue from the depression and onset of the Big War—so the tavern was practically given to him. Maxie spent months remodeling, trying to make it look like

35

an Irish pub, at least the way he remembered them.

The bar was below street level with a short flight of steps leading down from the sidewalk to the front door. Above the entry, a large sign was fixed to the wall that read "Maxie's Tavern."

The two exterior windows looked directly onto concrete wells, allowing minimal light to shine through the metal bars that guarded the window. It's really difficult to toss someone through a window with bars blocking a break in or break out.

Maxie owned the whole building, lived in one of the apartments over the bar, and let out the other three. Nice arrangement with great income potential. From time to time, I helped him out, especially when customers started to play rough in his joint or tried to skip out on their tabs. In return, he provided me insight into our corrupt legal system and gave me the scoop on the dirt he picked up from behind the bar. It was a great set up.

"Nice night last night. Did you get caught in the rain?" I asked as I walked into the tavern.

"What a dreich night!" he said. It has taken me a while to understand his Scottish idioms. Basically, he means, "What a dull, miserable, overcast, shitty night." I couldn't have agreed with him more.

"I get any calls?"

"Yeah, some guy called you about half an hour ago."

"Around ten?" Somewhere last night, I lost my watch. I stood in the middle of Maxie's joint, hunting the timepiece through the pockets of my "clean" suit jacket.

"Yeah, that's about right."

"Leave a name?"

"Yeah, it was Clay Morgan."

"How about a beer n' a burger?" The Danish didn't hold me very long. Hey, it was ten-thirty, and I was hungry.

"Sure, coming right up." Maxie disappeared into the kitchen.

I called back to him, "Mind if I use your phone?" After waiting 15 seconds I shouted, "Do you have a paper?" There was no reply to either question, so I started dialing.

O'MALLEY WAS STANDING OUTSIDE THE DOORWAY OF THE conference room Dingle was in, cleaning up reports and starting a file on the murder of Eloise Rumsfeld. O'Malley had been there for about three minutes, waiting for the lieutenant to finish up, when he finally leaned in and asked, "What's wrong with your friend, Lieutenant?"

"What's that, Sergeant? Is Dugan causing problems again?" Dingle put down his pencil and looked up from the paperwork.

"Sort of. He seems so disrespectin' of the law, more specifically, the force. His wisecracks last night kinda got the best of me. I might have been a little hard on him. How do you do it? Put up with his attitude and smart mouth, I mean." O'Malley appeared truly perplexed.

"Well, Sergeant, I guess there is cause for his attitude, but he was a damn good cop. Yup, damn good." Dingle looked at the ceiling, leaned back in his chair, and clasped his hands behind his head. "He has quite the nose for uncovering clues, but he rushes in based on hunches. Not all his moves are well calculated, and some can be downright rash, if you know what I mean. But last night was a perfect example."

"And yet you put up with his shenanigans. Why is that?"

"As I said, he was a damn good cop. In some respects, better than you or I ever will be." There was a moment of silence as the sergeant moved to an unoccupied chair in the conference room and sat down. "He was damaged goods after the war ended and he rejoined the force." Dingle paused for a second. The sergeant opened his mouth to ask a question, and Dingle raised his hand. "Wait a second. You wanted background. Let me tell you about Mr. Dugan. Before the Big War, Jamie and me served over in Brooklyn in the same precinct as partners for a few years. Then came Pearl Harbor. The next thing I know, Jamie signs up for the Marines."

O'Malley stared at the lieutenant, his mouth agape. "Marines? He fought the war with the Marines?"

"Yeah. They tried to make him a born-again killer. But you know the tough angle; it was kinda hard for the Marines to do that."

"Wow. That's a surprise! Where did he serve? France, Italy, MPs?"

"You're partially right," Dugan said. "He did get put in the MPs, but he fought like hell to get out. Finally, they reassigned him to the Second Division, Pacific Fleet, and he was sent to join his unit right after Guadalcanal."

Still amazed, O'Malley said, "Wasn't the Second Division part of the invasion group on Tarawa after Guadalcanal?"

"Yeah, they sure were. Dugan came away highly decorated, but scarred. He won't talk about it much, but I wouldn't push him too far. Underneath that mild Irish exterior is a wise-cracking PI with little regard for the team that deserted him when he got framed."

"What? What frame was that?" asked O'Malley

"Dugan was faced with the DeNato case, and even his superiors deserted him. He's a little erratic in his approach and quite angry. It was the DeNato case that did it. Put him over the top, I figure."

O'Malley looked puzzled. "DeNato case? I don't remember much about it other than Dugan got suspended for something, got cleared, and then zzzziiitt, gone from the force."

Dingle nodded. "Yeah, that was the DeNato case, but he wasn't guilty of anything. You see, during his off-duty hours, Dugan joined in a poker game. The force frowns upon these rovin' card games, especially when big money is involved. And there sat the force's highly decorated war hero and newest detective, right smack dab in the middle of one. Well, who is he playing cards with? None other than local gangster Rocky DeNato. Rocky lost a big pot to our friend. Unfortunately for Rocky, his newly imported Jaguar was part of the pot."

"So that's where he got that Jag. What's the harm, though? How could that lead to his suspension?"

Dingle waved away the question. "Rocky was a poor loser. He didn't just want his car back, he wanted to tarnish Dugan's reputation, ding it the way his was when he lost his new car. So two weeks later, Rocky framed Dugan for a heist that he and his boys pulled off. The cops from our precinct followed the clues, and they all led to Dugan. Someone spotted the Jag, Dugan's fedora was found at the scene, and footprints that matched Jamie's appeared in a grease slick in the parking lot behind the joint. Things like that."

"So how do you know it wasn't Dugan?"

Dingle looked at the sergeant. "He was at Maxie's Tavern over on 43rd, you know, where he currently hangs out, drinking beer and listening to Emily Ross. She was singing, Maxie was tending bar, and Jamie Dugan was drinking from six that night till one in the morning. We have the signed and sworn statements of thirty people covering the hours well before and after the crime occurred."

"He could've slipped out."

"Dugan is no good at tellin' lies. Oh, sure, he is known to fib a little and steal evidence every once in a while, but an out and out lie? Not part of his character. Nope, Dugan was there the whole time. Anyway, someone ratted out DeNato about a month after Dugan was suspended; only by then, we had no evidence to pin it on him. It was our informant's word against DeNato's, and the rat wouldn't be a witness for fear of being Rocky's next victim." Dingle shook his head and stood. "We told Dugan what we found. He listened, looked at his badge and gun lying on the captain's desk, and told him to go to hell. Dugan went back to his desk, cleaned out a few things, and left. He only comes around now when he needs something we have that nobody else does."

"How'd the Jag appear near the heist and what about the hat?"

"DeNato had more than one set of keys to the car. Most new cars come with two, you know. The hat is a popular brand that can be purchased at any number of shops in Manhattan. Footprints were taken off shoe size, and apparently, someone had broken into Dugan's place and lifted a pair of his shoes before the crime. The shoes mysteriously re-appeared after the crime and after we had been through his apartment, if you want to call that dump an apartment.

"It was a set up. You know the crazy thing? Not much was taken in the heist, just some old records on rental receipts for office space down in the financial district and some junk jewelry. You know—paste." Dingle looked at his sergeant, who was lost in thought. "Oh, and an old fountain pen with some initials on it. We never found the pen, although it was listed as a missing item."

The sergeant got up to go, but hesitated. "Did Dugan confront Rocky after he found out?"

The lieutenant smiled and nodded. He got up from his chair and moved to sit on the corner of the conference room table. "Oh, yeah. As the story goes, Dugan walked home from the precinct, carrying the box of trinkets from his desk, mulling over what the captain had told him about DeNato. When he entered the apartment, he dropped the box, went back to the street, and hailed a cab—"

"What happened to the Jag?" O'Malley asked.

"Anthony—you know, the mechanic—had it at his repair shop in Brooklyn. Someone crashed into it in a hit and run, but that is another story for another time. Anyway, without his precious car, Dugan was relying on cabs again. Rocky has an office, if you can believe that, down on Maiden Lane, near 24th. The cab dropped Dugan off in front of the building and he rode the elevator up with a guard who must have sensed his anger. On the way up, the guy frisked Dugan, a really thorough pat down. He deposited Dugan on DeNato's floor. Into the offices marched Jamie Dugan, like an army of one, all puffed up, neck muscles bulging, and blood racing through his veins. I guess he must have been three steps short of a stroke.

"There sat DeNato behind an oversized desk with only the morning news on it. DeNato's jacket was off, his expensive leather oxfords were up on the desk, and a fat cigar was clenched in his teeth. You know what he looks like—a six-foot wop, weighing in around two hundred and fifty pounds. Poor Dugan. He thinks he is a monster at six-two, but the weight difference really sets the two men apart. DeNato's eyebrows went up like railroad crossing gates as he watched Dugan come in.

"Dugan stopped about three feet in front of the desk and glared at Rocky. I guess you could see smoke coming out of his ears. But ever so calmly, he said, 'This ain't over by a long shot.' DeNato looked at Dugan and said, 'You into horse racing, Dugan?' Dugan nodded and said, 'You know I am. What's your point, DeNato?' 'Don't bet against the horse that has the lead.' DeNato raised his left hand and flicked two fingers in Dugan's direction, like someone asking for the garbage to be taken away or the dirty dishes moved out of sight. One of DeNato's goons came over to drag Dugan out, but Jamie didn't go quietly. He slipped the goon's grip and smashed him in the face with his elbow then mashed his heel on the guy's foot. The thug lurched forward, and Dugan hit him with a roundhouse that spun the guy half way across the room and into one of DeNato's fancy leather chairs, cracking it in four places, and left the thug sprawled on the floor."

O'Malley inched forward in his seat to speak, but Dingle said, "Let me finish, Sergeant." O'Malley raised his hands and sat back in his chair.

"So Dugan looked at Rocky and said, 'Don't send a mare to do a stud's job. You may find that being in the lead makes you blind to what is going on behind you.' And he turned and walked out of the office. Or so the story goes. They have been bitter enemies ever since. I, for one, would not want to find myself on the dark side of Dugan or DeNato. You catch my drift, Sergeant?"

Sergeant O'Malley got up and nodded. He turned to leave, but stopped short. "Yeah, I get you. You two must have been pretty close, you and Dugan." The sergeant walked out of the office, and Dingle returned to his paperwork.

"Yeah, we were really close." But O'Malley was already gone.

THE FIRST STOP I HAD TO MAKE WAS AT THE PRECINCT. QUES-
tions needed answers, and Dingle had some of them, although
they were incomplete. I figured that since it had been a few
hours, they might have the technical stuff: Time of death,
murder weapon confirmation, print results. You know, the
grunt work cops do.

The precinct was on 36th Street, off Madison, in a grey
building, with about thirty steps leading up to the entry foyer.
The police chief, Arthur W. Wallander, was an unusual guy.
I thought he might die of old age as our chief. His predeces-
sors had never lasted more than three years, or the term of
the incumbent mayor, whichever came first. Wallander had
made it through two administrations, mainly because of his
relationship with the mayor. I figured if he could do it, I could
leverage my relationship with Dingle and get the info out of
them. I just love New York politics, sometimes.

I knew the building well. Hell, I even knew Wallander,
not that I called him Arthur or Art, but I knew him. I had
lived within these grey walls for a lot of years. As I walked up
the steps to the oversized entry, the memories came rushing
back. It was as if I were on my first day on the job, a rookie.
Those were the days!

Before I joined the force, I'd gone to college for two years
and did pretty good. Then things got rough at home. Mom
started working two jobs and Dad lost his to the big lay-off
program we called the Great Depression. As a result, we
couldn't afford any more "luxury expenses," as Dad referred
to them. I had to go out and make a living, rather than pay
someone to teach us there weren't jobs for the highly educated.
Hell, there weren't jobs for the uneducated. Being a good
young man of ˥·ish descent whose grandfather, God rest his
soul, was a cop back in the old country and whose nephew

had been a cop in the Bronx, it made sense for me to become one of New York City's finest. Plus I had an in. The name Dugan meant something. There were lots of young guys who wanted work, and this was work, although the pay was lousy.

I did well during my first few years on the force, learned my beat, and faced a lot of problems I'm still trying to forget. I got to know people and made tons of connections, connections I still use. I never had to kill anybody, but I solved quite a few cases. I learned to follow orders real well, kept my mouth shut when I needed to, and applied some good old logic to crime investigation.

Then the war broke out—you know, the big war. When those bastards decided to launch a sneak attack on Pearl Harbor, I decided it was time I learned how to kill a man. I enlisted in the Marines, and after training, I was assigned to an MP division. It took me the better part of a year to get that changed to the infantry. After some additional training, I join the Second Marine Division in New Zealand after the boys took Guadalcanal. Yeah, I was part of the force that landed on Tarawa to take the island of Betio and so that our flyboys could get closer to Tojo and his home field. Come screw with us, will he? Home field advantage be damned, especially if you're from New York.

After the war, I came back to the city, decorated but damaged. NYPD held my job for me and welcomed me back. It was not long before I got my chance to advance. A spot opened for a detective's posting in Brooklyn and I aced my test scores for advancement. Once I made detective, my track record intact, ribbons and awards not withholding, I did the job. My first year was sort of like a honeymoon. Everything worked really swell. I bagged me some scum, shot a guy or two, but it was all I could do to keep from deleting dirt bags from the earth, or at least New York. Yes, sir, everything was going along really swell. But then came the year that things began to turn to shit. The year of DeNato.

I sauntered past the desk sergeant and waved. "Hey, Mack, how the kids?"

He waved back, looking a little dazed and confused. "Fine, Dugan. Just fine."

"Where's Dingle? I owe him a statement or something."

Mack got distracted by an arresting officer and his collar, so he just pointed in Dingle's general direction. I continued my journey up a set of stairs toward the lieutenant's desk.

I found myself on the second floor in a sea of dingy desks and chairs. The cops called it the "bullpen." Looked just the same as when I worked here. The windows were brown with dirt from the city, making them look like they were etched in the sewage the cops dealt with on a daily basis. Although the temps outside were in the mid-40s, the room was hot with steam pipes feeding the radiators that ran along the wall. One radiator hissed like a snake that had its tail stepped on. There were times I actually missed being here, feeling the camaraderie among the cops as we all suffered in this gloom. I didn't feel that way now. This was not a place I wanted to work anymore, let alone visit.

Three desks were arranged by the windows overlooking 36th Street. Two of the desks were occupied, one with a "customer" providing a statement; the other had Lieutenant Dingle buried deep in paperwork.

Dingle had a cleanish desk, in that his mess was more organized than most cops I know. He was filling out some form, probably one regarding last night's murder. Oh, God, what I wouldn't give to find out what happens to all that paperwork. When I was here, I figured the commissioner used my reports to feed the furnace. A summer feeding for the steamer that provided all this heat regardless of season.

I went up to his desk, sat in the chair that flanked it, took off my new fedora, and set it down on his desk. He looked up and said, "Take your hat off my desk."

"Is that a way to greet your old partner?" I asked.

"What brings you to my office, Dugan?"

"Office? This is just a desk in a sea of desks." I thought this might just be friendly banter, but it turned mean.

"Beats your office in a tavern. Now that really reflects well on the PI class of citizen in our city." Dingle looked down at his paperwork and exhaled.

"Well, my client got offed, so I can't get paid. I figure I gotta learn a few things to get my paycheck, like who is Rumsfeld's attorney."

"Oh, Jesus. We got a murder on our hands, and you're here asking me who the murder victim's lawyer is so you can get paid?" Dingle leaned back in his chair and looked at me like he did when we worked together. "Don't you think of anything but yourself? Go on, get out of here, and let me work, will ya? And take your hat off my desk." After a brief pause, Dingle looked up at me and said, "Why not ask your client's husband, maybe share one of your photos?"

"Aw, come on, Matt. I helped you out last night. At least you can give me a clue or two." I picked up my hat from the corner of the desk and put it on the back of my head, allowing my forehead to breathe.

"Damn it," Dingle said. "You're interrupting my report. The least you can do is buy me a decent cup of joe." Dingle got up from his desk and put on his coat, looking around the bullpen. He waved over a beat cop and told him we were stepping out for a few minutes.

We walked into a coffee shop across the street and ordered. Matt waited for me to pay and then sat down at a table along the wall where he could watch who came and went. I pulled up a chair.

"It's not Reggio's coffee," Dingle said. "But it's decent enough. Now what are you doin' on this case and how can I get you off it?"

"I just want to go my merry way, but there are expenses to be covered. I could make a few calls and find the lawyer, but I thought it would be easier if I went through proper channels so you guys don't get pissed at me again." I smiled, showing the cut up the left side of my face.

"Yeah, sorry 'bout that. O'Malley gets excited when he thinks he's got a lead."

"Yeah. Like a blood hound on the trail, running through walls, cars, and other people's faces."

"We caught up with Mr. Rumsfeld, and we've temporarily ruled out him and the girlfriend as primary suspects. Your photos helped clear that up. And from all indications, they were there, going at it, for at least eight hours."

I raised my eyebrows with that news. "Oh? Since when have you heard of a guy going at it for eight hours? Eight minutes is like a record of some kind."

Dingle looked at me with a sheepish grin. "The super said the noise from the room was nonstop. He had to go up there once to get them to quiet down. He said the girl answered the door and he heard a man in the background."

"Give the guy a medal for stamina. What kind of shoes was he wearing?" I asked.

47

"What kind of stupid question's that? How the hell do I know?"

"You're the cop. Were you able to determine if it really was Rumsfeld in there?"

Dingle didn't look at me, but said, "No, other than your photos. The cops I sent to the address just showed them around for confirmation. Why?"

"This is embarrassing, but I had taken my photos and I just wanted to see what happened after all the, you know, preliminaries. After the photo shoot, I was hungry and went to grab myself a deli sandwich. When I came back, Rumsfeld's car was gone. Presumably, he was driving it."

"Oh, now you tell me. Why didn't you say that last night?"

"Come on. You saw me. Your boys did a number on me and my car. The Jag will be scarred for life. Was the murder weapon the carving knife from the kitchen?"

"Yeah, it was confirmed this morning."

"Well, at least we know that whoever used the knife had some knowledge of the kitchen. That set of knives was not out in the open. I think that puts the hubby back in the limelight. How about prints?"

"None. Wiped clean. I'll have O'Malley question Rumsfeld again. I want you to stay out of this, though. Find the lawyer, get your money, and move on. Okay?"

"Sure, who's the lawyer?"

"I have no idea. You're a bright guy. You'll figure it out."

"Gee, thanks. I thought you made lieutenant, so what's with your office? You piss someone off? You gotta make captain now to get an office with a real door, or what?"

Dingle got up and grabbed his hat. "Screw you, Dugan." He walked out of the coffee shop and crossed the street back to the precinct.

I CHECKED AROUND FOR THE RUMSFELD ATTORNEY USING some contacts I had in financial circles downtown. The name that kept coming up was Bernie Clienfelter, a real jackleg. He reportedly dealt with uppity financial types who bought up real estate on the cheap, through foreclosure. Sounded like they were pretty successful. How or if this fit in with my deceased client, I had no idea.

Clienfelter put his shingle out on 50th, near 8th Avenue, not far from where the oh-so-avant-garde Port Authority Bus Terminal was being constructed. I left my office and headed to 50th to see Bernie about a will.

It was about noon when I arrived. The building was a reddish brown and looked like a converted tenement. It gave me the creeps just walking up to the front door. The wind had picked up again and the papers from the street were being tossed about like confetti. A gust ripped the entrance door from my weak grip and slammed the door shut behind me sending an echo throughout the first floor that momentarily drowned out the mechanical noises from the machinery outside.

A couple of hours before, I had taken my arm out of the sling to try to loosen it up. As I rotated the arm around my shoulder, I had concocted a few ways I could exact my revenge on that fat excuse for a public servant. Now I realized just how weak my grip and muscles were. I was hoping that my mental faculties were going to be up to the task.

In the dimly lit hallway just inside the door was a list of businesses occupying the building. The occupancy rate looked to be about fifty percent, with many upper floor offices being vacant. *I wonder what they charge for one of these offices. By the looks of things, the tenants probably get paid for using the space.*

I found the listing for Clienfelter's office. Third floor. Well, at least there was an elevator. I took it up, but couldn't help thinking I should have walked. I would have made it to the floor fifteen minutes earlier. I found a door with his name etched in smoked glass. Real class for a building dressed up to look respectable. I turned the doorknob and walked in.

"Is Mr. Clienfelter in, doll?"

The secretary was about forty-five and a little hefty. She wore her brown hair fashionably long so that it covered a short neck. Her round cheeks had been emphasized with additional make-up so she looked like an actual doll. Brown eyes took me in in one gaze.

Through smacking gum, she said, "Yeah, but he'll be a while. Ya wanna have a seat, hon?" She set back to work typing. I reclined in a comfy, well-worn couch and waited for about five minutes.

The office walls were cheap and thin, so it wasn't hard to overhear what was going on behind the secretary's desk. Voices climbed as a shouting match climaxed and a tearful, red-faced woman flung the door open.

"You are a son of a bitch, Clienfelter. Nasty, nasty man," she sobbed in a Brooklyn accent, maybe the Bronx. "I hope you melt in hell." She moved off with her proud head up and a tan felt hat in her hand. Her brown frock dragged across the office floor. It was just a little bit longer than it needed to be, as if she purchased it off a rack down at the Salvation Army store.

Bernie Clienfelter shrugged as he watched her storm out. He had a mean look of determination as he turned his gaze toward his secretary.

"There is a man to see you." She jabbed a thumb in my direction.

"Huh? Yeah, sure, come on in, if this won't take long." Clienfelter beckoned to me with his hand, then turned back to his office and disappeared from sight.

I pushed up from the overused sofa, grabbed my fedora, and headed after him. I thanked the secretary, who replied with a few smacks and pops of chewing gum and a smile that quickly melted into a bored grimace as she began typing again.

Clienfelter's office was a small space. Bookcases on two walls. Open windows along a third of the wall offered a nice but chilly breeze for the cramped space. The desk, littered with folders, was oversized for the room. I parked myself in a wooden chair and looked about the room. I'd almost missed the small closet door next to the outer wall. I smiled up at Clienfelter, who hadn't sat yet.

"You settin' up camp here?" he asked. He was about 6'4" and very thin. He had a trashy, light brown mustache that looked to be the best he could do at growing facial hair. It went from his nose to his upper lip and moved like a centipede as he talked. He was bald except for the "abbot ring" above the ears, which looked like the doors of a stopped taxi letting out passengers. I didn't know if I should laugh or shake my head. I did neither.

"I only have a few minutes before my next client shows up, so don't get too comfy," he said.

"I just wanted to know if you're the attorney handling the Rumsfeld will." I studied him for any telltale signs.

"I might be. Why do you ask?"

He was the guy.

"You know, she got bumped off last night."

"No, I had no idea." Surprised, he sat down in his plush chair and gazed up at the ceiling. After a few moments, he straightened. "What does this have to do with you and me?"

51

His eyes settled on mine, as if prepared for some sort of battle.

I took out my pre-WWII NYPD badge, which I'd held onto for times like this. "I'm investigating the death," I said.

"Oh." His gaze rested on the badge for a few seconds and then he looked back at me.

Relics like this badge really do come in handy, I thought. "Anything unusual go on between Mr. and Mrs. Rumsfeld lately? Any changes to either's will?"

"Yeah, now that you mention it. I just received an outline for a codicil to Mrs. Rumsfeld's will. She was supposed to be down this morning for the final signature and witnessing. She was due here in a few minutes."

"Oh, yeah? What about the codicil? What'd it say?"

"I just took a quick look before my secretary typed it up, but she was adding another person to share in her estate. Most of the property and money was hers."

"Now what happens?" I asked, trying not to show my surprise.

"It all goes to the husband."

Now that's interesting, I thought, seeing the emergence of a motive. "So the codicil's not legally binding?"

"Nope. No signatures. It could be contested, I guess, but it will all eventually go to Mr. Rumsfeld." He emphasized "Mr."

"Thanks." I stood to leave. "Who was being added to the estate?"

Clienfelter looked at me and shook his head. "That is client privilege."

"Your client is dead, Mr. Clienfelter. Please, just give me the name."

"Get your court order, and I'll be glad to give it to you." Clienfelter was standing pat, and I had no real jurisdiction. I shouldn't have even been there. I smiled as I thought of Dingle catching me impersonating a police officer in front of a lawyer.

I walked out of the office, completely forgetting about my expenses. That would have gone over really well. First, I tell him I'm a cop and then strong-arm him for my fee. I left quietly.

CLIENFELTER FOLLOWED DUGAN OUT OF HIS OFFICE. As Dugan disappeared into the hallway, Clienfelter turned to his secretary. "Where do these people come from? That's what I want to know." Clienfelter handed her a manila file with "Rumsfeld" typed on the tab. "File this in the client safe, will ya?"

"Yeah, sure," Delores said. "Must be pretty important."

"Mrs. Rumsfeld got herself murdered, and I don't want our living client's reputation getting soiled."

"You don't think Mr. Rumsfeld's mixed up in this, do ya?"

"Not sure, but I'm going to do some checking around. Maybe you can make a few calls and see what you can gather about him? Let me know right away if you dig up anything." Clienfelter stood, staring at the door, as if he expected someone to walk in. "I have a few calls to make on my own."

The secretary started going through her Rolodex, looking for contacts that might shed some light on Vernon Rumsfeld.

THE PIECES WERE NOT ADDING UP THE WAY I HOPED, EVEN though a theory had begun to form somewhere in the fog of my brain. I had just one thing left to nail down, and if it turned out the way I thought, case solved, or so it appeared.

I didn't like where all of this was going, though. So I headed back to my "office" for a bite.

Two gin and tonics and a chicken sandwich later, I walked to the bar and asked Maxie for the phone. I called Clay to see if we could get together for a few beers tomorrow afternoon around five. I made a few more calls, put the booze and sandwich on my tab, and then asked for my briefcase, which I usually kept stashed behind the bar.

"Here. It is a wee bit heavy," Maxie said, letting his faint Scottish accent roll with his words.

I took the case and pulled out my .38 Police Special and a box of ammo. "This thing makes it a tad heavy." Maxie winced and went back to cleaning up behind the bar while I placed the loaded gun back into the briefcase.

"You aren't planning to use that thing are you, Jamie lad?" It seemed a curious question, especially from Maxie.

"It's just for protection, Maxie. Just protection. Let's hope it doesn't go off."

I walked over to where I had left my fedora, placed it on my head, and exited the bar.

It felt funny carrying that old briefcase again. It had been quite a while since I last used it. You'd think in my line of work, I would go to bed with my gun, but I'm not really much of a gun-guy. Don't get me wrong; every so often they come in handy in my line of work. Other than sitting behind Maxie's bar, the last time I carried this case was after the war as I walked around with my discharge papers from the Army. This time there were no papers, just something that could be discharged.

The wind had died down and the sun was poking through the clouds, giving the early afternoon a warm-up. If it weren't for all the crooks, this would be a real nice city. Of course then I wouldn't have much of a job.

I climbed into my Jag and drove back up to 78th, windows down so I could listen to the purr of the finely tuned English engine and enjoy the background of the city noise.

———◆——◆——◆———

THE SUPER ANSWERED THE DOOR TO HIS APARTMENT ALMOST as soon as I stopped knocking. He yanked open his door hard and fast as if he was trying to surprise whomever and keep them from bothering him with some trivial request. He leaned against the doorjamb and chewed on a cigar that looked and smelled as if it hadn't been lit for days. It needed to be lit just to put it out of its misery. His T-shirt was sweat stained, and his jeans had mud on the legs, as if he had been working in a garden or lost a dirt-throwing fight. He stood there in soiled socks and no shoes. He could have used a shave and a haircut. Long brown hair hung over his ears even though he kept pushing it back so he could see. Not only did he need a haircut, but a shave would have been a nice touch too. The word "unkempt" came to mind.

After a bit of chitchat about the neighborhood, I held up a photo of Mr. Rumsfeld and asked, "Is this the man who was in the second-floor apartment the other night?"

"Who are you, another cop? I can't seem to keep you guys away."

Avoiding the question, I responded, "Listen, I've got to do this follow-up work or the lieutenant will be pissed I might have missed something. Will ya help me out and answer the question?"

"I don't know. I didn't see the guy that night. I didn't see you with the other cops. They've been crawling all over this place, ya know."

"Have you ever seen this guy?" I flashed a photo of Clay Morgan.

"Yeah, he's been around."

"Who is on the lease for the apartment?" I pushed my fedora back on my head and grinned at the super.

"Why are you asking so many damn questions? I gotta see a badge before I go any further." He shifted the cigar in his mouth and hardened his gaze. I hardened my stare right back at him.

"I'm looking for a killer," I said, putting my NYPD badge to use again.

"Murder? Whose murder? Say, weren't ya here around noon a day or two back? How come I didn't see ya when the police were asking questions?"

"Those were some of my underlings. Now what's the name on the lease?" I pulled a twenty-dollar bill from my wallet and dangled it in front of him. "I'll let you buy a new T-shirt."

"Clay. Clay Morgan." He grabbed the twenty and slammed the door in my face.

"You're welcome," I muttered.

A resident walked up, turned her key in the lock, and let herself in. I stuck my foot in the door just as it was about to shut and watched her walk down the hall and up the stairs before I entered the building.

The second-floor hallway was clean, painted in off-white. Nice fluorescents lit the hall and a brown, short-napped rug helped dampen the sound of footfalls down the corridor. The floor had a small, probably one-bedroom flat near the back of the building, and one larger toward the street side. It reminded me of a typical railway flat. With the apartment as narrow as it was, I pictured the rooms running off an interior hallway.

When I got to the apartment in question, I knocked and rang the doorbell. I even showed some patience, waited, and then knocked again a little louder. It seemed nobody was home, so I got out my tools to jimmy the lock. I got the doorknob unlocked, but there was a deadbolt that I couldn't budge.

"Hey, you. What ya doin' there?" A young broad had her head poking around the stairway from the floor above, looking down at me.

"I have a message for the woman who lives here. Do ya know if she's in?"

"No. She works from about nine to six." The tenant stepped down the last few steps and into the hallway. "Matter of fact, they are usually at work during the day."

"Huh?" I was stunned for a second. "There are two dames livin' in this apartment, Miss—ah? What did you say your name was?"

"Me? I'm Rachel. Who are you lookin' for?" She was a lot cuter when she wasn't hiding in the stairs. She was thin with long, straight, black hair with curls that flipped up at the ends. She was dressed in jeans and a long-sleeved white shirt with the sleeves rolled up just short of her elbow. She had a scarf knotted about her neck, a very patriotic red, white, and blue scarf.

"The dame who holds this lease, the primary resident. Do you know if she was working last week, Rachel?"

"Yup, all week, except for Sunday. She works down at city hall as a court clerk. You want to leave me the message for her?"

"That's okay. It's kinda personal. I'll try her on Sunday. Thanks for your help. What did you say her name was?"

"You really don't know who lives here, do you?" Rachel

gave me a skeptical eye and placed a hand on her hip.

"Okay, you got me. I'm investigating a murder." I flashed my badge one more time. It was coming in real handy. "A possible suspect in the case may have been in this apartment."

"The killer?" The girl stood there, awestruck. I had gone and scared her. Just what this apartment needs, some broad in her late teens running around telling everyone there's a murderer living here. "What murder?"

"Nothing in your neighborhood. Just someone who might have seen a person possibly involved. It's a lead I am trying to run down, you understand? No stone left unturned?" She relaxed a little, like a quivering leaf downshifting to just shaking.

"Yeah, sure. I understand. I guarantee you neither of those ladies had anything to do with any person involved in a murder." She pushed back a stray strand of hair, curling it behind her ear, and tried to force a smile.

"How can you be so certain? You friends with them or something?" I asked.

"Yes, actually. I know them both. We get together when I'm not in class and looking for some place to put my feet up for a while. Beats sitting alone in my unit upstairs. They're really nice. Sweethearts."

"You were going to tell me the name of the owner of the apartment."

"Oh, yes, sure. It's Amanda." She looked at me kinda funny. "Amanda Morgan. You can't really think she's involved, can you?"

Amanda? I thought Clay was on the lease. What gives? He got a sister or mother living here? "Thanks for the info. Try not to go blabbing the murder story around, would ya? I don't want the super and residents to get upset," I said, brushing away her question.

"Sure. Murder suspect in my apartment building. Imagine that. That explains why all the police were here the other day," she murmured as she wandered back up the stairs, shaking her head. I guess everyone needs to be proud of something these days.

I left the apartment building and returned to my car. The conversation I'd just had was going to run around the neighborhood, growing and shifting with each re-telling.

Guiding my Jag through traffic back to my office, I considered each bit of evidence. How neat it all seemed. Everything pointed in one direction. To one person. To put this case to bed, all I needed was a confession. I could send a bill to my client's estate, pay the rest of my bar bill, and get the Jag repaired. I might have some extra scratch to put on the ponies. The answer seemed plain as the nose on Maxie's face, but my conscience was in turmoil. Something didn't add up. The evidence pointed to the wrong man, and I knew it. I just couldn't prove it, yet. I figured I knew who the killer was. All I had to do was smoke him out.

Morgan arrived at Maxie's right on time.

<hr />

"Now that's an interestin' story," Clay said, a long set of Southern vowels on "interesting" dragged out the word as if he was thinking. He showed a lopsided smile, but his eyes were as soft as a kitten's.

"Yeah, not quite the Sunday comics."

Clay looked at me and said, "Y'all going to have to tell me how it turns out."

I let out a long sigh and looked up at Clay. "Sure you wanna hear the rest?"

I set my fedora on the bench beside me and looked into Morgan's sad, blue eyes.

"Y'all can't frame me, James," he said. "I didn't do anything wrong. Shoot, I lost my job and got kicked out of my apartment. If you did your homework, you know my name's on the lease, for Christ's sake."

"Sorry, Clay." It was Matt Dingle's voice.

I was surprised to see the lieutenant standing there, staring at Clay, O'Malley a few paces behind him, holding a set of handcuffs.

"How long you been here, Matt?" I asked.

"I wanted to hear what you had to say, Jamie, in case there was incriminating evidence we could use against you," Dingle chuckled. Turning to Morgan, he said, "Now come along peacefully, Clay, while we sort this whole thing out."

Dingle looked back at me and added, "Mr. PI, thanks for all the leg work implicating your friend here. By the way, I'll need that badge."

I felt like a schmuck.

O'Malley stood there with a shit-eating grin on his face. He cuffed Morgan and looked at me. Didn't say a word, just smiled. The scene made me want to pop him in his smug face, the big, overgrown, fat cop. He still had it in for me for some reason.

The sergeant grabbed Clay and spun him toward the door. "He won't be botherin' you for some time, Dugan." O'Malley ushered Clay out of Maxie's as Dingle looked on.

I was reaching into my coat pocket for my PI/NYPD ID when Morgan yelled, "No. Wait." Clay turned his head back in my direction. "I didn't do it. You gotta believe me, James."

O'Malley shoved Clay toward the door. I stood as Dingle came over and put a hand on my shoulder.

In desperation, Clay turned to me again. "Talk with Vernon Rumsfeld, will ya? He'll clear me, James. Please."

I don't know why Clay keeps calling me James. All it does is piss me off, but not this time. Somehow, it left me upset. Real upset, but not with Clay.

I looked up to see Maxie holding the door open for Morgan and O'Malley. Dingle trailed closely behind, forgetting the badge. The noise from the street was muted by the sudden shock of my friend being taken to jail. The three disappeared into the bright afternoon sunlight as Maxie closed the door behind them and darkness crept back into Maxie's Tavern.

You know the evidence is stacked against him. You know he's being framed. I said to myself. *I know they have the wrong guy.*

It had been a slow day at the Clienfelter Law Agency. Bernie got up from his desk and entered the outer office, where Delores Young sat scribbling in her legal pad. The phone was perched between her ear and shoulder.

"Uh-huh. Yeah. Got it. Okay, thanks, Mr. Glibner. I'll let Mr. Clienfelter know." There was a brief pause. "Okay. Well, goodbye, then." She hung up and made some final notes in her legal pad.

Bernie anxiously shifted his weight from one leg to the other as he waited for his secretary to finish. "Was that about Rumsfeld?"

A little surprised he was there, Delores looked into her boss's face. "Yeah. Mr. Glibner represented the previous owners of the Baker Building. He gave me some background on the settlement."

"Let's take this conversation into my office, shall we? Make sure the front door is locked so we don't get any surprise visitors."

A few moments later, Delores was seated in front of her boss's desk smoothing her skirt over her legs and knees.

"A consortium originally bought the Baker Building—five men, to be exact. Vernon Rumsfeld was one of the five," Delores began.

"That much I know," Bernie interjected.

Delores continued, "They owned it about five years before the Depression hit. Each of the partners passed away in unusual circumstances over the next four years, eventually leaving Mr. Rumsfeld the sole owner of the property."

"I didn't realize they'd all died. I thought they sold their shares to Rumsfeld. How did these people die? Did Glibner say?"

"He gave me two of them. He said they didn't sound that questionable as stand-alone deaths, but when you put it all together, it began to look suspicious. The first was Robert Banks. Mr. Banks committed suicide in November of 1928 by jumping out a fifteenth-floor window. He checked into the Moravian Hotel that morning and jumped that afternoon."

"The Moravian?" Clienfelter said, trying to place its location.

"It's on 37th and Lexington. I think it changed hands a few times since the suicide. Glibner didn't give me the latest name, but I didn't think it was important. It's one of those luxury places with a spa hot tub, outings to golf courses in the area, and great lunch and dinner menus. Real upscale."

Clienfelter scratched his mustache a few times. "Not the type of place one would check into to commit suicide, I would think."

"The second death was a hit and run. Mister Colin Bertrade was struck and killed by an unknown assailant in April 1929. Apparently, he was coming out of a late meeting with some of the partners. The death occurred on 36th and Fourth Avenue. Nobody saw or heard anything. Each of the remaining three partners had alibis, as they were all in the same meeting, and Mr. Bertrade was the first to leave."

"Murder?" Clienfelter leaned back in his chair. "I know the Bertrade name from somewhere. It's familiar."

"It should be. It's Clive Montfort's middle name. Bertrade was his uncle. Bertrade is supposedly some kind of royalty, so Montfort changed his birth given name to Bertrade as his middle name to capitalize on the perks that might come with the name association or recognition," said Delores, looking over her notes again.

"You're telling me someone killed Montfort's uncle, and it could have been Rumsfeld?" Clienfelter popped forward in his chair as if he was about to pounce. His eyes were wild with excitement. Delores inched away.

"That's the way it looks. Rumsfeld was in the meeting that Bertrade left early, but he could have hired someone to do his dirty work for him. So, yes; that's exactly what it looks like," Delores said quietly. She went back to her notes, trying to ignore her boss's movements. She flipped a few pages to make sure she left nothing out, and then looked back at Clienfelter. "Rumsfeld and the rest of the owners made an arrangement when they originally bought the property. If one died, his portion would transfer to the surviving owners. By 1931, Rumsfeld was the lone survivor and took possession of the Baker Building, or at least that portion the five owned with the bank. He, Mr. Rumsfeld that is, fell behind on the loan payments. And, the bank trying to offset carrying the red ink on their books, eventually sold the delinquent mortgage to Clive Montfort. You know the rest; Mr. Montfort moved to foreclose on the building, taking possession himself after satisfying the remainder of the mortgage.

"Apparently, the Depression had a heavy impact on the rental incomes for the Baker Building and Mr. Rumsfeld. According to my notes, Mr. Rumsfeld was in hock up to his neck to the bank, so it was easy for Mr. Montfort to gain control and foreclose." Delores looked over her notes to see if she had missed something germane to the issue. With nothing more to say, she closed her notebook and tidied up the papers under its cover. Looking up into her boss's eyes, she felt satisfied with herself. In the span of just a few hours she had pulled all the strings together. *Let's see what Clienfelter has to say to that*, she thought to herself. *He was involved in the end of this "deal".*

"I remember the paperwork on that case. I did the deed transfer and the rest of the filings. But I never knew…" Clienfelter stopped and leaned back in his chair. "We had better be very careful with this information. Type up your notes and put them in the safe—uh, our hidden safe—for the time being."

Delores moved back to her desk while Clienfelter tried to figure a way to leverage this information and avoid unfortunate accidents like the ones Misters Banks and Bertrade met fifteen years ago. "I wonder who the other partners were," Clienfelter mumbled. "Delores, can you find out who the other partners were with Rumsfeld when they first bought the Baker Building?" There was a mischievous smile that formed on Bernie's face.

"You got it," came the secretary's response from the outer office.

AFTER DARK, MAXIE USUALLY TRIED TO HAVE LOCAL TALENT come in and provide entertainment for his customers. On this particular evening, Maxie booked one of his favorite trios to do a set or two.

I was staring at the empty seat where Clay had been three hours ago when the band came in and began their set up. A quiet murmur ran through the crowd in anticipation of the music to come. Each member of the trio tried out his instrument, much to the delight of the quieting drinkers. Maxie had a wide grin on his face and more rounds of drinks were ordered to hold tables for the first set.

"I don't think you should have anything more, laddie." I guess Maxie thought I was a little drunker than I did. He looked at me with real concern. After I didn't answer, he asked, "What ya goin' to do, Jamie, lad?"

"You like the bum, huh?" I asked.

"Yeah, seems like a regular guy, an' aren't you two friends?"

"Yeah, I guess we were. Good friends. Real good friends, until this happened. That's going to sour our relationship." I looked at Maxie. "How about some food and coffee? Say, a burger, slightly well done, with onions and ketchup and some fries."

"You got it. Stayin' for the music?" Maxie asked, beaming again.

"Yeah, I just might. Is Emily coming tonight?" Emily Ross was a sultry jazz singer who sometimes stopped by and joined the trio for a few tunes. She was a real looker and held my interest for reasons entirely unrelated to music. She was a great singer, too.

"Don't know. I told her the band would be in tonight."

Maxie took a few steps away then turned back to give me a wink.

Maxie usually ended up losing a few tables to make room for the trio, and if there was a singer like Emily, the tables got real crowded, as everyone loved to hear Emily Ross sing the torchlight jazz tunes. The tavern generally ended up with standing room only and much longer bar bills.

Maxie's layout is such that the actual bar is located on the left side of the joint as you walk in. Six booths run along the far left wall up to the bar's imposing mass. The bar itself is worn, dark mahogany and sports a brass foot and handrail. When Maxie redid the space, he found this old bar in a secondhand kitchen equipment store in Queens and refurbished it himself. My booth is perched just behind the bend in the bar as it heads toward the kitchen. On the right side of the tavern, tables crowd a narrow aisle that leads to the massive bar. A space was set-aside for combos to set up for their gigs at the right rear of the joint.

After devouring my burger and downing a few cups of coffee, the band began serving up light jazz. I was watching the front door when Emily flowed in through the smoky blue haze. She was dressed in a full-length maroon dress that hugged her body like my Jag hugs the road. She had long, dark brown hair that fell behind her shoulders and ran toward the small of her back. A couple of guys fell out of their chairs, staring, as she wound her way to my booth. I saw envy in male faces as they watched her move into the seat across from me. The female clientele pulled out their little mirrors to check their make up as Emily walked by. With swift and well-placed kicks, the ladies struggled to refocus their dates' attention to the business at hand—them.

"Hi, Jamie. Long time no see," she said in a breathy voice.

"You are a sight for sore eyes, doll. What brings you to my neighborhood?" I am a real natural with words.

"I was hoping you were here. Do you still call this bar your office?" She made air-quotes around the word.

"Yeah. Can't afford rent yet."

Emily actually had permanent work as a reporter for a small newspaper in the Village. She wrote the Local Scene section of the paper's Thursday edition, covering major and not-so-major events in and around the Village. She also did some freelancing for other rags in the city, covering the "hip" parts of town. When she wasn't getting ink on her fingers for various papers, she did ghostwriting for some of the classier authors who resided right here in New York City. But what she really loved was singing. She had her own blend of bluesy-jazz with a sultry twist. And the locals loved it.

She smiled at me, and my heart melted. "I was devastated to hear about Clay. Murder?" Her eyebrows knitted. "You are going to prove him innocent, right? That guy and I go way back to our college days. You and I both know he didn't, *he couldn't*, murder anybody."

"Wow, bad news travels fast around here. How'd you hear about it?"

She leaned all the way back in the booth. "A little birdie told me about it. I've got to go warm up and do a few numbers. You goin' to stick around? I want to talk to you about something after my first set."

"For your first set, you better believe it. I'll be here." I stood as Emily left the booth and moved off to meet with the band.

Maxie came by, and I asked him for my briefcase.

"Sure. Where you goin'?" he asked. "Aren't you goin' to listen to Emily sing?"

"Yeah. I told her I'd listen to the first set, but it looks like I still got a murder to solve." I sat back down as the band kicked it up a notch.

I listened to Emily weave through a few old standards that she'd updated to better fit her style. The trio let her voice carry over their instruments, and the effect mesmerized the audience. Emily finished with "I Can Dream, Can't I?" As she sweetly sang, "You'll never be mine, but I can dream, can't I," I thought I saw a tear spill down her cheek. I didn't know if she was thinking of me or Morgan. But I can dream, can't I?

I hated to run out on the dame, but the murder had created a pall over the evening and I had plenty to do.

I grabbed my fedora, threw some bills on the table, and muttered, "Now, where'd I park my Jag?" as I slid out of the booth and left Maxie's through his kitchen.

———✦———

IT WAS NOT TOO LATE TO FIND A QUIET PLACE WITH NO DIS-tractions, so I headed to Harlem and parked around the corner from a less familiar haunt, the Downbeat. It was a great nightclub with plenty of jazz and few people that knew me. From the outside, it looked like a rundown tenement building. Its entrance was about four or five steps down into a cellar. Anyone could tell the place was jumping as the music leaped out of the building, rising and falling with its trumpet players and pianists. On Thursdays, a group of local artists tried to outdo each other by coming up on a small stage and taking command of an instrument, like the piano, bass, guitar or trumpet. Inside, the crowd was gathered in front of the band, dancing in a fog of smoke and the smell of booze and beer. I moved to a table against a far wall that was filled with empty glasses and cocktail napkins. There was no coat or sweater on the chairs. I gambled and sat. I pushed my fedora back on my head and a second later felt a heavy hand land on my shoulder, then watched as a frosted glass of beer found its way to rest in front of me.

"Ain't seen you in quite a while. What brings you to Harlem, man?"

"Just out for some fresh air. Got any?" I heard his quiet chuckle and Yarrow stepped around from behind me and sat in the chair on the other side of the table. "This place is really jumping tonight."

"You got that right. The who's-who's been here o'er the past three days. Art Tatum left the stage about fifteen minutes ago, and the place erupted. It was out of sight, man. He can really tickle the ivory." Yarrow was a big man with a broad set of hands stretched from years of blues playing on the piano. He had a fine ear and a great appreciation for any man with dancing hands on the ebony and ivory. "You don't come here just to listen to the music, man. What's the prob, besides all those bruises and nasty marks on your face? You been straying outside your foxhole again?"

"I'm being led through the murder of a client, and early signs are not what they are supposed to be," I told him. "I don't like being fed crap like this. Someone's fixing the deck."

"So how can I help ya, man?" Yarrow spread his hands, palms up, like a Jewish delicatessen owner trying to explain why his prices went up. A smile crossed his lips. "Sorry," he said. "This must be serious."

"Yeah." I drew a deep breath and continued. "You've heard of the Rumsfeld murder, no doubt." I looked at the nodding Yarrow. "Well, she's the client. Anything you can gather from the street would be welcome, from the smallest whisper on up to the most obvious shout. I think I know who did her in. Just don't know why."

"And that's got you creeped out, right? I'll ask around. How can I reach you?"

"Maybe it would be better the other way around. Let me give you a call in a few days."

"Make it the end of the weekend. Sunday is quiet until about five or so." Yarrow looked around and spotted something that got him a little edgy. "Gotta split, man." And he was gone.

There are not that many folks I would walk into their place of work and ask for help, but Yarrow was a special friend, one that shared a cruel and punishing past with me. A friend that came to my rescue and one that I fought to save. A friendship forged out of bloodshed and war.

I sucked down the beer, put a Jackson on the table, and got up. The small band was rocking to an up-beat version of "Rent Party." There was hardly space on the floor to move, but move they did. The crowd swayed to the rising and falling of the beat and the seduction of the instruments like palm trees rooted too close together in a strong breeze. Shouts were barely audible over the blaring of the trumpets and wails of the saxophones. Sweat mingled with sweat, eyes locked on their partners' like a hunter to a prey. With the thoughts of Emily still fresh in my mind, I watched couples wrap themselves around each other as a prelude to what I am sure they were anticipating at the end of the evening. It was more than I cared to watch, so I made for the door and the cool, quiet night.

IT WAS CHILLY WHEN I STEPPED OUT OF YARROW'S PLACE ONTO

the sidewalk. Chilly and dark. There was a street lamp across the boulevard, but someone had taken the time to douse its light. Dim neon sporadically reflected off the early morning damp concrete from the Downbeat and a few of the closed-up stores, but that was about it. I pulled my collar up on my jacket and tugged my fedora further down on my brow. I stood there for a second, lost in thoughts of faraway places and distant times that had changed my life forever.

It was about this time of day, but without the chill, that I met up with the fellas of the 2nd Marine Division, and it wouldn't be long before we were tested in battle as men, as Marines, *as survivors*. During this first taste of battle, I watched men die while I took a life or two. It was where I met Yarrow and spent the next three and a half days with the man who became a lifelong friend. But that's another story, and a not very pleasant one, either.

FRIDAY

My first stop was at the QuickPic, over on 41st and 3rd. I had to get my negatives and the rest of the photos I had taken for the late Mrs. Rumsfeld. The building, a one-story grey hunk of concrete with a big bay window in the front, had been there at least thirty years, and from the outside, it looked like it could use some refurbishing. Inside was different. Ma and Pa Chiang—that's what I called them, since I had no idea how to pronounce their given Chinese names—had cleaned up the joint and installed a dark room in the back. That's where the quickpic'ing took place.

The front of the store had a table with three chairs around it. When the table was occupied, it gave the illusion the store was busy. The table provided a place for people to look at their photographic genius before ordering the enlargement they wanted, all while overlooking 41st Street. The entrance was on the left side of the store and along that wall was a long counter filled with cameras, lenses, and other equipment. Along the opposite wall were camera bags and inexpensive frames for that successful black and white you just enlarged to put on your wall or give to your sweetheart.

Ma and Pa were born and bred New Yorkers, like me, but had lived with Mrs. Chiang's family north of the island for eighteen years before moving back into the city about five years ago. That is when I first got to know them, right about the time I left the force. They wanted to fit in with the local Anglos, and so they had adopted Anglo-sounding names, like Alice and Bob. But I told them that was demeaning, not that calling them Ma and Pa wasn't.

The Chiangs and I swapped deals a while back, and I

called in a favor on the Rumsfeld case, getting them to turn two quick developments for me. The first were the photos O'Malley found in the boot of my Jag. The other was the complete roll of film I left with them with instructions to develop another copy of the ones I originally took to Mrs. R's house. I'd figured my client wouldn't want to give back the mattes I'd have given her had she been alive.

I was at the QP about the time they opened, and seeing me come in, Pa Chiang went to retrieve the photos and negatives.

"That'll be six dollars for the job," Ma Chiang told me. "You want it on account, or can you pay up now?"

"I got the six dollars, but if I give it to ya, I won't be able to eat much for dinner. Can you wait 'til I collect from my client? Say two weeks?" Delving into how I was going to collect from a dead client and through such a jackleg lawyer would have sent the Chiang's over the edge and forced me to pay up front, before I got the photos. Don't get me wrong, the Chiang's are nice enough folks, just not all that trusting in others.

"Ya, sure. We can wait, but no more than two weeks, okay?" she replied as her husband arrived with the photos.

"Deal." I extended my hand for the oversized envelope.

Moving to the table, I sat on the stool against a wall. I get nervous when someone can sneak up on me. I spilled the contents on the table, looking for something I might have missed. There were seven photos in all, two copies of what O'Malley filched from me, and an additional five I hadn't seen yet. I flipped through the fresh five before I looked at the steamers Joey appropriated from the Jag. The apartment looked like I remembered it. Since the building was a railroad flat, there were basically two apartments on each floor, the one in the front overlooking the street, and one in the back that had a gorgeous view of the alley. Rumsfeld was lucky. He got not only the girl, but access to the street-view apartment. Boy, this brought back the memories. And that really was some zoom lens I had. A couple photos in, the blonde minx had already lost her blouse and bra, and based on the look in ole Vernon's eyes, he was clearly interested.

By the time I got to the fourth photo, I noticed some interesting shadows that got me wondering if there might be other rooms I hadn't accounted for. When I turned to the last of the newer shots, I wrenched my gaze from the pair's interesting position and noticed that, sure enough, there was a door partially open. A second bedroom? Maybe a bathroom? Made sense, didn't Rachael say *there were two of them in the apartment*?

"Nice pictures, Mr. D." Pa Chiang came over and smiled like the lecherous old man he was. I was staring at the shadows, and Pa had his eyes on the blonde's alabaster breasts. As revealing as the photos were, they did not do her justice.

Ma came up from behind and whacked him with a fly swatter she used to control the pest infiltration. "You get back to work. Don't interrupt Mr. Dugan. Those photographs are no good for you! I should have never let you develop them." English turned to Chinese, and Pa Chiang hung his head and fled to the storeroom under a storm of swats and the continued berating of Ma Chiang.

"Goodbye, Mr. Dugan," Pa Chiang said in a sad voice, loud enough for me to hear as he ducked off.

"Yeah, right. See ya later." My voice drifted off as I considered the possibilities of the second bedroom. *Just how many people lived in the apartment? Rachel did say there were at least two, right? And, was it Amanda Morgan in that compromising position? I had no idea what she looked like. Clay, yes, I knew him, but Amanda? I had never laid eyes on her. Was she blonde sort of like Clay and...* There came a tapping at the bay window of the QuickPic that interrupted my mental image of the beautiful blonde as Clay's sister.

Tap, tap, tap. There it was again. I heard some murmuring through the glass and looked up to see Matt Dingle standing on the street, motioning me to come outside. I stuffed the pictures back into the envelope, pulled my fedora over my brow, and went out to see what the lieutenant wanted.

"Hey, Dingle, what ya doing over in this neck of the woods?" I asked as I exited the store.

"Something you said keeps nagging at me." Dingle's look was accented with a push back of his fedora and kneaded eyebrows.

"What could I possibly say to a police lieutenant that would leave 'im worried?"

"You asked if I was sure it was Rumsfeld at the apartment the other night, so I went back to the super and found out you'd been there askin' questions, and lo and behold, he confides in me that he'd seen Rumsfeld leaving around two-fifteen that afternoon." Dingle shoots me an all-knowing smile.

"Well, I'll be..." I just let it hang there. This was news to me as well, since the super never said anything about recognizing or seeing Rumsfeld. I enjoyed watching Dingle struggle through the pause, waiting to see what I might surprise him with next.

"That's all you gotta say for yourself, Dugan?"

"Yeah, unless I can come up with something snappier. You got anything else?"

"We tracked down the Rumsfeld lawyer, and apparently you've been there as well." Dingle's look got more serious.

"What did he have ta say?"

"He didn't know Mrs. Rumsfeld was dead until you told him. Said you were some kind of cop and showed him a badge. Please tell me you turned your badge into the precinct when I asked you to."

I waved away Dingle's concerns and asked, "What did ya say that lawyer's name is?"

"Enough playing coy," Dingle said, starting to get serious. He pulled his hat toward his eyes. "Who else did you call on, Dugan?"

"That's about it. How is our Southern reporter friend, anyway?" I smiled and shifted the envelope to the other hand.

"Looks like we're gonna release him soon."

"I think the guy is clean, too," I said.

"That's what we came up with. Zilch. Apparently, he was in a downtown apartment when the crime was committed, and as you told him, it was a tough night for getting around. We're still checkin' out a few other leads, so he should be released either later this PM or tomorrow."

"That's good to hear. Well, gotta go." I turned to leave, but Dingle grabbed my arm. "What ya got there? More photos?" If Dingle hadn't noticed the envelope before, he had zeroed in on it now.

"Yeah, but for another case. You'd be surprised how much infidelity is going around our fair city these days. Give my regards to Clay." I shifted my fedora and turned to walk away.

"You take care, Dugan. Rumor has it someone is looking for you. Apparently, you are raising eyebrows with your prying. And Dugan, if you still have your badge, turn it in before you get arrested for impersonating an officer." Dingle grinned, doffed his hat, turned, and walked away.

I made my way back to my Jag. This time, I pushed the pics

under the cushions on the passenger side, just below the springs. "Let's see if anyone can find these," I murmured to myself.

I THOUGHT ABOUT GOING UP TO THE MORGAN APARTMENT on 78th, but it was too early. Amanda Morgan wouldn't be home until after six. So I turned the Jag downtown, toward the financial district and the Baker Building on Pine Street. It sometimes took a long time getting to the financial district with traffic and all, so I took the quickest way that I could think of, down the FDR. The traffic was typical for a New York Friday, and I got to Pine by eleven-fifteen. I hate parking in garages, but at this time of day, I had no choice. The one I selected left me five blocks from my destination, and I walked in the front door about eleven-forty. From there it wasn't hard to find Vernon Rumsfeld's office; all the floor marshals knew where it was. I didn't know if he was in or not, and no one else seemed to know, either. I decided since I was there and paying for parking, I would roll the dice and see.

The building was about fifty years old, and the lobby was cramped. There were three banks of elevators, each servicing its own set of floors. Off to the side of the lobby was a shoe-shine man with his stand next to a deli that served early lunch to workers in the building. He beckoned me over for a shine, but I waved him off and headed for the elevators instead.

Rumsfeld had his office on the twenty-seventh floor. It was a sweet location with a great view of the crowded down-town skyline. I came in through an outer office where his secretary usually sat, though it now was vacant. It was pan-eled in oak, to my untrained eye, and the carpets were short napped in an off-white color. The door to Rumsfeld's office

77

was ajar. I took off my fedora and moved from the outer office toward the inner-sanctum of the Baker Building manager.

I had forgotten Rumsfeld didn't know me, although by then, I felt like I knew him quite well, maybe to an uncomfortable degree.

"Yes?" Rumsfeld looked up from his desk. He wore a dark gray suit and a white shirt with a loud red power tie. His clothes said work, but his face said something else. It looked like he had aged twenty years. His cheeks were ashen and the bags under his eyes didn't help his look. Even his mustache was a little grayer. It was either the loss of his wife, which I had trouble believing, or something else was eating him up.

"Mr. Rumsfeld, the name's Dugan, Jamie Dugan. I'm a PI. Your wife hired me a while back. I'd like to talk with you for a minute." I approached his oversized desk. Made me wonder if he was over-compensating for something.

Rumsfeld eased the glasses off his face and stared. He stood as I approached his desk and sized me up.

We measured each other for a minute. He looked like he belonged in the financial district. He was slightly stooped, like a CPA, and had un-callused hands with well-manicured fingers. I bet he got them treated, or whatever they do to fingers these days, at least weekly. His body looked as though it was made to sit. I doubt he ever handled a shovel or hoe. But he looked just like the man I spied with my zoom lens.

"What do you want, Mr. Dugan? Is this some kind of shake down?"

"No," I said, moving to a chair. "I wanted to meet you and ask a few questions. You see, a friend of mine is being held for your wife's murder. I don't think he did it."

"Oh, that's too bad. What you want me to do about it, bust him out?" The sarcasm dripped from his words like honey, only it wasn't sweet to my ears.

"Naw, I think you could buy his way out, but break him out? I doubt it," I said. "I do think you know something that might help find the real killer or killers."

"Who do you think did it, Mr. Dugan?" Rumsfeld reclined in his chair.

"There are plenty of suspects. You, for one. You had time and, apparently, motivation. Your little love triangle with your wife and that blonde bombshell would be a real motivator."

"How do you know about Miss Somers?" Rumsfeld asked, blurting her name.

"Your wife hired me to follow you and see what you were up to. Apparently, Mr. Rumsfeld, she didn't trust you, and for good reason, I might add," I said calmly.

"So that's where the cops got the photos of me and Mary Jane. I should have realized someone like you would turn them over to the police, Mr. Dugan."

"She's quite the number. You ought to be proud. How'd you two meet?"

"I already told the cops everything. Why don't you ask them?"

"I could do that, but I'd probably misread their information and jump to the wrong conclusion. That's one thing I would prefer not to do. It's always better to get your answers straight from the horse's mouth." I tried to sound like I wanted to believe anything he might tell me, in hopes that he would open up. I didn't expect him to spill his guts, but out it came. I felt like the good Father in a confessional, but I didn't know if it was fact or fiction.

"It was purely by chance." Rumsfeld got out of his chair with an air of resignation and moved from behind his desk to a large bookshelf. It looked custom made for the space. He opened the center door to reveal a built-in bar, complete with a sink and refrigerator, and pulled out two glasses and a bottle of scotch. He lifted the scotch in my direction, and I shook my head. Hell, it wasn't even noon, and I hadn't checked the track sheets yet for Saturday's races. There is a certain level of sobriety required in selecting the day's winner.

He continued. "I usually lunch at a small deli not far from here, and in she came one day and literally knocked me over." Rumsfeld chuckled as he recalled the event. After the collision, he said, she helped him up and offered to buy him an "I'm-so-sorry" drink at a pub overlooking the East River. A few days later, they shared a hotel room in SoHo. All that was about a month ago. Rumsfeld began to get nervous about seeing her, but she persisted. She finally convinced him to come to her apartment for the afternoon, that Wednesday when his wife was taken out, to put it callously.

"That was the day before yesterday, the day Eloise was killed," Rumsfeld said. "She begged me to come up to her place. You know where it is." I nodded. "I got there around ten AM and stayed for some of the afternoon. After that, I drove back to my office. That time with Ms. Somers really put me behind. I had to reschedule a tour of the building for a possible tenant."

"You mean this building?"

"Yes. Eloise owns the building, but I am the property manager. We had lost a really solid tenant when they moved their operations to Delaware. That left the building less than sixty-five percent rented. We don't turn a decent profit until we go over seventy-eight percent occupancy, so I was eager to lease to this prospect. He wanted about half a floor and I just happened to have the space available." Rumsfeld looked almost giddy with his alibi.

"Miss Somers must have made quite a case for you to leave your office and drive all the way up to 78th Street," I said.

Rumsfeld blushed, coughed, and continued, "Just about the time Ms. Somers started getting rid of the lunch left-overs, in comes this guy, Clay Morgan. He starts carrying on, asking who I was and what was I doing in his apartment. Mary Jane retreated to a bedroom. I kinda lost track of her. She had originally asked me to stay 'til about five and go out for an early dinner, but I couldn't do that. She had told me it was her apartment, so Morgan's entry was a surprise. When he arrived and started fuming, I got out as quickly as I could before things got out of hand, and raced back down to Pine. That's the truth." He turned and looked at me after he spewed out his alibi.

"So what time did you actually leave the apartment?"

"You were watching. Don't you know?"

"I figured it was about three or so. That makes for a late lunch." I was fishing since I had gone for a bite about the time he was saying he left—plenty of time to commit the crime.

"No, it was closer to four-thirty. I'd had one of my employees pick up my car so I had to take a cab back downtown."

Warning bells went off. Why would he have an employee pick up his car while he was having an affair?

"Do you think her meeting you was an accident? The initial meeting at the deli, I mean."

"You make it sound like it was on purpose." At least I got a rise out of the creep.

"A set-up, yeah." I kept probing, mainly because I didn't believe him. It's said that the best lie is wrapped in a grain of truth, and I had a feeling that I had been fed the grain along with a shovel full of BS.

"Well, she's very good, if it was just a pick up." He seemed deflated. It looked like Rumsfeld had run out of gas as he sank into a chair on the other side of his desk. He was either a good actor or I was missing something. I waited while he took a long pull on his scotch.

"When did you get home?" I asked.

"Around eleven-thirty PM. The client and I went for drinks and a bite to eat after I gave them the tour and we negotiated the rent. By the time I arrived home, there were police waiting for me at the front door. When they gave me the news, I was shocked. I still am." He downed his glass and made for the bottle again. Once his drink was refilled, he came back to his seat.

"Didn't the cops try to contact you at your office before you got home?" I asked, remembering what Dingle told me when the body was first discovered.

Rumsfeld stared at his drink for a minute. "Yeah, that might be true. I really can't remember. It was all such a shock." He let out a long sigh.

"At least you have an alibi for the time of your wife's death." I was getting edgy, watching the way he consumed whiskey. *If he killed his wife over a building, one apparently just breaking even, and with just a few drinks in him, what else might he do? And to think it was not even lunchtime yet.* The day was still young, I reminded myself.

"Did you and Mrs. Rumsfeld have any children?"

"No. Why do you ask?" Rumsfeld seemed to be battling multiple demons—whiskey, death, an affair, and accusations. He looked at me with sad eyes and shook his head. "Actually, Eloise never talked of it, but she had a daughter with her first husband. He had sole custody. It was a real sore point for her. That girl would be nineteen or twenty about now."

"Who was Mrs. Rumsfeld married to back then?" I was

beginning to wear on Rumsfeld, and my time was running out.

"You're some PI. Don't you know?" Rumsfeld swirled the booze around in his glass and looked up at me.

"I'd just like to hear it from you," I tipped my hat in his direction. Hell, much of this information was news to me. First his wife owned the building and now I learn the blond is not Amanda Morgan. *How am I going to keep all the players straight?* I thought to myself. I reached into my coat pocket and pulled out a small black covered notebook to write down some of the items I learned. No pen. Rats.

"Mind?" I asked as I reached on to Rumsfeld's desk for a pen within reach.

He just smiled and shook his head. "Help your self." He made no move to help or hinder.

"Clive Montfort, a Wall Street financier. A real bastard, from what I've heard." Rumsfeld's voice turned monotone, like all his emotions had been drained. He looked at me, as if he realized he left his car running or the refrigerator door open.

"I'll get out of your hair real quick. The police found some men's clothing and toiletries in your wife's bedroom the night of her death. Was she having an affair that you were aware of?"

"No. The police asked me that same question. I don't think she was, but I guess we really never know anybody, even after years of marriage. Passion wasn't Eloise's defining characteristic, if you know what I mean. I never thought she would take a lover."

"What was her defining characteristic, Mr. Rumsfeld?"

"Money management. She knew how to make and retain wealth. She was a Depression survivor, Mr. Dugan. A real survivor. Any more questions?" He opened his hands, like he was going to offer me the deal of a lifetime.

"Yeah. Did all the partners in your consortium really die, giving you sole ownership of this building before it was foreclosed on?" It was the wrong time, but the question had to be asked.

"That is public information, Mr. Dugan. You can look it up if you like." Anger began to seep into his eyes and jaw. It was time to leave.

"Thanks. If I think of anything else, I'll let you know." I got up and took in the scene. It all looked so nice. Vernon Rumsfeld behind that big, clean desk that had maybe one or two measly pieces of paper on it. Then I remembered the sheet I lifted from his desk at their home. Rents. "How has business been, Mr. Rumsfeld?"

"Huh?" He looked at me and stuttered, "Fine, just fine. Now if you don't mind, I'd like to get back to work. Can you see yourself out?"

I took five steps toward the door then he stopped me.

"Mr. Dugan, if you wouldn't mind, I would like to have your assurances that you'll destroy any photographs you have featuring Ms. Somers and me. I wouldn't want to have to sue you for ~~liable~~ libel or slander. Do you understand?"

"I'll just hold them for a while. There might be a demand for them by the NYPD," I answered, and then I turned on my heel and walked out. Something deep down inside of me said he was withholding a big chunk of story.

I was in deep thought, digesting the latest information as I walked back to the parking garage. That comment about Eloise's lack of passion echoed what Mrs. R said about him during my last meeting with her. She said he "lacked passion" toward her. There was a mismatch somewhere. *What did Eloise Rumsfeld really want me to find out while shadowing her husband? Could the romance have been as fresh as Vernon indicated? And who is this Rachel, anyway? Could she be another lost soul in the city or the woman I met from the apartment above Amanda Morgan's? Naw, that would be too easy.*

I pulled out into the street, questions thick in my mind, and headed back to my office.

As I glided in and out of traffic on my way to Maxie's, I thought about when Eloise Rumsfeld first approached me about taking the case. I was sitting in Maxie's on a slow day, checking out the fifth race at Aqueduct while running up my tab with another beer.

She was attractive in a mature kinda way. At first glance, it was clear she had some mileage on her, but with good maintenance, she didn't look a day over forty-five. She had on a red, knee-length spring coat. The hem of her black dress hung just below it. Black leather gloves and a black felt hat with broad brim and a short black veil rounded out the outfit. The hat was tilted to one side, obscuring an eye. She must have been a knockout in her day.

"You are Mr. Jamie Dugan, are you not?" She had a stern tone and a satiny voice.

"Yeah, uh, yes, that would be me. What can I do for ya?"

She slid into my office-booth and removed her gloves. I removed my fedora and watched. The gloves are off, whoever she is after, I thought.

"My name is Eloise Rumsfeld, Mr. Dugan. I feel strange coming to you like this. I tried to reach you before just showing up, but you're a hard man to contact."

"Sorry about that. My work schedule can make it difficult

to pin me down. Well, you found me." I gave her my best reassuring look.

"I have a feeling my husband is having an affair," she said in a hushed voice as she gazed around the room. "And I would like to know about it. Who she is. Where she lives. That sort of thing."

"Why do you think he's cheatin' on ya?" I asked. But let me tell you, when the suspicion is there, I've come to learn, the fella or lady is stepping out ninety-nine times out of a hundred. Nowadays, it seems everyone is getting extra on the side.

"It's a sense. It's like he's gone numb." She got lost in her thoughts for a second and then came back to our conversation.

"When we were first married, Mr. Rumsfeld made a real effort to be home on time." Her face grew more serious as she leaned toward me. "He always showed me attention and affection. Now I'm lucky if I see or hear from him during the day. Even on the weekends, he is running out some place." Once again, she scanned the faces of the other customers and the bar workers. When she looked back at me, I nodded that I got her drift. "He even moved into the guest room. Privacy, he said. He wanted his privacy. Ha!"

"It started about two months ago. I sensed it immediately." There was a pause as she gathered herself. "I know there's another woman, and I want you to find her!" She was agitated, like a storm was blowing in.

"What's the real reason, Mrs. Rumsfeld? Why do you really want me to watch your husband?"

"What are you talking about? I know he is having an affair. I want you to catch him in the act and give me the name of the woman. Is that so hard, Mr. Dugan?" Her voice got louder as she finished her sentence. Her temples bulged and cheeks reddened.

"Okay, have it your way. How did you get my name, anyway?" I usually get referrals from either a client or someone who knew one of my jobs.

"You came highly recommended from a friend, who would rather not be mentioned." She took a long breath and composed herself. "I will pay you well, Mr. Dugan. Here's a thousand dollars. It should cover the first week, at least." She pushed an envelope across the table.

I sat there, staring at the envelope, not moving a muscle to retrieve it. "That's a lot of money. How do you know I'll deliver?"

"My source says you'll get the job done and that you're a man of your word, an unusual quality in this town. Will you take the job?"

Okay, so I had about ten bucks to my name and no jobs lined up. Maxie was breathing down my neck to pay my tab, and the Jag was dented and needed a tune-up. It seemed like an easy enough task—take the pics and give them to the dame. What was there to lose?

"Yeah, okay." I took the money. "But what you'll get are photos. A name and address, if I can get them, will be my bonus to you."

"No," she said. "I want all of it. Her name, where she lives, and whoever put her up to this—I want that person's name and address, too." She was used to ordering people around, and I was tiring of her attitude.

More often than not, these cases usually ended up at seedy motels with a Mr. and Mrs. John Doe at the register for a name. No real names. No real addresses. I really didn't like infidelity-tracker work and was tempted to walk away from this one. "If you want a complete background check on the floozy your husband is running around with, you can contact the police. That's their specialty. I can even give you references and contacts."

Mrs. Rumsfeld persisted. "I am sure you can figure out what the lady's name is with some digging around. I'll give you a bonus. Let's say two hundred and fifty dollars for the name and another two-fifty for the address. There's more if others are involved and you can uncover them. Of course, with names and addresses, say an additional $500 apiece. Agreed?"

"I'm on your case, but we'll have to see about those bonuses. I can give you a report in a week and see where you want to go from there. First I need a photo of your husband, where he works, and a sample of his routine, as best you know it."

She looked at me, trying to decide if the compromise I offered was acceptable then nodded. "Okay, we'll try it your way, but I really want the name, so try to deliver as much of the package as possible."

Eloise rummaged through her purse and pulled out a framed photo of a dapper-looking guy. He was about fifty-five, with a full head of neatly combed graying hair and a well-salted pencil thin mustache. His pipe was clenched tightly between his teeth, and although he didn't wear glasses in the photo, there were creases from where the frame's temples ran up to the one ear that showed. He wore a three-piece suit with a diamond tiepin. Classy, real classy kind of guy. I wondered *if just oozed into that three-piece or it was standard apparel. He* *wasn't wearing one today*, that's for sure. She took the photo out of the frame and handed it to me. After looking it over for a few seconds, I pocketed it.

"In case this job drags on longer than we figure, I charge two hundred a day plus expenses. A day is eight hours of work. If I go over, I charge overtime. If I don't, I'll give a pro rata rate, which is a percentage of the…"

"I know what pro rata means, Mr. Dugan. Your rates are fine." She closed her purse and looked around Maxie's one more time. Her gaze settled on Maxie, and I wondered if she was giving him the eye or if she was fixed on something else.

"Mr. Rumsfeld has his office at the Baker Building on Pine Street. He usually leaves the house around eight-thirty in the morning and gets home about six. He must eat lunch downtown somewhere, but I am afraid I do not know his schedule when he is at work. Lately, he has been coming home around nine. He calls me most afternoons to claim he has to work late. He manages the Baker Building, among other things. Right now, he is working to fill some vacancies that occurred over the last four to six months."

"Where do you live, Mrs. Rumsfeld?"

"Why do you need to know, Mr. Dugan?"

"Might have to follow him to or from home."

She nodded. "In Chelsea, near 23rd and Second." She gave me the brownstone's street number. "When may I expect to hear from you again, Mr. Dugan?"

"As I mentioned, in about a week," I reminded her. "Shall I just stop by your house or give you a call?"

"Here is our home number, but please respect the delicate nature of my inquiry and limit your calls from nine AM to three PM. And please, try to ensure that Vernon is out of the house before you call." She inched out of my office-booth. "Good day, Mr. Dugan. I look forward to hearing from you in the near future." She turned, put her gloves back on, and disappeared through Maxie's front door.

It was getting on toward evening, and there was a tide change in the city. Millions who worked in the city were trying to leave for a weekend out of town, and those intent on visiting were trying to get in. New York was one big traffic jam. The good part was that the change momentarily left a few parking spaces open for the Jag, and I took advantage. I found a spot behind another gin joint about four blocks away from Maxie's. By the time I got to my office—ah, Maxie's—it was almost three PM.

"You know, Maxie, I'm thinkin' of looking for an office. Not that you haven't got a classy place, but I was thinking that I need my own space. You know what I mean? One that comes with a parking space for the Jag." I was sitting up at the bar, letting my feet dangle, when the phone rang. Maxie picked it up, said, "Uh-huh" a few times, and handed it to me, shrugging.

"Yeah? Dugan here."

"Dugan, I want ya to listen and listen good." It was a gruff, familiar sounding voice on the other end. I'm real good with voices. I hear them all the time.

"Yeah, you got a name?"

"Never mind that. You back off and back off now. Stop nosin' around the Rumsfeld dame's death. Capisci? If you don't, and I know you probably won't, things will start happening that ain't so good for your health, if you know what I mean. And don't go thinkin' you can disappear; I know you, what you drive, where you hang out, and who your friends are. This is your first and last warning."

Then "click" and a dial tone. The first name that came to mind was Rocky. Followed by a second, DeNato.

Before the Jaguar, before the card game, I knew Rocky DeNato. I saw him rise up as a two-time hood, going from purse snatching to armed robbery to murder. He was really good at it, too. Dingle and I tried to nail him on one thing or another, but his lawyers always found an out for him. One time we had ourselves an eyewitness to a murder he committed, and he sat across from me in the interview room just as cool as a cucumber. That night, we took our witness to a safe house in Connecticut and stationed two guards around the house and one inside. The next morning, the witness and the guard inside the house were dead and the other two guards were missing. We never found their bodies. I couldn't figure if they sold out the witness and fled to a warmer location or met their ends, too.

The weird thing about DeNato was that he was not part of one of the New York mobs. He held himself in higher esteem. I thought one day that would get him killed, that the mob would come looking for him and end his career for us. Instead, he became a hired gun available to the highest bidder and stayed out of the mob's way. I hadn't heard from him for a while and figured he was doing small-time stuff with the sewer rats. But now it sounded like he was running with the big dogs.

Eloise Rumsfeld's murder was in a class by itself. She was a wealthy dame with plenty of sway. People looked out for her interests, at least up until a few nights ago. Rocky DeNato was in on this murder in some way. How, I wasn't sure, but I felt it in my bones. I knew he wasn't bluffing, but I was in this hand all the way.

"You need to find someone to screen our calls, Maxie," I said as I handed back the receiver.

"Who was that, Jamie?" Maxie asked.

"Some hood trying to scare me off this case. I'm beginning to think I might be getting close to something." I pushed my fedora back and scratched my head. "Hey, Maxie, did you ever think of putting one of those television sets behind the bar so customers can watch a game or news on it? I hear the Yankees are having a great spring training."

"Huh?"

"Ah, forget it. It was just an idea." I slid off the stool and made for the door.

I WAS BEGINNING TO FEEL LIKE A RESIDENT OF THE APARTMENT building on 78th. I found a parking place about a block away and metered the Jag. I turned my left wrist to look at my watch, but realized I still hadn't found it. *I've got to find my watch or get another.* I knew it was late in the afternoon, almost time for the early eaters to sit down to dinner. Foot traffic had picked up on Second Avenue, and the aroma of various blue-plate specials filled the air. I just needed it to be after six PM so I could try to catch the residents in the apartment. Well, Amanda Morgan needed to be in, for starters.

I crossed the street and hesitated, trying to time it so I could follow someone with a key into the building. Once inside, I headed to the apartment on the second floor and knocked. This time, I got an answer.

The door opened, and an attractive brunette stood in front of me. She wore matching gray plaid skirt and jacket, just like she was home from the office. And if she wasn't cute enough standing there in her stocking feet with a cocktail in her hand, the sultry look on her face said *come on in* but not in a nice way, more like a challenge. She was kind of short, about five-five or so, with a real nice figure. Sultry soon turned to puzzlement as she uttered, "Yes?" I suspected she thought I was someone else knocking at her door.

"Evening, ma'am. My name is Jamie Dugan." I held my badge at my side. I decided not to play that card unless it was actually needed.

"You're the one who framed my brother!" She started to slam the door in my face, but I got the toe of my shoe between the door and the jam. *What happened to sultry and inviting?*

"Brother?"

She had no southern drawl, and any similarity between Clay and her was undetectable. She was quite attractive, and Clay? Well, Clay was Clay.

Now, I've known Clay Morgan for quite a while now, for at least a year or so after he moved to the city. That'd be four or five years now. We met not long after I left the force; he wanted to do an interview with me to expose misconduct by anyone on the force that I might have a grudge with. After we sat down and had a beer or two, I realized he was trying to land a job at a local rag and they were looking for all the dirt they could get on the in-town PD.

Clay wandered the streets looking for human-interest and crime stories. Murder was not his cup of tea. He preferred the cerebral kind of crime—you know, the kind where someone thought about what they were trying to do and then left some dumb telltale sign that got him, Clay, sniffing in the right direction. Embezzling, extortion, some racketeering, even limited mob activity. He usually left the mob stuff to the cops for fear of retribution. Apparently, he had had some experience with retribution that helped him decide to leave his hometown and venture to the Big Apple. Typically, Clay did a good and thorough job, which left a few local hoods really sore or heading under the covers for a while, sore and angry from his "insights."

Clay and I got along well, and then we kind of stumbled onto a murder scene and worked out most of the clues, giving them to Dingle. Dingle got credit for the collar, Clay got his story posted in the morning newspaper he was working for, and my relationship with O'Malley began to go south. Clay and I became real chums after that, but he never confided in me that he had a sister, and a cute one at that. Right now, I was feeling bad about Clay being run in and spending a night on the city.

"Aw, come on, lady. I'm working to figure out what really happened. Will ya let me in, please?" I leaned on the door, trying to save my toes.

"Give me one good reason why."

"Vernon Rumsfeld was having an affair with some doll, and they were in this apartment doin' the dance of twenty toes. Apparently, your brother caught whoever was in here doing the rumba with Vernon, and it resulted in an argument. That didn't look very good for him, wouldn't ya say, Miss Morgan?" I hoped my words would have some effect so I could at least get inside the place.

The door slowly eased open, and Amanda Morgan walked into the short entry hall. The apartment was larger than I thought. She led me toward the lounge, or parlor, for those with more than one room in their apartment.

Off to the left was a small dinette, beyond which was a galley kitchen. To the right was a long hallway with three or four doors. My guess was two bedrooms and two baths, with one of the baths in the master, if they were lucky. Dark wooden floors ran throughout the apartment with an occasional throw rug—one in the lounge, one in the dinette area, and a runner down the hall. Amanda must have some job to afford all this square footage. I wondered who had the room at the end of the hall and if they knew what had been going on in there, or who the participants were. I needed some way of opening up the conversation …

When we reached the lounge, I asked, "So, how do you do it?"

"Do what?" She turned and stared at me.

"You must be workin' long hours to pay for this place and keep up with some torrid affair. Maybe he's your sugar-daddy, huh?"

"What?" she almost screamed at me in disbelief. She reeled around, swinging an open-handed slap at my five o'clock shadow. I ducked the incoming palm.

"You know, the affair with Vernon? The married Mister Rumsfeld." I smiled and pushed back my fedora on my head. I wanted a reaction and got it. Now what?

"First of all, and most importantly, I am not carrying on an affair with anyone. I don't know anyone named Vernon Whatever. Second, I work for the circuit court in lower Manhattan, which keeps me very busy. I have no time for such things as an affair with this, this guy." She was spitting mad and working hard to find the right words, but it was not coming out well. I guess I had chosen the wrong tack in getting Amanda to talk to me. After all I had the name of the broad involved. I amazed myself at how I can launch into trouble without really giving it much thought. Now I needed to defuse the bomb I'd lit before it went off and closed our conversation.

"I was tracking some dame, a blonde who met Vernon here. It might have been a rug she wore, and since there are no other dames—ah, ladies—living here…"

95

"Stop. Stop right there. Did you take photos of a blonde woman in this apartment?"

"Wow, that's some leap you made." I thought I had said "tracking." Tracking was the operative word here up until the photo thing came up. I swallowed. "But yeah, I took a few photos for my client, Vernon's wife. I'll show you later, if you're interested. The camera angle did not give me the full face of the doll, but at first glance, with a blonde wig, it might be you."

"Well! There are two tenants living here, as of the end of the month. It coulda been—" She stopped for a second and then continued. "Anyone who's got a key to this place could have used it. So, it coulda been any one of a number of people. How do you know it was anyone living here? The super coulda let someone in. Hell, I don't know."

"Ma'am, if the shoe fits, wear it. He was here, in this apartment, with some blonde broad, and she lived here, trust me. She seemed plenty comfortable with the layout."

"You were watching? You're some kind of pervert. I'm going to have to ask you to leave, Mr. Dugan." Amanda folded her arms and stared at me.

"Let's call a truce, okay? I'm sorry for barging in here and accusing you right off the bat. Bad form on my part. I am not a pervert. I snapped a few pics after I determined it was the husband and tried to get a facial of the lady for future ID. I didn't get it. Truce?"

Amanda looked at the floor and then nodded.

"So you got a roommate, ah, another dame living here?"

"I needed to take on some boarders to cover the rent since Clay lost his job and he can no longer pay his share." She caught her breath. "Tell me again, Mr. PI, how you go about detecting. My brother is really up the creek if he is relying on you to sort things out. He could be in jail for a long time."

"Did he move out or was he pushed?" I asked, annoyed I didn't already know the answer. I hated to admit it, but it had been about two or three months since I had last seen Clay. Then he called, and Dingle and O'Malley hauled him away.

"He moved on his own accord about two or three weeks ago. I think he moved in with some reporter he used to work with." Amanda looked around the room. "I wish I hadn't asked him to go, but I was desperate for a roommate who could help make the rent, and it was clear Clay wasn't going to. You see, I found this flat and got Clay to co-sign the lease, which made it terrible having to ask him to find another apartment."

"So this other roommate, who is she? Mary Jane Somers, by chance?" I needed some names to help restore my sanity. I was batting zero on my detective work.

"Oh, no, you don't. I'm not getting her involved in whatever you and Clay are into." Amanda stood there defiantly, hands on hips.

Just then, I heard a key in the lock. Amanda let out a sigh, and in walked the blonde from the photo shoot. She took two steps in, threw her coat on the nearest chair, and kicked her shoes into a corner of the entranceway. "What a rugged day this has been. I could really use a glass of—" Then she saw me for the first time. "Hello, there, tough guy. What's with the cuts and bruises? You a cop?"

I'd forgotten I still looked like Dick the Bruiser. I hadn't thought about the cop look, though.

"Nothin' a week of good rest won't cure. What's your name, gorgeous?"

"Who's the lug, Amanda? Did I interrupt something?" The blond gave Amanda a wink.

Amanda sighed. "Mary Jane, this is Jamie Dugan. Mr. Dugan is the private eye who had Clay thrown in jail after his crack detective work."

The room fell silent, which gave me a minute to take in Mary Jane Somers. She stood about five-foot-three in her stocking feet and wore a sleeveless yellow dress that had narrow straps and caressed her body like the hands of the dancers at the Downbeat. The dress hung just below the knees, giving me and Jesus a full view of her calves and ankles. Her lips were painted bright red, focusing my attention on her mouth, and she smelled like you'd expect one of those gorgeous models do, you know, the one's who do advertisements in *Life*. She was a knockout, and I saw why Vernon was so drawn to her. Why she was so drawn to Vernon? I didn't have the answer to that.

"Wait a minute. That wasn't my fault. All the evidence in this case points to your brother. And in a murder case, the cops like holding suspects to keep them from disappearing, as they have a tendency to do." I stood there with my fedora in hand, defending the New York City Police Department. What a strange situation this was becoming.

"Yeah, I'm sure it was planted, whatever it was," Amanda said.

"Well, I got stuff to do, and my feet are killing me," Mary Jane said. "It's nice to meet ya, Mr. Dugan." She gathered up her coat, shoes, and purse and walked toward the hall. She stopped and turned around. "You look familiar. Do I know you?"

"I don't know. Let me think. What's your last name?"

"Somers. Mary Jane Somers."

"You work in this neighborhood?" I asked. I made the mistake of looking at Amanda, who gave me a look that said, *Don't go there. Don't even think about it.*

"No, I actually work down on 34th at Macy's, in the fragrance department. Maybe that's where I've seen you." She turned to go down the hall.

I left it there and nodded. I tried another question before she disappeared. "Is there another tenant living here?"

Mary Jane called back over her shoulder. "No. But there is a young lady who visits us quite a bit from upstairs. What is her name, Amanda? Rachel something or other."

Amanda stood with her back to Mary Jane, staring at me. "That's quite enough, Mr. Dugan. Let's leave our friends out of this, shall we?"

Not hearing Amanda, Mary Jane stopped in front of one of the doors. "Montfort. Rachel Montfort. I knew I would get it sooner or later."

Man, Mary Jane was just loaded with information. I watched Mary Jane unzip her dress, reaching around to her back, as she walked into her room. It made me want to follow her and dig for more clues.

Amanda sighed again and added, "She has been staying upstairs for about a month or more now. We gave her a key to our apartment. She seems so lonely upstairs. It must be terrible. She comes down here from time to time and looks after things for us, like plants."

I looked around the flat to see what kind of plants they had. They were the rare, non-existent kind. Maybe they were in the bedroom.

"She's a great kid. You leave her out of this, okay, Mr. Dugan?" Amanda said. "She's just trying to get through college and doesn't need you getting in her way or causing any problems."

"Yeah, that's her, a real sweet girl," Mary Jane yelled from her room. "Fix yourself a drink. I'll be out and join you in a second." I heard the door close as Mary Jane started to change into something more comfortable. I was so tempted to…

"You've got the information you're after. Please leave," Amanda said.

Bummer, I thought.

"That's a lot of dough for a college kid, Miss Morgan. You know, renting an apartment and all while attending college. How'd she come by that money, if you don't mind my asking?"

"I don't know. Maybe she has a rich daddy." Amanda threw the comment out, but I should have listened and followed the clue. "She mentioned someone that matches your description stopped by not long ago looking for us. That was you, wasn't it?"

"Your brother is being released by the police today or tomorrow. If you see him, tell him to look me up. He knows where my office is." I headed for the door. "And please, tell Ms. Somers I gotta take a rain check."

"Goodbye," Amanda said as I left. I heard relief in her voice. She closed the door behind me and the deadbolt slid into place. I don't think I made a good impression.

"See ya around," I said to no one in particular and tipped my fedora. I took some mental pictures of the apartment's layout and headed back downtown while mulling all the juicy facts I'd just learned.

I DROVE BACK DOWN TO MAXIE'S AND COULDN'T FIND A PARK-ing place, so I circled the block a few times until I found a spot in a back alley behind the same gin joint. It was late when I got back to Maxie's, and I hadn't eaten for some time. Maxie had closed the grill, so I had to settle for a cold sandwich and beer while I pondered where this case was taking me.

"Hey, there, copper." I turned toward the familiar voice and looked into Clay Morgan's blue eyes. He slid into the bench across from me and shouted at Maxie for a beer. "Y'all are buying," he said sliding strands of hair back into place on the top of his brow. He offered me a slight grin and continued, "Well?"

"So the inspector couldn't stand having you around anymore and threw you out, huh?" I waved to Maxie then began finishing my sandwich, all the while watching my friend with one eye. The other was on my food. "Where you been? Cops don't let their perps out after nine."

"Here and there. I really am innocent, you know." It was the look of a friend, a tired and frustrated one, at that.

"Yeah, I know. Someone set you up," I said.

"I had a lot of time to think while cooped up in that cell. For instance, why are both of us involved? Couldn't just be convenience, ya think?"

"I think you are involved for just that reason. Convenience. Someone went through a great deal of work and pressure to put you in the right position to be compromised, shall we say. You're now unemployed, thrown out of your apartment, by your sister of all people, and God knows where you are these nights when you're not being put up by our city. Someone went through a lot of work to get you where he or she wanted you. And me? They're just leading me around like a dog on a false scent. They must think I'm dumb. That was, until I got the call from a DeNato voice over."

"DeNato? How'd he get involved?"

"That's a question I can't answer, but I'm working on it."

Pondering, Morgan said, "I want to find this killer. What can I do? Or do I have to go out on my own?"

"I have two things in mind, and I think you are the right person for the job." Maxie appeared at the table with Clay's beer, and I held up a hand to stop him for a second. "Clay, you need a bite to eat?" He nodded vigorously, while gulping down half of his beer. Maxie just shrugged his shoulders and went off to warm up the flat iron.

Our conversation lasted an hour. I shared it all. Details from the crime scene, the steamers, my conversation with Rumsfeld, my visit to Amanda's. All of it, except the stop at the Downbeat. I didn't want lay all my cards on the table. I have to hold something back; after all, I am the private eye here.

"Tell ole Clay how ya think I can help." A big smile crossed his face as we finished the sandwiches and beer. Maxie smiled from behind the bar and gave me a wink. Everyone was happy again, except me. I was confused by how this case was unraveling.

"Something about my discussion with Rumsfeld didn't sit right. He's passing himself off as an office property manager, saying his wife had all the wealth. I have trouble believing that. I need you to find out what he really does, and look for anything out of the ordinary that may influence his actions in any way. The other thing might be more tricky."

"Yeah? What's that?"

"I need you to dig up whatever you can on those ladies in your old apartment. Also, there's another, younger dame who lives in the same building, see what you can learn about her. A Rachel Montfort." Morgan looked at me kinda funny, so I added, "Yeah, your sister, too, but not too deep, I think she's clean. She's a wacko, like you, but I think innocent. I just need you to dot the 'i,' so to speak."

"You really think I'll find anything on my sister?"

"Don't know yet, but I would like to be sure. I'm most curious about Mary Jane Somers. I did get to meet Rachel Montfort, but only in passing. That last name sounds familiar, but I can't place it, unless …."

"What?" Clay looked at me. "Unless what?"

"Oh, nothing." I tried to wave off Clay's interest in my connecting the pieces of the case. "My mind is trying to make connections that might not be there. After you check on those folks, I might have a theory to share."

"What are you looking for?"

"Anything you can find. How can Somers afford to pay her share of the rent working in Macy's fragrance department? How did she find the rental opening? What did she do before working at Macy's? Who is Rachel Montfort, and what is her connection to Rumsfeld? My gut tells me there's a connection. How'd that dame, a college kid, pony up two month's rent all at once for her own apartment?" I looked at Clay. "I have no idea if your sister is in any of this, but I don't want to leave any information out. If it makes you uncomfortable, I'll find somebody else." I realized that I needed to keep Clay busy doing something before he got himself killed or something. Research and background checks were right up his reporter-ally.

"No, no, no. I understand." Clay held up a hand. "I'll dig around. But I'm here to say Amanda is clean as clean can be. She works for a circuit court, for Christ's sake." Morgan shook his head. "What y'all going to do if I'm doin' all this grunt work?"

"For starters, I'm gonna nose around why you were let go from your last employer. One day you're working, the next you're not, and then Vernon's ladylove swoops into your old apartment room while you're out looking for a meal and a job. Sounds a little too coincidental to me."

"Yeah, I've been thinking about that a lot." Clay's face grew tight, and the muscles on his jaw pulsed. I could hear his teeth grind from across the table. "I've still got a few pals at the paper. I'll ask around, too. I imagine it will be easier for me to find out why the axe flew than you. I'll get back to you on that, as well."

"I have to get a copy of the will, and I doubt Dingle has one to lend me. I have ta go back to Clienfelter's office, anyway. The last time I was there, I forgot to collect my fee for expenses. This case is beginning to eat into my profits." I lifted my fedora to scratch my head and then lowered the grey hat to the bench. "Something else just occurred to me."

"Yeah, what?" Morgan asked.

"When Eloise Rumsfeld hired me, she said her husband had stopped being interested in her physically, and that was one of the telltale signs of his infidelity."

"Yeah, so?"

"Well, Vernon revealed that she was not a passionate woman, if you know what I mean. So who is telling the truth? Vernon has nothing to lose. Why lie?"

"On the other hand," Clay said, "Mrs. Rumsfeld was trying to pique your interest and persuade you to take the case. Maybe they were both convinced the other had gone cold. Or maybe she was lying." Clay looked down at his empty plate then eyed my cold French fries.

"Take them." I motioned to the fries and pushed the plate closer to him. "This thing about physical attraction might explain why Rumsfeld strayed, but doesn't say a thing about the men's clothes or cologne in the missus's bedroom and bath."

I listened to Morgan devour my fries, and another thought occurred to me. "There's somebody else behind this. I just got this feeling. A woman working in Macy's doesn't go to the financial district for lunch on a whim. We find out who's pulling the strings, and we are that much closer to the killer's motives."

"Now you're grasping at straws," Clay said with some exasperation in his voice. "There is no dark underworld lord here, just a plain and simple murder and I think you know who did it. All you need is the why."

I unrolled a twenty, went to the bar, and gave it to Maxie. "This is a start for settling my bill. Keep the change."

"Gee, thanks. Your bill came to twenty-two bucks. You still owe me two dollars."

I peeled off another twenty from the cash Mrs. Rumsfeld gave me.

"Satisfied?" I flashed Maxie a wide grin and left.

CLAY'S TAXI PULLED UP IN FRONT OF THE GREENWICH VILLAGE brownstone. He was headed toward a cozy, two-bedroom flat warmed by Emily Ross's feminine touches. It was an interesting, but not intimate arrangement. Emily had laid down the law on times for bathroom usage and created a regimen for Clay. As much as he hated to admit it, the Rumsfeld case was more than a great distraction, especially if he could make a few bucks off it.

Opening the entry door of the brownstone, Clay relaxed. He gazed up the stairs. In seventeen steps, he would be there, with a place to kick off his shoes, hang his jacket, and take a load off for a while before having to go back out and pull his butt out of the fire.

The apartment door opened into a comfortable but tight

living area. The centerpiece was a gray sofa draped with a maroon afghan. It was "to add color," Emily had said, "and on cold nights, I like to curl up in it while I read." In front of the sofa was an oversized wooden coffee table that Clay figured she'd picked up at a rummage sale. Stacked on the table were a number of manuscripts that Emily had been asked to review or rewrite. Two chairs stood across the table from the sofa, there was a table and lamp in between the chairs. Perched in one of the chairs was Emily, marking up a manuscript. Her red pen glided over the page as she scanned the text, stopping to make a mark here and there, her creative process at work.

Clay closed the door with a thud that surprised Emily, who looked up from her work then turned back to her assignment, trying to collect herself from the intrusion. Clay moved over to the sofa, kicked off his shoes, and removed his jacket. He loosened his tie as Emily continued to work. Realizing it might be several minutes before she finished, Clay rose and got himself a glass of wine from the refrigerator. Clay was not really into this wine stuff; he preferred a good beer or hard liquor, but Emily only had wine on hand, most of it white or this pink crap. He tolerated it just so he could force more alcohol into his body. After Clay consumed a long sip, Emily looked up from her manuscript and sized him up, as if he were a page that needed rewriting.

"Tough day?" she asked.

"You said it." There was exasperation in his voice.

Emily marked her place in the manuscript and closed the document. She reached for a half-finished glass of blush wine that had reached room temperature. After a sip, she made a face and put the glass back down.

"I see Jamie finally got you out of the slammer." Her tone was mild.

"Naw, not really. The cops couldn't find enough to hold me. Dingle inferred that it looked like a frame job." Clay exhaled. "He patted me on the butt and sent me on my way with a warning to stay out of the case." He looked across the room at Emily.

"You and Jamie still looking into the murder or have you heeded Lieutenant Dingle's request?"

"You know Dugan. Once he digs his teeth into something, he won't let go until it's put to rest or he gets beaten into submission." There was a short pause. "Of course, I've never actually seen him beaten into submission, but there's always a first time."

"Clay, don't talk like that. Deep down, Jamie is a caring, sweet guy who gets a little overprotective from time to time, but the big lug is nice."

Emily reached for her wine glass again, forgetting what happened the last time she had a sip.

"Why do you buy this pink piss, Em?"

"Cause I like it." Emily picked up the glass and took a large swallow, trying to hide her distaste for the warmed rosé. "Besides, someone gave me the bottle, so we're drinking for free. Enjoy."

"They must really hate you to give you this." Clay took one more swig and then set the glass down. The two laughed and then lapsed back into silence.

They had met at college in Charleston, South Carolina. They dated for a few months but soon found that, although there was physical attraction and they shared an interest in journalism, they were headed in different directions.

In college, Clay had a nose for trouble and was usually in it, whether he went looking for it or not. He had a wide circle of friends and knew folks from all sides of the tracks. He was well versed on underground politics, and he saw a political set up or power grab through the eyes of those grievously affected, almost invariably the poor. It was only because of his family's position in the city that he was able to prosper, especially early in his career, when he worked for the local newspaper as a street reporter.

Emily was a year behind Clay, and upon graduating, took up a position writing a social column in her hometown newspaper in Summerville, a western suburb of Charleston about fifteen miles away. It didn't pay much, but it afforded her the opportunity to try other things. The paper had a small staff, and she was often forced into writing bits in other sections, such as sports, obits, and town hall meetings. Both Clay and Emily had a knack for putting words to paper. Clay often added a little of his own sweat and blood, but it was Emily that had the real flair for writing.

After their romance went up in flames, they remained good friends, often using each other as sounding boards. Clay was first to move to New York, but Emily followed within six months, after hearing Clay talk about how exciting the "Yankee" city was. There were other reasons for her move. She missed the guy. She hated to admit it, but she still had a soft spot for Clay Morgan, though she couldn't really call it love. More of a physical attraction, and his good looks didn't hurt, either.

"So, where do you two stand on this murder?" she asked.

"I think Dugan knows more than he's telling." Clay was dying to know what Dugan was withholding, but didn't want to press him for it. He gazed at the door, trying to pin the crime on one of the few suspects his mind could conjure up, using the criteria Dugan kept pressing: motive, opportunity, and method. MOM.

He felt Emily eyeing him with uncomfortable interest

and so blurted out a question. "So where did you and Jamie Dugan meet?"

Emily leaned back in her chair to reflect. She reached for her wine and drank, despite the warmth. "We met at Maxie's, of course. I think that's where everything in Jamie's life happens, don't you? I was struggling to make ends meet, and I applied for evening work as a singer. This small group was looking for a voice. Apparently, they had had one or two gigs, and the crowds, although appreciative, were not flocking to hear them. So I hired on for their first show at Maxie's." She paused, seemingly to reminisce about those early days before continuing.

"A few gigs later, we'd begun to develop a following. One night, the band and I were into our third and last set when three hoods came into the bar and began to break things up. The audience scattered, women screaming, guys heading to the hills. Out of nowhere, this guy came up to one hood and flattened him. The leader of the crew had Maxie by his shirt, yelling at him to play ball or else. The second hood turned into an oncoming right cross, and got his nose flattened. The guy walked up to the thug holding Maxie and leveled him with a punch to the kidneys. There he was, Jamie Dugan, standing over the criminal like Superman in the comics, still wearing his fedora. Jamie picked the gangster up and shook him till his gun rattled to the floor. Then he landed a few more punches to his face and stomach until the baddie was nearly unconscious. One of the other two thugs began to stir, but Maxie crowned him with a bottle of whiskey." Emily paused and smiled, remembering Maxie grabbing a bottle, recognizing it as an expensive brand, putting it down, and lifting a cheaper brand's bottle instead.

"Maxie and Jamie dragged the three to the front door

to throw them into the street. I thought it was over until we heard shots. Apparently, two more hoods were waiting in their car next to the curb. I guess they expected to make a quick getaway. They grabbed for their guns as they exited their car, but a witness later said that Jamie dropped the first one with a recovered gun and took out the other hood's knee cap."

Clay was enraptured. "I had heard that there had been problems at Maxie's before, but never imagined—"

"Yeah. Well, when Jamie finished, he brought all five back to the front of the tavern while Maxie called the police. Sergeant O'Malley showed up, and boy, was he mad."

"At who?"

"Dugan! It was as if O'Malley wanted them to succeed in the shakedown. It was fifteen minutes before Dingle showed up. The police eventually took the five down to the precinct. I never did find out what happened to those guys, but Jamie saved the day. He and Maxie apologized to everyone and got us to play an additional set. Drinks on the house. You know, I never heard of another incident like that at Maxie's. After we finished the set, Jamie and I had a drink before he called me a cab. What an evening." Emily sighed.

"I guess Dugan is Maxie's protector, sort of Maxie's muscle." Morgan chuckled, while Emily shook her head.

"He is one tough guy, but he has a soft spot for the underdog."

"He might be the underdog in this case. As best I can see it, he's got his hands full. Mind if I make a few calls? I have some digging to do."

"Go ahead. I've a manuscript to finish." She waved at the small table sitting by the hallway that led to the bedrooms. There was a black rotary phone on the table with a note pad and pencil.

Clay went to the refrigerator, got the bottle of wine and

walked over to the chair where Emily was sitting. Emily picked up her glass and handed it in his direction. He topped it off and said, "Thanks, Em. You really saved my bacon here."

Emily placed her refilled glass on the table next to her chair. Morgan leaned over and placed the moist bottle on the table near her glass. She started to tell Clay to put the bottle up, that it would leave a moisture ring on the table, but before she could get the words out, Clay leaned in closer to her and put his lips on hers. They were warm and soft and she found herself drawn further into his charms. He smelled of a manly musk scent that was intermingled with sweat. Craning her neck further back, she engaged to deepen the kiss and felt his lips part. She responded in kind feeling his breathe gently against her skin. Clay's tongue eased into her mouth and she began to gently suck on it as it slowly moved between her lips and teeth seeking out her tongue.

Clay's hands moved down to her ribcage as he held her then lifted her out of her chair and into his arms. As she rose she could feel Clay's hand move up her ribs to her breast, gently crossing over an erect nipple tightly restrained by her bra. Emily let out a low moan letting her hand reach for his chest.

Finally, Clay came up for air and softly whispered, "Maybe we should take this to somewhere more comfortable."

Emily just nodded as Clay led her back to the bedroom. "What about your calls," she asked suddenly remembering the case.

"They'll have to wait until I've had my way with you," Clay said with a lecherous grin.

Emily smiled, "I like the sound of that."

SATURDAY

I have found that the first stages of investigating a crime are like being in a fog, the kind that envelopes three city blocks. There are no definitions, just a lot of haze. You have to work to give things shape. It's not like the seedy clarity you get when tracking a panderer. Lust leads to big, stupid, Times Square billboard-sized mistakes. Murder, particularly of the premeditated variety, ain't that easy. There's a lot of careful covering up of foot and fingerprints, not quite like trying to frame a guy, but the same difference. But even when the perpetrator tries to hide his crime, there's always evidence, something that links events together like a piece of string through freshly popped popcorn on Christmas Eve. The only problem is finding the evidence before it is destroyed, disposed of, or lost. This means a lot of legwork, usually with many dead ends and a forceful discussion or two with folks unwilling to share their knowledge.

On the positive side of the Rumsfeld case, the list of suspects was getting shorter. But with Clay no longer locked up, and Rumsfeld looking like his alibi might put him in the clear, there were a lot of unanswered questions. Right now, the big question was whether Clienfelter was going to cooperate and pony up a check so I had cash for my surefire winner in the fifth race this afternoon. Of course, I kept asking myself, could I get to the track in time for the fifth race? It was Saturday, and I never missed the fifth race on Saturday, regardless of which track was open. Hell, I've placed bets on fillies running in the fifth in Southern California on a Saturday.

I arrived at Clienfelter's office around nine-thirty Saturday

112

morning to find his secretary sitting behind her desk, probably working on the same piece of gum from the last time I was here. She hardly glanced up from her notepad while her fingers flew over the typewriter. I took the time to read the nameplate on her desk. Delores Young.

"Hi, Delores. Your boss has you workin' weekends? That's a bummer. A looker like you should be taking the time off and sleepin' in. You know, beauty rest and all."

Delores looked up and smiled. "Don't you know it?" She turned back to her typewriter and handwritten notes, trying to find her place.

"Delores, is Mr. Clienfelter in?" I asked cheerfully.

"No. He must be runnin' late. He hasn't called me to let me know when he would be in, but he's expected," the secretary said in her distinguished Brooklyn accent.

"Did he have any appointments this morning that might cause him to run late?" It was worth a shot.

Delores stopped typing again and looked at his calendar. "Nope." She immediately returned to her work.

"Mind if I have a seat and wait a while?"

"Naw, help yourself. There is some coffee two doors down the hall in the break room, if ya want." Delores said as she kept on typing.

I hotfooted down the hall and got myself a cup of joe. I checked the break room for other forms of entertainment and found *The Herald* crossword from the day before. I took it back to the outer office and got comfortable on the worn leather sofa, while Delores made music with her typewriter.

Around eleven-thirty, Clienfelter showed, looking a little frazzled and on edge. He walked through the reception area so fast he almost missed seeing me, but he stopped short. He slowly took his hand off the doorknob, turned, and stared at me, dismay in his eyes. I sat there, deadpan, crossword puzzle still in my hand, unsolved.

"I know you," he said. "You're that Dugan fellow who was here a day or two ago. What the hell do you want now?"

"I had a contract with Mrs. Rumsfeld, which I fulfilled. I am here to get paid. According to my math, she, or her estate, still owes me three hundred dollars. Since she is no longer living, I thought I would collect from you." I got up and took a step toward him. "You are still their lawyer, right?"

"Get the hell out of my office before I call the cops. The real cops. You lied to me. You're not a cop, and I'm not talking to you about nothin'." It wasn't the most irate statement I've heard, but I got his drift. He was a little upset.

"Let's just step into your office for a second." I gently led him into his office by the arm of his coat, giving him a lift when he seemed to slow a bit. I set him down tenderly near his desk, even smoothed out his coat, and then kicked the door closed with my heel. The slam echoed in the outer office and brought his attention back to my face.

"Mr. Clienfelter, I'm a reasonable man, and you seem to be a reasonable guy. Why don't we just sit down and talk this out? I need the three hundred to pay bills and satisfy creditors from this case. And then there's the other thing." I smoothed out the lapels of his jacket, picked some imaginary lint from the shoulder, and helped him sit in his chair. *Gently*, I thought.

"What other thing?" Clienfelter looked nervous.

"We'll get to that." I laid a torn piece of paper borrowed from Maxie's bookkeeping records on Clienfelter's desk. I had scribbled on it, very legit like, to make it legal for the jackleg. "Here's your receipt for the three hundred."

"You can't scare me, Dugan. I know my rights. I'm a lawyer, for God's sake. Why don't you leave before I call the police?" He was shaking, really shaking.

"Let's start with you writing me a check from Mrs. R's estate, and then we can talk about the other thing." With a gentle shove, I helped him sit back a little farther in his chair and took a step back. "Write!" I said, in a not so pleasant voice.

I raised my voice to get him to respond, and it worked. Clienfelter pulled out his checkbook and wrote the check. He handed me the check, which I double-checked and stuffed in my shirt pocket. "Thanks. Now the other thing."

He looked at me nervously, like he expected me to pull a gun or something.

"Relax. Give me a copy of Mrs. R's will, and we'll part friends. Maybe not best friends, but at least we'll be friends." My comments fell on deaf ears.

"No way. You'll have to fight for it in court." Clienfelter's face turned bright red. I figured he could have a coronary any minute.

"Who are you workin' for, Clienfelter? You're not just protecting a client, are ya? Who's the other party?" I must have struck a nerve. Clienfelter's gaze dropped to the floor, and he shook his head. Someone had him more afraid than I did. Not good.

"Okay, then at least tell me who Mrs. R tried to add to her will." I leaned with both my hands on the leather top of the desk. "Give me a name." I raised my voice again. Hell, if it worked once, why not try it again, right?

"Rachel. Rachel Montfort. That's all I know. Really." Clienfelter cowered. "You've got your money, now get out, and stay out of my office!" His voice rose nervously and cracked into a falsetto about an octave above his usual voice, like an alto choirboy testing the upper reaches of his range. His whole body shook with adrenaline.

"Miss Young," he shouted to his secretary. "Call the police. Now!"

I touched my breast pocket, where the check rested, tipped my fedora, and walked out of his office. When I passed Delores's desk, she had the phone to her ear. I tipped my hat in her direction and she looked up with a crooked smile, exposing her teeth and a well-worked piece of gum. I heard Clienfelter's voice in the background as he tried to regain his composure.

"Toodles," I said and left.

RACHEL MONTFORT. THERE WAS THAT NAME AGAIN. IT POPPED up like a bad penny. First at the apartment and now in the will. Nobody at the apartment seemed to know much about her other than she was a college student apparently funded by her mommy and daddy. But the name Montfort rang a bell. I don't run around in classy circles, strange as it may seem, but I do read the paper a lot, sometimes even beyond the racing sheets. So every once in a while, extraneous items get lodged in my brain. I drove toward Maxie's, looking for a place to park again. Nothing. I guess the tide of out-of-town visitors was in. So the Jag found its way to the back of the same gin joint I could never remember the name of. My spot was still available, so I parked and locked up. I might have to leave the Jag here for the weekend, I thought. Nothing like April in New York, at least to a tourist.

The early lunch crowd was flowing out of Maxie's when I arrived. I waved at Maxie and signaled for a cold beer. The temperature outside was on the rise, heading toward seventy degrees, and with the city's humidity, it could be tough in my wool suit. It was only going to get hotter, especially for the rest of the folks involved in this case. Wool in summer—who needs it?

I sat in my booth, wondering how I could reach Clay, when Maxie arrived with my beer. "People been looking for ya, laddie," Maxie said in a hushed tone. "I don't know what ya been doin', but you have them stirred up. Watch yourself."

About ten minutes later, I'd put together a list of things that had piqued my interest:

1. Who is Montfort?

2. What's up with Mary Jane Somers? She sweet on Rumsfeld, or is she gaming him?

3. Clienfelter seemed shaken. Did he come from a scary meeting? With whom? Why so nervous?

4. Vernon Rumsfeld didn't seem bothered about wife's death. He's lying about something. Is his alibi BS? (need to check out further)

"What a wonderful world we live in." Morgan's southern drawl floated across my booth. "Do you realize that someone has invented a machine the size of a room that does mathematical calculations in seconds? Now why would anyone go and do that?" Clay slid in across from me. "I bet these 'computers' can't help you find a winning horse."

"Yeah, but they might improve my odds." I countered with a grin. "I read the newspapers, too, you know. Is that the investigative report for the day, or is there more to come?"

"Oh, you're gonna be tickled pink when you hear the rest I've gleaned today." Clay's face practically lit up the dark recesses of the tavern. "Apparently, Vernon Rumsfeld is not a wealthy man, but has extensive gambling debts. A man after your own heart. His problem is the stock market, not the ponies, though." Clay leaned back in the booth, looking very proud. "Made some terrible miscalculations with his puts and calls."

"Really? You don't say." I pushed my fedora back and leaned forward on my elbows. "Why don't you tell me more on our way to the track? You can start by explaining what those puts and calls are."

Clay and I got up, left Maxie's, and hailed a cab. I thought about driving, but there'd never be a space for the Jag when we got back, and I hate large parking lots; nobody watches what's around them when they open their doors.

We got to the Big A, or Aqueduct Raceway, part way into the fourth race. It was like returning to a shrine. Built in Queens's South Ozone Park in 1894, the structure stood like an old friend, ready to take my money and provide all the heartache I could stand. I loved the smell, especially when my bet was in and I was next to the track watching the horses head for the starting gate. A mixture of freshly raked soil, horse manure, and booze combined to bring my senses alive. When the colors of the silks were added into the equation, it was as close as I could get to heaven—or hell, where I end up when the results come in.

I was able to get to the window to put my bet down before the fifth race started. Then Clay and I headed to a spot just outside the stables in time to see the jockeys adjusting their silks, putting their goggles on their helmets, and watching the finishing touches on saddling the fillies. I waved to a jockey friend, Angel Carbanos. Angel was a different kind of guy. He had changed his name from Richard Mawk to catch the eye of a trainer or two when he first started. He told me that the best riders used names like "Angel"; it helped their mounts fly past the competition and into the winner's circle.

He liked riding for trainer Michael Rubio. And Rubio's horses had been good to me the past three years.

Angel mounted his ride and brought her over to where we were standing. "Hope you picked the right horse, Dugan."

"I'd say I did, but then you might think I had a bundle ridin' on ya." I smiled up at Angel. "Did Mike pick up anything in the claiming race today?" I'm always interested to see if there's a "maiden" that Rubio thinks can break into the big time.

"No, but he got Pistol Whipped claimed away from him." I never did like that gelding.

"Good luck and hope to see you in the winner's circle." I waved to Angel and he led his mount to toward the track and their escort.

"You got him for this race?" Clay asked.

"Naw, that's a nag. Stiletto couldn't find her own rump with both hind hooves. Let's go to the rail and look at the rest of the runners."

We fought our way through the crowd and found an opening three quarters of the way down the homestretch, where we could get a good view of the nags coming out of the turn and thundering past us to the finish line.

We could barely see the horses getting into the gate when I turned to Clay. "You mentioned the Baker Building. Isn't that where Rumsfeld works?"

"He used to own it. Back in 1930 or '31, as best as can be determined, he owned the building outright after sharing ownership with four other fellows. With the Depression, ole Vernon amassed so many debts the Baker ended up getting foreclosed on. Guess who took it over?

"Clive Montfort?" I asked.

"Yeah, and for a song." Clay looked as if I had let the air

out of his discovery. He continued his story in a much more monotone voice. "According to my source, the building was practically empty, no tenants. You know, the result of the Depression and all." He tried to smile, but it didn't work. Not even his dimples made a showing. "How'd you know that?"

The last of the thoroughbreds was stuffed into the gate for the start of the race. I was lost in the moment, until Clay nudged me a few times to bring me back to earth.

"I repeat. How'd you know that?"

"I remembered where I saw Montfort's name. Now that creates the question of what does the will say?"

"Didn't you get a copy of it?" A cloud of concern began to rain on his mood. Having crashed his positive attitude once, I tried to redeem myself.

"No. Clienfelter was most uncooperative. However, I did get my three hundred dollars."

"That's all? Listen here, it's my neck on the line. You got to do better than that."

Clay's neck veins were starting to pop. Where had his jovial personality gone? My redemption seemed lost. Oh, well.

"And I hope that three hundred isn't on some flea-bitten nag." He shook his head.

"I did get a name, the person Mrs. R. tried to add to the will. Rachel Montfort. Sound familiar?" I looked back to the starting gate, wondering what was taking so long. This case was becoming a distraction.

"First name doesn't, but the last name sure enough does. Montfort was the partner at the brokerage firm that Rumsfeld lost his building to. He's the man that took over Vernon's building."

I continued checking out the track until the light bulb went off in Morgan's head.

"You mean the same Rachel Montfort that is staying above Amanda and that Somers woman?"

I nodded. It was like discovering the world is round and the sun doesn't circle the earth. Clay stared at me and mouthed, "Wow."

"And they're off," came a booming voice over the loudspeaker. I strained to watch the horses make the clubhouse turn. Down the backstretch, I saw my horse running comfortably in third. Third? That's not comfortable. By the time the pack of leaders made their turn home, my horse was just barely in second, whiskers ahead of Stiletto, who was running third with Angel showing his whip to his ride. It looked like my nag was making a move on the leader. My luck might be changing.

The thunder of hooves was getting louder and the roar of the crowd was almost deafening as the horses began their charge to the finish.

"Come on, *Gumshoe*!" I shouted. My heart pounded.

"*Gumshoe*?" Clay shouted back at me. "*Gumshoe*? Get serious."

At that moment, I swear, Angel gave Stiletto a break from the crop and took a swing at *Gumshoe's* jockey, knocking him out of the saddle and onto the turf, where he was practically trampled to death. Stiletto catapulted into the lead, and the crowd went quiet as they stared at the fallen jockey. It seemed like ten minutes before we heard the scream of an ambulance racing to where the poor man lay. There were a few trainers, other jockeys, and would-be physicians around the body. The top three finishers didn't include the riderless *Gumshoe*. She'd wandered into the infield through a break in the fence and stood there munching on the sweet grass and emerging dandelions.

I quietly watched the ambulance leave the scene of the crime and begged the track gods to post a foul on the results board—my last gasp at redemption. When none came, I threw my tickets onto the track, disgusted with the whole affair, and grabbed Clay. "Let's get a drink," I said as I pulled him toward a fancy track tavern overlooking the homestretch.

I knew most of the track's employees, so there was no problem getting in. The problem was finding an empty table, which we finally did with the help of a few waiters and a couple of five-dollar bills.

Clay and I ordered a round of drinks and some lunch. I was tempted to hand Clay the remaining hundred dollars for safekeeping and keep it out of the hands of people I didn't owe money to yet, but thought better of it.

"I hope you're through for the day," he said. "With the state of your financial affairs, you can't afford any more flops." Clay got a thoughtful look on his face. "Maybe you should have bet on Angel's horse."

I wondered how Angel could whip my jockey off his horse and not get caught. I sucked down the remainder of my scotch and soda, trying to calm down and get back to the case. So far, the connection between Somers and Rumsfeld looked like chance, but that didn't feel right. I asked Clay to do some more digging around Montfort. See if we could find any threads to pull there.

About two minutes after Clay got up to make a few calls, a hot, familiar dame slid into the chair Clay had just vacated and pushed his half-eaten sandwich aside. She was dressed for Ascot Downs more than Aqueduct, with her makeup piled on and wearing a matronly dress. She looked like an actress who was trying to play older than she should have.

"Mr. Dugan?"

"Yeah, long time no see, doll."

"You remember me? Amanda told me about your visit. She said that you stopped by their apartment asking a lot of questions, trying to free her brother from jail or something."

"Miss Montfort," I nodded. "Mr. Morgan is right over there." I pointed to Clay standing at a bank of phones. "What brings you out to the track on a beautiful Saturday?"

"Vernon—Mr. Rumsfeld—called and asked if I had seen his wife's diary. He said some private detective had been asking about it. I take it that was you?"

Interesting question, I thought. "Yeah, that was me. Do you know anything about the diary, Miss Montfort?"

"You made it sound important to Mr. Rumsfeld, so I thought I would find you and see if I could help your investigation. You are investigating the murder of Eloise Rumsfeld, aren't you? Isn't that what Mr. Morgan was charged with?"

"Yes and no. What's your point? I am off duty right now, tryin' to relax with a quiet day at the track. Did you bring the diary?" I asked. *There is no way she would have brought the diary down here to Aqueduct*, I thought.

"Amanda seemed pretty adamant that you were going to help her brother, and according to her, you are real stubborn."

"How did you find me? At the track, I mean."

"A lot of people seem to know you, Mr. Dugan. I called Maxie's Tavern and talked with the bartender. He told me you were out here. This is a big arena, Mr. Dugan. I have been all over it trying to find you. I was about to give up." Rachel almost looked upset with all the work she'd done locating me.

"It's called a track, Miss Montfort, and yes, it is big. They call it the Big A."

"You must know by now, of course, that Eloise was my mother," Rachel said nonchalantly.

"Mother?" You could have knocked me over with a gentle whiff of bourbon. "Eloise Rumsfeld was your mother? And your father, biological father, is…"

"That's right, Mr. Dugan. You can say it. Clive Montfort."

I leaned back in the chair, took off my fedora, and scratched my head. "Well, I'll be. Is your father involved in stocks and bonds? Like a broker?"

"Not just a broker. He is the senior partner in the firm of Berkley, Owens, Montfort, and Burrows. Have you heard of the firm or my father, Mr. Dugan?"

"The firm, yes, but the man, not until very recently. But I am interested in meeting such an influential citizen of our fair city."

"Excuse me, miss." Clay was standing to the side, looking down at Rachel. "You are sittin' in front of my ham and swiss on rye." Rachel looked up, reddened, and began to slide into the next chair. "Don't you bother none, little lady. I'll just sit down over here." With his southern drawl dripping honey, Clay pulled up another chair. "You all right there, Jamie?"

I guess my color hadn't returned.

"Sorry. Rachel, this is Clay Morgan. Clay, this is Rachel Montfort." I caught my breath and continued. "Rachel here was telling me that she's the daughter of Clive Montfort and Eloise Rumsfeld."

"Yeah, I just found out," Clay said quietly. "That kinda changes the playing field." Clay stood and took Rachel's hand in a modified, genteel grip.

"It's my pleasure, Miss Montfort," Clay said and sat back down.

"So you're the one the police arrested for Mom's murder. How did you get out?" She didn't seem too bothered by the fact that she was sitting thigh to thigh with a man accused of murdering her mother.

"Sorry to disappoint, Miss Rachel. But the police realized I'm no killer and let me go." Clay's southern ease made him sound so innocent. He leaned toward her. "Miss Rachel—ah, Miss Montfort, what is it that you do for a livin? I thought you were going to college somewhere in the city."

"I am going to NYU. Daddy pays for my room and board. He doesn't really know where I am living. When I got the chance, I moved out and got him to pay for my rent until I finish getting my education."

"Those are nice apartments," I said. "And with such great downstairs neighbors."

"I have one morning class, but most of my classes are in the afternoon. When I am not in class, I stay on campus studying or with my boyfriend at his apartment." She blushed. "Since I don't have roommates, I spend quite a bit of time with your sister, Mr. Morgan. Your sister and Miss Somers are like having two mothers living on the floor below." She paused and looked from Clay's face to mine, as if she expected some type of reaction.

"I thought the modern generation found the older generation boring, out of touch," I said. Clay nodded.

"Boring? Sorry. Although we don't share a lot of the same interests, they do offer me a great spot to unwind and relax. Their stories are interesting. I hope my life will be as interesting as your sister's." She looked at Clay.

"So why are you here?" I asked.

"Oh, to give you this." And with that, she handed her mother's diary over to me. This was a day for stunning turn-arounds, and I was speechless.

She looked so young and innocent. As I said, I had never

graduated from college, but it was nice to dream. Rachel stood and said, "I have got to go. Would you mind letting me out, Mr. Morgan? I'll tell Amanda that I saw you and you're all right." As she pushed back her chair with Clay's help, she turned back to me and said, "I think it is a complete diary, though I haven't had a chance to read it yet. I hope that doesn't interfere with your investigation, Mr. Dugan."

Clay looked down at me as Rachel Montfort walked away. He sat back down expectantly and then pointed to the diary. "Well? Aren't you going to read it?"

"I have a better idea. Let's take it back to Maxie's. Too many prying eyes for us to be reading it here." I called the waiter over, settled our bill, and we left, looking for a taxi back to Midtown.

———◆———

THERE IS NO EASY WAY TO OR FROM AQUEDUCT RACEWAY unless you drive or take a cab, so Clay hailed a hack for the long ride back to Maxie's. I sat next to him in the backseat, mulling over the case. I couldn't bear to think any more about my jockey being unseated so close to the finish line. Christ, there went half my paycheck.

"Did you lose a pair of shoes over this past week or so?" I asked Clay.

"You mean the ones you found at Rumsfeld's place? Yeah, I bet they're mine."

"And the cologne?"

"Yeah, that's probably mine as well."

"How do you figure someone got a hold of that stuff?"

"Beats me. But I'm guessing it happened after Mary Jane moved in."

126

"If I were a bettin' man, and clearly I am, I'd say there are a number of parties in on this murder. And the suspect list keeps right on stretching. For instance, I had Rumsfeld figured for taking your stuff, but now, I don't know. And what's Somers's role? She could have taken stuff you left behind after moving out of the flat."

"Yeah. But at least there seems to be a limited number of people on the suspect list. Better than half the population of Manhattan."

The cab stopped moving about five blocks from Maxie's in gridlocked traffic.

The cabdriver turned toward the back seat. "There are cops and a fire truck up ahead. It looks like they've got this street closed down. You guys wanna walk or wait this out?"

Almost in unison, we replied, "We'll walk."

Clay looked at the meter and said, "He'll pay." He jumped out to wait for me.

We avoided the crowded sidewalk and headed down one of the auto lanes to get a look-see at what happened. About two blocks from where the red pump truck was parked stood one of my snitches, Rattling Rufus. When Rufus got excited, he sounded like a rattlesnake, releasing words rapid-fire in a high-pitched, nasal tone. Rufus is short, but easy to pick out due to a watch cap he wears pulled down over his ears regardless of the temps. I have seen him in that thing in late July with the temps in the mid-nineties and climbing. He provides great insight into street gangs and the mafia's foot soldiers.

"Rufus, what's happening down there?" I nodded in the direction of the pumper.

"Man, you don't wanna see. Someone torched a Jag, and it's in bad shape."

I must have looked like Walter Houston in *And Then There*

Were None when he starts discovering bodies. I felt the color drain from my face, and I had to work to close my mouth.

"That's where I parked my car." I took off down the street, leaving Rufus to rattle on to Clay about what he saw, or thought he saw.

Sure enough, there it sat between two older jalopies, the Jag's paint blistered and charred, the interior still smoldering, destroyed, hacked to death by the overzealous NYFD. The cars next to mine showed blistering paint on the sides facing the Jag, innocent bystanders wounded for their proximity to the target.

Firemen stood near the charred remains. Two manned a hose as the water trickled from the nozzle; the third had an ax. They looked at each other, nodded, then began to put up their equipment. I walked over to the one with the ax, another city employee set to have a go at my car with a heavy implement. It was obvious he enjoyed his work.

"What happened here?" I asked. "That's my car."

"It looks like it was a nice one, too," the guy with the ax said. "Jaguar, was it?" For a public servant, he was surly.

Out of breath, Clay came up next to me just in time to grab my arm before I could get a punch in. "Just tell me what happened," I demanded.

"When we arrived, your car was in flames. That's about it. We put it out."

Nonchalant jerk.

"Did anyone see who did this?"

"Don't know, but you might ask that nice policeman over there." He pointed towards a plain-clothed man who was interviewing a bystander. Dingle. O'Malley was within shouting range of the lieutenant, moving a group of gawkers out of the alley.

Clay held back to talk to the fireman as I approached Dingle. When I arrived, he was finishing his interview.

"So you saw a man in a gray trench coat and a dark derby walkin' out of the 9th Avenue side of the alley?"

"Yeah, walkin' real slow. Looked like there were two or three of them, but he's the only one I got a good look at," the interviewee said.

Dingle turned to face me. "I don't think you heard the bit about this guy being on the hefty side. And he wore tan leather oxfords."

I started to open my mouth, and Dingle raised his hand. "I know, it sounds like DeNato, but let's not jump to conclusions. There's a real good chance there's more than one heavy guy in this city who shares DeNato's taste in clothes."

"Fine, do it your way. Do you mind if I just go and ask Rocky a few questions, nice like?" I calmly asked.

"Yeah, I got a problem with that. You don't ask nicely. Stay away or he'll tap you next. I told you there were folks getting nervous with you asking all those questions. This is probably a message for you to stay away. So back off and let us do our job. Or have you forgotten what that is?"

When Dingle and I were paired up, we dealt with many angry victims of gifts like this—torched cars, broken storefronts, all sorts of message-from-the-mob kind of crimes—and Matt and I always told them, "Let us do our job." It was strange to have it directed at me this time.

"Let me tell you, their strategy just backfired. I'm more determined to find the killer and solve this case than—"

"Dugan. Enough. I don't want to solve your murder as well." Dingle's voice got steelier with every word.

I tried to calm down. I knew if I continued, I might get a permanent tail by the NYPD. Or worse, thrown in jail until I cooled off. At least, that's what I'd have done if I were Dingle. "Well, it looks like I'm cabbing it permanently now." My voice was bitter, and I could hear it as the words came out, short and clipped.

"Don't forget to get your car towed, or I'll have it impounded," O'Malley reminded me with a big grin.

"Yeah, yeah. On second thought, impounding it might not be a bad idea. At least I'd have a parking spot for the remains." The look on Dingle's face went from smiles to don't-you-dare.

I checked the interior of the Jag. The front seats were torn up and charred. The little storage area behind the front bucket seats was burned, but not as badly as I suspected. Everything was dripping wet from the fire hose, and the ax work didn't look too good, either. I shook my head. I was pretty used to having the Jag as my means of transportation. I was going to miss all the looks I got from jealous guys and good lookin' chicks as I hustled around town.

I checked for my baggage under the seat. It had flown, part of the personal portfolio of the arsonist—probably DeNato.

"Damn," I muttered as I took another look at the seats. "Does everybody know all the good hiding places?" I pivoted and walked back to Maxie's. Clay was nowhere to be seen.

I SAT AT THE BAR, A RARITY. MAXIE CAME OVER AND WIPED the space in front of me. "I'm sorry 'bout yer car, laddie. What kin I get fer ya?" For some reason, his Scottish accent seemed just a little bit harsher, more Scottish.

"How about a scotch, straight up with a twist. Naw, forget

the twist. Just give me a double, no ice, just booze. I need to use your phone. Will ya pass it over? And Maxie, will you put this in a safe spot for me? Thanks." I handed him the diary.

Maxie gave me the phone then sauntered away, but not too far. The mechanic who maintains my British machine is Anthony, and I was hoping he would be in for a possible re-build. I had met Anthony once before, in another life. His full name was Anthony Nunyos. He's a Puerto Rican New Yorker with a shop over in Brooklyn, on McDonald Avenue. When I finally reached him, I asked him to send a tow truck to collect the rubble and told him I'd be in touch in a day or so for his recommendation on whether to fix it or junk it. I think I already knew the answer, but I wanted his opinion.

As soon as I hung up, the phone rang. I answered.

"Yeah?" I breathed into the speaker.

"I heard your car got toasted today. That's a shame, a real shame."

"Who is this? You got a name?" But I already knew it.

"This is your second warning, Dugan. Unless you want your so-called office to receive the same, lay off the Rumsfeld case. You got it?"

I looked in the mirror in front of me and scanned the room. A lot of love went into this place. Maxie had built it from next to nothing. "Yeah, I hear ya."

"Good," the voice said. "If you play nice, you might live to work another case. And then, maybe not." A soft chuckle came from the other end of the phone, and it just chapped me. But deep in the recesses of my numbed mind, the voice sounded familiar.

"Don't go being so generous." And I hung up the phone just about the time Maxie delivered the scotch.

"You want your brief case?" Maxie asked.

"No. Hold it for a while, will ya? Here." I threw down the scotch in one gulp and shivered as I felt the warm liquid light up my body. "I'm heading back to my apartment for a shower and some clearer thinking." I turned to exit, waving at Maxie as I left.

"You want the drink on your tab?" I thought I heard him ask. I didn't respond. He already knew the answer to the question. I was becoming a regular clairvoyant.

UNBEKNOWNST TO ME, CLAY HAD TALKED WITH THE FIRE-fighters who doused the flames on the Jag and had learned the same thing about the probable arsonist, only quicker than I did. He made off down the alley after the perps and caught a glimpse of DeNato's car making a turn off 8th Avenue, about three stoplights away. Apparently, he was cutting across toward Times Square, like he was heading back toward 6th Avenue. With what we knew of the case, Clay made some assumptions, hailed a cab, and told the cabbie 32nd and 6th. He told the driver he was a reporter hot on a murder lead, so the cabbie, in fine New York fashion, zipped through traffic and arrived at Clay's destination in record time.

Clay and I knew there had to be multiple parties involved in this murder. We just weren't sure what the target or reward was. DeNato was easy—money. We couldn't figure if Somers was involved, but we had our suspicions. Clienfelter, he was up to his eyeballs in this, and survival was his only reward. Clay's hunch was that DeNato was headed back to the boss man. Since 6th had two-way traffic and a direct line to the popular high-rises, Clay gambled, hoping DeNato would pass his cab, if he'd been fast enough to get ahead of him.

When the cab pulled over to the curb at 32nd and 6th, Clay checked uptown to see if DeNato's Packard was traveling down 6th, and much to his amazement, it was. He acted as if he was fumbling for the fare with his head down, obscured, and watched DeNato's car go by.

"Follow that Packard, will ya?" Clay said. The cabbie re-engaged the meter and followed the car for eleven more blocks, then DeNato's car turned on 23rd, running toward Madison. Clay's cab stopped in an open spot on 5th, across from Madison Square Park, and Clay let the meter run while he watched the Packard pull up in front of an office building on the other side of the park.

When he first came to the city, Morgan used to get confused with the locations of the park and Madison Square Garden sports arena. He would give the cabbie the location of Madison Square Park, thinking he was heading for the arena and would get out on 23rd, nowhere near where he wanted to be.

Clay paid the cabbie his fare plus a handsome tip, then followed DeNato and his cronies into the building. By the time Clay reached the lobby, DeNato was nowhere to be seen. Figuring that he had taken an elevator to one of the offices, Clay checked the occupying company names on the marquee and tried to reach me at Maxie's. Maxie informed me I was headed home to get some shut-eye.

I AMBLED DOWN THE HALL OF MY TENEMENT BUILDING UNTIL I faced the door to my apartment, a place I could rest in safety and comfort. The key eased into the lock, and the door opened without a sound. I stepped in and felt along the wall for the light switch. Suddenly, someone grabbed my wrist and spun me around to his waiting fist. When I opened my eyes, the lights were on, and two goons were staring down at me. One guy pulled me up by my lapels. I couldn't tell if it was him or me, but someone smelled like he'd been living in his suit for a week. I was convinced there was a clove of garlic in the suit pocket as well.

"We just want a make sure you get the message. Stay off the Rumsfeld case, or the next visit we pay you will be yer last." The mug didn't look friendly, even though he tried to smile.

"You've got really bad breath. Have you tried changing your toothpaste?" It was an innocent observation. "Maybe you should floss more."

He responded by smashing me in the face again. I spun into the arms of the other goon, who proceeded to tap dance on my kidneys, with what felt like two blocks of concrete. I collapsed to the floor.

"He's goin' to be pissin' blood for a while," the kidney-tapper said.

"You need to find a maid. This place is a wreck," the first gorilla said as he smashed my coffee table against the wall. "You betta hope you don't see us again. This time, you need a maid. If we come back, you'll need a coroner. Have a nice day, Dugan."

As they exited, Goon 2 gave me a forget-me-not kick to the stomach. Already curled into the fetal position, I lay there not thinking, not moving, just listening to my apartment door open and close.

I have been beat up before, and it is not a nice feeling. Only one time in my life have I ever begged to pass out, and this was it. When Yarrow and I were on that beach trying to take Tarawa, I took a bullet in my side and thought for sure I would be buried on that mound of bloody sand. I passed out then, too, but not because I hurt so bad. It was loss of blood. I tried to stay awake and pull that trigger one more time, just to nail one of those yellow bastards. It was the feeling of "vengeance is mine." The black came quietly then.

Now it was just pure pain. My chest ached with every breath, and my kidneys felt as though they would never function again. My stomach screamed in pain. You know how people say it gets dark, or some such crap, before passing out? Well, let me tell you, as I lay there, the world got deathly silent and the room went into a tailspin. It was then, wrapped in pain, that I slipped from consciousness into blessed sleep.

SUNDAY

After coming to, sometime in the middle of the night, I lay on the carpet for what seemed like an eternity. I tried to get up, but the slightest movement sent waves of pain surging through my stomach and rib cage while the room circled above. It was with the hope of eventually taking revenge that I was able to crawl to my sofa and pull myself into a sitting position on the floor using the sofa cushion as a backrest. *It was like Tarawa all over again*, I thought as my body slid down the side of the sofa and I passed out on the floor.

WHEN I WOKE, I FOUND I'D TIPPED OVER AND WAS LYING ON my side next to the sofa. With shards of sunlight beginning to seep into my apartment came a faint knocking at my door. My struggle to sit up began anew. I shook my head to clear it of the cobwebs that had formed.

"Mr. Dugan? Mr. Dugan, it's Marge, Marge Stewart from down the hall."

Marge Stewart was the first person I met when I moved in. She was a seventy-year-old grandmother who'd taken me under her wing. She was a thin, gray-haired lady who stood all of five-foot-three with heels on. She looked like an angel to me. Her endearing features included a pair of twinkling, dark brown eyes, and a perpetual smile. Her chocolate skin was a nice contrast to all that white hair.

Everyone in the building knew about my squalid little apartment—no stove, and a view of an adjacent apartment building out my only window. But Mrs. Stewart was the only one who took pity on me and from time to time invited me over for a meal. "Corn bread, fried catfish, and butter beans... eat real good," she would say.

"Mr. Dugan, you have a call from a Mr. Morgan. Hello? Are you there, Mr. Dugan?" Another gentle rap at the door.

She also let me use her phone from time to time. I can't afford the luxury of a home phone. Besides, I'm never home.

I moaned and tried to sit up once more. "Mrs. Stewart, I'm here. Give me a minute, will you?" I rolled over and crawled onto the sofa, eventually pulling myself up to stand. My left arm was wrapped around my waist trying to hold in what remained of my stomach as I sort of limped to the door and, with much pain, twisted the knob. I must have been quite a sight to my kindly neighbor, who stood there with her jaw hanging open.

"Oh, my. Are you all right?" A worried frown creased her face.

"Oh, sorry. Just some rowdy visitors. They shouldn't be back. What was it you wanted?"

"You have a call, a Mr. Morgan." She looked at me like one might give a bum a once over.

"What time is it?"

"It's seven o'clock. Are you sure you are all right? I can call an ambulance. It will be here in minutes."

"Give me a second, and I'll be down to your apartment, Mrs. Stewart. Okay?"

She nodded, and I slowly closed the door. I had to test my kidneys and see what color my urine was going to be, plus throw some water on my face and stop the world from its gentle spin. I tried not to look into the mirror, but it was right there over my sink. The left side of my lip was split open and there was a black and blue berry growing on the outside of my right eye socket where I caught a really solid blow. It looked like my nose might be broken, and blood was caked inside my left nostril. The thug was definitely right handed, but of course, better than half the world's population is right handed. My left ear was cut, but the bleeding had stopped thanks to coagulation and the carpet, I guessed. Some sight, I thought. Now I'll have to get my carpet cleaned.

All the splashing around in the sink cleared some of my cobwebs and reduced the amount of blood caked on my face. Five minutes later, I was cradling what was left of my stomach in my left arm again and inching down the hall to Mrs. Stewart's apartment. I dragged my left shoulder along the wall for three points of support rather than two. I gently knocked on the door, and she must have been standing right there because it opened before I could rap my knuckles a second time.

"You said something about a call?"

As I said, she was a tiny woman, but she acted as my crutch, helping me limp toward her phone. I collapsed into an overstuffed chair and grabbed the receiver from the end table, where it was waiting patiently.

"Dugan, is that you? Finally!"

"Where the hell have you been? I thought the sight of Dingle made you run for the hills."

I looked up at Mrs. Stewart and mouthed, "Sorry."

"Oh, no. I caught up with the guy who torched your car and tailed him, first to his office, then to his flat. I'm just outside the lobby of his office building now and thought you'd wanna come over and wait for him with me. You can buy me a cup of coffee and a Danish while you tell me what a swell guy I am for tracking him down. And oh, yeah, you owe me ten bucks for cab fare and tip."

"Huh? Cab fare? Give me a few minutes. I have to pull myself together here. It might take me a while. Two goons paid me a visit last night, and I have to tape up what remains of my ribs and stomach. Are you at the offices down near 24th and 5th?"

"Yeah, that's it. How'd you know?"

"I'll tell you later." I heard Morgan hang up, and I did likewise.

Mrs. Stewart gave me moist towels to clean the blood from my lips and jaw that had re-emerged since I washed up. She also wrapped a towel around my forehead and fed me a cup of coffee. All that kindness felt pretty damn foreign, but oh, so welcome.

I looked over at Miss Stewart. "You mind if I make a phone call? I might need some help getting to my appointment."

Mrs. Stewart smiled, like she knew I was calling for re-enforcements and nodded. "Go right ahead, young man."

I quickly dialed the one friend that I considered my cavalry, and he promised to meet me in thirty minutes outside of Maxie's.

About ten minutes later, I was on my way to my office to pick up my briefcase before rendezvousing with Clay. I just couldn't figure out what to do with DeNato's body once I filled it full of lead. Then it dawned on me.

Outside of Maxie's, a "race car" roared up and stopped near the front door. When I was on the force, I had seen some outrageous automobiles, but none that rivaled this tan death trap, the Crosley Hotshot. From what I remember of an article I read about the car, the description went something like this:

The Crosley Hotshot was the first sports car produced in post-World War II America, and it was considered by most

139

automotive connoisseurs a major hunk of junk. It weighed in at 1,100 pounds and measured 145 inches long. (Hotshot was actually a minor hunk of junk, but at least it was slow and dangerous). The Hotshot was the handiwork of consumer products pioneer Powel Crosley Jr., of Cincinnati, Ohio. What Crosley really wanted to do was build cars, which he did with middling failure. The Hotshot was a pinnacle of his failing achievements. This roadster puttered around at an average top speed of 52 mph. The engine of the Hotshot was powered by a dual-overhead cam .75-liter four-cylinder engine, not cast in iron but brazed together from pieces of stamped tin. When these brazed welds let go, as they often did, things quickly got noisy, and hot.

The Hotshot was a real flamethrower if you catch my meaning. But the car looked really sharp.

As I walked out of Maxie's den and into the bright sunlight of the mid-morning, this sight greeted me. Already badly beaten and trying to recover, my pain was forgotten as my eyes took in the sight. In the driver's seat was Yarrow. He wore a large, dark brown fur hat that didn't go with his black trench coat. The steering wheel of his Hotshot had a pink wrap around on it that didn't mask his large, mocha-colored hands. Car and driver were definitely not camouflaged. Two fuzzy dice hung from a dash-mounted review mirror. They bumped against the dash as he drove over the city's potholes. The tan car had a red leather interior. Unfortunately, the color palette of Yarrow's outfit clashed with the car's, making me wonder how far off we might be seen as we drove downtown.

I shook my head, said a silent prayer, and climbed into the passenger side of the automotive coffin. I closed my eyes and gave Yarrow the address that Clay had confirmed with me over the phone, then waited for the surge of power as the Hotshot puttered to our next destination.

"This can't be your car," I said.

"Nope, belongs to a buddy of mine who owes me a favor," Yarrow responded as he turned to me with a sly grin.

"He still owes you," I muttered.

I BEGGED YARROW TO PARK THE CAR A FEW BLOCKS AWAY, SO our arrival would not be a complete give away. All we would need then would be a band and a few floats. When we approached the building on foot, I spotted Clay standing by an outside phone, where he had a good view of the lobby. I hurried to join him so I could use the public telephone service and call Anthony, who'd hopefully had a chance to look at my Jag and had a slightly larger and faster auto than my man Yarrow. It was about nine-thirty, and I doubted Anthony was at his shop, but I thought I'd go through the motions, just in case I got lucky. On the third ring, Anthony picked up and proceeded to tell me that my car was a total loss. Couldn't even be used for scrap. My blood pressure soared with the news, and my knuckles turned white as I gripped the phone.

I talked Anthony into giving me a loaner, telling him I had an emergency. He agreed to look around his shop and see what he could send.

Yarrow and Clay introduced themselves to each other and waited for me to join them. We sat just outside the lobby, looking for both DeNato and the loaner car to arrive. While we waited, I relayed the sordid tale of meeting the muscle in my apartment the night before and how I practically crawled down the hall to get Clay's call. I appreciated Clay's efforts to

141

find and keep tabs on DeNato, but I didn't want him to get a big head, so I smiled and nodded.

"What's the plan?" asked Yarrow.

"I'm working on it," I answered. I was filled with enough rage that planning was the last thing on my mind, just revenge. Lucky for us, the loaner showed up first.

By now, it was close to ten-thirty, maybe even eleven, and since there were no Sunday workers coming to the building, anyone looking for a parking place wouldn't have a problem. I watched as the loaner pulled up, not believing the state of the jalopy.

"Is this the best you guys got?" I asked.

"This old truck is the *only* thing we got," the tall, thin driver said. He was in gray overalls with grease stains on the knees and down the sides.

"You got a key to the lot so I can drop it back at the shop?"

"The shop is closed for the weekend, but we should be open on Monday. You don't really need a key. Plus, Anthony will kill me if I gave you mine."

"After, say, two this afternoon, I won't need it anymore, and I don't wanna leave this fine vehicle sitting out on the street where some reckless driver could do it harm, you know? Just give me your key, and I'll put it under the front floor mat for you."

"Anthony's Repairs" was stitched on the overalls, and just below that, the name "Vinnie."

"Look, Vinnie. Here's twenty dollars for your help. And another twenty dollars for a deposit on your key. When I return it, just keep the first twenty as my token of good faith in you and the shop. Okay?"

I held out the forty dollars to Vinnie, which he immediately snatched. He handed me the keys to the shop and truck. "Don't let on to Anthony that I lent it to ya, capisci?"

"Thanks, Vinnie. It'll be under the floor mat. Trust me."

What a great city to work in, and I had all the best of intentions.

I looked at my loaner again, a '42 Ford pick-up truck with "Anthony's Repairs, Brooklyn, New York" stenciled on the door. What a come down from the Jag, but it was a definite lift from the Hotshot. Clay caught my eye and nodded toward the Packard pulling up in front of my loaner. Two goons got out of the Packard and headed toward the building to collect DeNato and escort him to his ride and next destination. I ducked behind my ride, trying to go unnoticed. *Must be nice to catch such a ride. Won't Rocky be surprised?*

After they passed, I went up to the driver's side of the Packard and motioned to the driver to roll down the window. He did as I asked and received my pistol across his left cheek as a reward. He crumpled lower in the seat, and I leaned in to borrow the keys to his car. I was committed to my somewhat half-baked plan, which was starting to come into focus.

I returned to the office building, where DeNato's thugs were waiting for him to appear in the lobby by way of the elevator. I joined Clay, who was hiding off to one side behind a fake plastic bush that's supposed to bring the green in from the outside. Yarrow was nowhere to be seen.

I leaned in close and whispered. "Those are the fellas who paid me the visit earlier. Where's Yarrow?"

Clay shrugged and casually walked to a newsstand alcove that had a few vending machines and tried to look like he was getting a Sunday paper from a machine.

One of the thugs made for the bathroom. I pulled my hat low and followed him into the men's room. Five minutes later, I joined Clay at the newsstand.

"I found Yarrow," I told him.

The other thug looked at his watch and then to the door of the bathroom. This reminded me I still hadn't found my watch. Then an elevator ding echoed in the nearly vacant lobby and DeNato emerged.

DeNato's playmate said something quietly to him. "Well, go check on him, now!" DeNato said. The hood left for the bathroom in a hurry.

"Now's our chance," I said to Clay, and the two of us flanked Rocky DeNato.

"Hey, Rocky, how's it hangin?" I asked.

He looked up, startled, and reached for his coat pocket. I already had my gun out.

"Easy, big boy," I said. "Get the rod, will ya?" I asked Clay. And the three of us exited the lobby and headed for our get-away pick-up truck.

"You'll never get away with this, boys," DeNato said.

I cuffed DeNato and led him to the back of the truck. "Get in," I said. "We're gonna have a little ride and then a nice talk."

He sat on the tailgate then I lifted his legs and spun him around so his back was toward me, and clocked him. "Sweet dreams, chump." I covered Rocky with a tarp in the truck bed, making sure he was comfy and tucked in for the ride ahead of us.

About that time, another hood came running out of the building looking for Rocky. He pulled out his gun and ran for the truck and us.

I tossed the keys to Clay. "Drive," I said.

"How bout the other guy? Shouldn't we take care of him so he doesn't follow?"

"That limo can't be driven, at least for the time being. He

better have cab fare." I dangled the Packard's keys in Clay's direction as I ducked low in the passenger seat.

"Where to?"

"Brooklyn," I said as a hail of bullets rang into our fender. "And make it snappy."

As we pulled away, Clay asked, "What about your friend, Yarrow?"

"Oh, yeah," I muttered. "Aw, he'll get by. You should see his neat getaway car."

———◆———

WE GOT TO ANTHONY'S GARAGE AROUND NOON, AND THE place was deserted. Looking up and down McDonough Street for stray cars, I unlocked the gate. Clay pulled the truck around back, and Morgan and I found a small handcart that we poured DeNato into. We wheeled him into the garage and with much effort and additional pain propped him up in a metal chair. Moving the fat hood around didn't make my body feel any better, but it did make me more eager for our conversation.

"Did ya have to knock him out?"

"Sorry," I said, wiping the sweat from my brow. I moved to another chair to catch my breath and find some relief.

"You okay? You look terrible. You need to see a doctor."

"I think our time with DeNato will help me start feeling better. Let's hoist this guy up so he doesn't hurt himself in the shop by banging anything."

Using a chain lift, Clay and I pulled DeNato up by his cuffed wrists, but not before I relieved Rocky of his watch. We raised him high enough to get his feet off the ground. I let him dangle there for a few minutes while I considered our next move and inspected the watch.

I patted him down and found a bulge in his coat. I reached into his breast pocket and pulled out an envelope. "Whew, there's a lotta cash here. You must be very careful carrying this amount of cash around in the city, Rocky. You never know who might want to take it from you. I'll just hold it for you until you're in a better spot." DeNato didn't answer, so I took that as an okay.

I'd never seen so much cash. I counted out thirty thousand for the Jag and another five grand for Clay's troubles. Clay put out his hand for his, cuffing his fingers, as if that would get the cash flowing his way. I stuffed it in my hip pocket.

"Hey," Clay said loudly. "Where's mine?"

I waved him away for the time being.

"That still leaves you with, wow, twenty-five thousand. You must have gotten a bonus for the fine work you've been doin'. Let me just hold this for you while we have our discussion." I pocketed the envelope holding the other twenty-five grand and started looking for water to throw in his face.

Clay poked at DeNato with a broom handle. "How come you pocketed the cash for my arrest? Shouldn't I get that?"

"What? You get it? I was the one who was worried. And I had to take abuse from your sister while you were in the care of our public servants with free meals. Right? Free bed and, I might add, a free toilet. All provided to the man who was thrown out of his own apartment and needed a place to stay. At least you had somewhere to lay your head."

"You ever use a toilet when there's no door or toilet paper?" Our conversation would have continued, but DeNato was beginning to stir, thanks to the overly stimulated poking from Clay.

"You still owe me for the cab fare," Clay demanded.

"What the hell is going on here?" DeNato demanded as he came to. In vile, coarse terms, he asked that we put him down. He peppered his comments with swearing and threats of separating our bodies from their more predominant parts. He got so agitated that he began to jangle like a piñata at a birthday party, his legs flailing away on the hunt for solid ground. With a little help from Clay, he began to spin in midair.

"Okay, reporter guy, here's a C-note. That should cover the cab and incidentals." I looked at Clay like I had just done him the biggest favor in the world. Then I turned to Rocky DeNato.

"Rocky," I said. "What do you call a horse that gets boxed in going down the stretch?"

"What do ya mugs want?" Rocky asked as he spun, his face turning crimson with anger. The spin wasn't fast, but it was entertaining.

"Just want to know who your employer is," Clay said.

"You boys are goin' to pay for this!" Rocky's voice boomed. "You can take your questions and go to hell."

"Aw, and I was going to let you stand on this here chair," Clay said as he kicked it a few yards further away from DeNato.

"This is a real nice watch, Rocky. Where did you get such an expensive timepiece? Oh, look, Clay. It's a Rolex." I buckled it on my wrist. "Looks real nice, huh?" I was starting to feel pretty good about my retribution for all the abuse I'd been taking on this case.

"You're goin' to give me my due here," Clay said, partially to Rocky and partially to me. "I took the fall for this murderer, ya know." Suddenly, he stopped talking. There was noise outside.

"I heard that, too. We got company." I looked around the shop and pointed to an almost empty grease pit.

"Yeah," Clay whispered and nodded.

DeNato had been watching us, and he began to grin. "In here, boys," he yelled.

"I wouldn't be yellin there, big guy," Clay said as he moved down the four steps into the bay's grease pit. "You don't know who's out there. They might start shootin' and not care who they hit."

The two of us backed into the grease pit, keeping our eyes on DeNato and the direction of the noise. I had my pistol aimed at the bay door, and Clay struggled to set up an old toolkit as a makeshift barricade, should there be an exchange of gunfire.

Then glass shattered and a spray of bullets ricocheted within the metal fabrication of the repair shop. It sounded like a broadside from a pirate frigate. Glass everywhere, light streaming through bullet holes in the building's sheet metal. Everything crashing, ripped apart from the devastation of the Tommy guns. The noise was deafening. We dove for the pit floor and stretched out on our stomachs with hands over our heads, smelling the grease and oil from many a day's work. Bullets hit our toolkit and opened the drawers with a crash, scattering wrenches, screwdrivers, and hammers onto our legs and backs.

Clay looked up at DeNato and tapped me on the shoulder. We watched in awe as his body spun like a punching bag being mauled by an angry heavyweight.

After what seemed an eternity, the shooting stopped and an eerie silence took over. A bottle with a lit wick came through a glass-free window and exploded against a stack of paint cans. It was followed by another and finally a third.

DeNato didn't care anymore. His life was gone, blood pooled on the greasy floor beneath him.

Clay and I continued to hover low in the pit as the flames licked at the walls. I thought I heard more gunfire, but I was partially deaf from the earlier barrage, and the added roar from the fire wiped out any exterior noise.

"We gotta get the hell outta here, or we'll be as toasty as fried chicken," Clay said.

I stuck my head up to see which doors provided our best escape from the flames. Clay slapped my arm and pointed toward one of the bays that had been pulled wide open, and there stood O'Malley yelling something into the garage. I grabbed Clay, and we dashed for the door as an explosion ripped open the back end of another bay. Metal went flying, and Clay sprinted by me into the open lot. Still limping from last night's beating, I wasn't about to win any races, even with flames licking at my heels. Then, adding to my injury, my shoe snagged a jack handle and I went sprawling across the floor. As I struggled to stand, a pair of giant hands grabbed my jacket and shirt and carried me out to Anthony's truck, where I was deposited on top of DeNato's old sleeping bag.

"We gotta stop meetin' like this, big guy." I looked up into the face of the cop who'd carried me back at the Rumsfeld brownstone. He grinned and dusted off his blue jacket, as if I'd mussed it up.

Clay smiled at O'Malley. "Did ya get 'em all, Sarge?"

Dingle walked over and holstered his weapon. He looked at Morgan, then at me, and shook his head. "I should have known it was you two. Is anyone else in there?"

"Yeah," I said. "But I think he's cooked by now."

"DeNato?" Dingle asked.

"Yes, sir," Clay said. "I think he's got a few holes in him, too."

"Oh, shit," I said. "I forgot to give this back to him while we were talkin.'" I pulled the envelope from my breast pocket and handed Dingle the twenty-five thousand.

"What's this?" Dingle looked inside and whistled.

"We figure that's the payoff for the car fire." Clay's southern drawl elongated each word.

I crawled slowly out of the back of the truck. I was too sore and tired to dust myself off. I did note the dirt and grime ground into my suit again. "If this keeps up, I'm going to have ta buy another suit or start working in my skivvies."

"Maxie probably won't let you into his bar lookin' like that. You'll have to find another office." Clay smiled and shook his head.

"Maybe blue jeans would be more your style," Dingle said with a grin.

"Dingle, could you lend me a hundred as suit-money from that wad?"

"No," came the terse reply.

"I should have asked DeNato."

"Speaking of DeNato, there goes your lead into the Rumsfeld murder," O'Malley said to Dingle. "I checked the body hanging in there, and he's not talking to nobody."

"At least we still have the diary," Clay blurted.

I covered my head and turned away from Dingle and Morgan.

"Ah, what diary?" Dingle asked.

"Diary, did I say diary?" Clay stammered.

"What kinda mess did you fools get into here?" Dingle said. "Are you holdin' out on me? You have evidence that should be in the hands of the NYPD?" Dingle put his hands on his hips, a natural position when people talk to me these days. "I have a lot of cleaning up to do here, but I'm coming down to Maxie's and we're going to talk through what happened. Got it? And I want you to dig up all evidence that needs to be turned over to us. All of it." Dingle paused for a second and his face got contorted. "What in the heck were you guys doing here with DeNato, anyway? How did he get hung up in the bay?"

"Let's just run it all through at Maxie's. I'll give you a statement and we can catch up on old times," I offered. "How did you know we were here?"

"McFarland got an anonymous tip, and we scrambled. O'Malley was first to arrive on the scene, weren't you, Sarge?" Dingle asked.

O'Malley nodded.

"Wow, you got here fast, Sarge," I said. "Did you shoot a lot of bad guys protecting us?"

"Get," was all I got from Dingle and a mean stare from O'Malley.

"Morgan, you still got the keys to the truck?" I asked and he nodded. "Then drive us to Maxie's." I turned to Dingle to say something, but thought better of it.

"Get out of here, both of you. I'll see you in a couple of hours, and don't forget the diary." Dingle waved his arm toward the gate. Cops, fire trucks, and fire fighters were all over the place, like ants over a dying grasshopper. He shook his head. "Anthony is going to drop you as a customer."

Clay got behind the wheel and I slid into the suicide seat. "Any holes on your side?" he asked.

"Yeah, two. How about yours?"

"Four over here. Anthony's truck shot up and his repair shop melted down. No way you'll be redeeming this friendship. You're going to need another mechanic."

By the time we got to Maxie's, it was five in the afternoon. The joint was just beginning to fill up for an early Sunday afternoon burger and beer. Maxie had scheduled another trio to play that evening in an attempt to drum up more business. It was a test.

I had to oust a couple guys sitting in my office. We ordered beers, and I slipped Maxie a twenty; in return, he handed me the diary. He eyed my suit, greasy face and hands, and all the scrapes and clotted blood on my face, and shook his head. Maxie handed me his table cleaning rag and walked away without a word. Clay said the smell from my suit was like early forest fire with an overwhelming odor of burnt oil and paint. Definitely not the right combination for making friends and influencing people.

I opened the diary and began to read excerpts to Clay. Then I got to where Mrs. R. had met and fallen in love with Clive Montfort:

May 1927, the world is anxiously awaiting the flight of C. Lindbergh from Roosevelt Field to Paris. Things are looking up. Found the love of my life in Clive Montfort. Wealthy stockbroker with seemingly endless connections.

June 7, 1927, C. Lindbergh landed in Germany yesterday, and Clive proposes marriage. Happiest day of my life.

And so it went, through the first few years of the marriage between Clive and Eloise Montfort. Then I got to a part of the diary with a lot of missing pages. I could see where the torn sheets use to be.

I looked up at Morgan. "What do you think of that?" I asked. "The rest of the diary seems to have been ripped out. Rachel said it was intact. What happened?"

"Don't look at me. You're the one with the diary. I'm still upset you didn't share any of the cash you took from DeNato. It would go a long way in squaring my rent with my flat mate."

"Hush a minute. Let me think. When we got the diary, Rachel said that she thought it was all there. No one has had it except…"

"What? Who?" asked Morgan.

"Maxie. But why would he—"

"Here're ye beers, boys. Want something to eat?" Maxie leaned over the table while he lowered the beers in front of us.

"Yeah, I'll have the fish and chips," said Clay.

"Hold on," I interjected. "Could anyone have gotten to the diary while we were out?" I looked up at Maxie, waiting for a calculated response.

"Nope, except for the half hour I had Jerry tend the bar alone while I had a bite." Jerry was like a mechanized server, not someone you could tell your troubles to, and definitely not someone you would want to take home.

"Where'd you keep it?" I asked.

"Keep what?" answered Maxie. "What's the matter, laddie? You're acting like someone took it or something."

"Exactly." I stared at Maxie.

"You accusing me of takin' what exactly?"

"You know, the diary pages," I answered.

"Why would I be interested in some damn book? I kept it under the cash register where I usually park your brief case, which by the way, you walked in without."

I was tired and in pain. What I thought was going to be our big breakthrough was a bust, and now I had lost my brief case and rod. I hate Sundays. "Sorry, pal. It has been a rotten end to a very long day. Make that two fish and chips and another round of beer, will ya?" I shrugged humbly.

Maxie shook his head and retreated to the bar and kitchen, mumbling.

"What's with you, man?" Clay asked. "He could poison us. You know that temper of his."

"I gotta make a call." I got up, went over to the bar, reached over the counter, and picked up the phone. It was maybe six inches from where my briefcase usually rested. Anyone could have grabbed the diary. *But if they did, why rip out the pages and put it back? Why not just keep it?*

I dialed Yarrow at the Downbeat, and he picked up on the first ring.

"I was hoping it was you. Did the cavalry come to your rescue?"

"Yeah, thanks. Good thing you stayed in the men's room, huh?"

"Well, it worked out for the best, anyway. Let me give you what I have so far. It seems like there is more to come." I sat and listened for a few minutes then hung up and returned to the table just as our fish and chips did.

"What do you know about the Depression?" I asked Morgan.

"Those were tough times. Some fifteen million people were out of work during the early 1930s. There were suicides. It was hard. People did strange things in order to survive. I read somewhere that a woman sold her child just to get something to eat."

"No, I mean what do you know about Clive and how he handled the divorce during the Depression?" I waited for Morgan to stop eating and answer my question.

It was as if the stairwell to his brain had closed down momentarily in order to stuff food in his face. There are times I think his mental processing gyrates between "limping slowly along" and "decided not to move at all." It all depended on how far he was from his next meal.

"There's not too much on the affairs of Clive Montfort during the Depression in the papers that I remember. Why do you ask?" Morgan said between the bites of fish and French fry.

"A little bird just told me that Clive and Eloise got divorced during the Depression, and Eloise traded her daughter for a building. The Baker Building."

Morgan stopped chewing and began to pucker to whistle then thought better of it. "Wow. I didn't know," Morgan said as he wiped his mouth with a napkin. "That seems hard, but it fits with what I heard about selling children for food. A building, huh?"

"There's more," I said as I forked apart my fish into smaller pieces. I told Morgan that she and Clive had signed a prenuptial agreement and that since Eloise pushed for the divorce, she was left with next to nothing. Clive, feeling sorry for her, gave her a building with just under break-even rents so she could eat for a while, but she had to give up their daughter. Without the building, mother and daughter would starve unless someone came to her rescue, and during the Depression, that was unlikely. I told Morgan that my sources were still working on the story, but it looked like we had a good motive, at least on the surface.

"He sounds like a creep to me, but I think he could have gotten away with that sole custody thing, given that Eloise could not survive what was going on back then. Thousands of banks went under after the panic ended, and she would have had no job and no place to live. Sounds like she made the right sacrifice." Morgan began to drift into a self-imposed daze.

"At least we know how she acquired the Baker Building."
I was starting to see the trend.

"So Rachel finds her mother and Mom feels guilty about
all this and tries to make it up to her by adding her to the
will. I wonder how Rachel knew where to look for her, what
name to ask for." Clay's voice drifted off.

I looked over at Morgan. "Clay, are you with us?"

"Yes, sir, Mr. Jamie. I was just digesting the latest. Did
your source say anything about Vernon's debts? Something
just ain't right, as my grandma used to say when there was
a storm a-brew'n." He looked at me from across the booth
table. "You know what I think?" The drawl suddenly left. "I
think that the debt, the girlfriend, and the fact that daughter
and mother are suddenly reunited are not just a coincidence."

"Like I said, 'Someone is pullin' the strings,' manipulating
the events from behind the scenes." I perked up. At least we
were thinking the same thing.

"Someone with a lot of connections!" Morgan said.

I guess there is an elevator after all in that noggin.

"I think it's time we pay Mr. Montfort a visit, but there
are a few things we need to take care of. Rocky was one thing,
even though it ended badly. But Montfort will have a platoon
guarding him. We won't be able to just waltz in on him." I
was wondering how to get close to Montfort when Dingle
and O'Malley walked into Maxie's and approached my table.

My briefcase appeared on the table with a thud. I looked
at the charred leather luggage with the straps halfway singed
off from the fire at Anthony's.

"You had best take better care of your things there, Mr.
PI," said Dingle. "Especially your piece." He gently laid my
rod on the remains of my briefcase.

"Thanks," I murmured.

"You got that diary, Dugan?" Dingle asked.

"Yup, right here." I handed it over to the detective. "I promised Rachel I would have it back in her hands tomorrow. Is it all right if I tell her you bullied me into giving it to you?"

"Whatever. What, if anything, did you two learn from this?" Dingle pulled up a chair and sat at the end of the booth looking from Morgan to me. "Aw, c'mon, you can save me a lot of work if you just tell me what I'm going to be reading."

I yawned. "It's been a long day, Detective, but here goes…" I fed Dingle the background from the diary right up until we discovered the ripped out pages.

"And after that entry, the next seven or more pages have been torn out of the diary, making it useless for the investigation. Who did the rippin' and tearin', I have no idea. 'When' is also a big question." Exasperated, I looked from Morgan to O'Malley. Morgan was still in his coma, but O'Malley had a sly grin on his face, kinda like he already knew it would be a waste of time to read the diary. Interesting.

Finally, Morgan said, "All the answers you are lookin' fer were in this here book." The rich southern accent was back.

Dingle rose. "I still need a statement, Dugan. How about stopping down at the station and givin' O'Malley here one before you leave town or get smoked." It was not a question. "The sooner the better."

O'Malley looked at us, and with a serious face said, "I'll be at the ol' precinct, waitin on ya." And with that, they left the bar, diary in hand.

"What was that all about, Clay?" I asked.

"I think we both know what happened and who did what to whom. It is just a matter of nailing down those last loose ends," Clay explained.

"I have an idea how we can figure out those loose ends,"

I said. "Why don't you call Amanda and see if we can come over for breakfast tomorrow morning? Ask if she can get the other two to be there as well."

Clay smiled and nodded back to me. "Two?"

"Yeah, Rachel and Mary Jane. You have to get Rachel there. I think she and Mary Jane are key for us."

Clay left the booth and made the call. He turned back to me with a thumbs-up then proceeded to make another call. He returned to the booth and stood next to where he'd been sitting. "Well, I'm bushed, and think I'm going to head back to my friend's apartment for a nap." He began to turn.

"Hold on. We're going up to see your sister tomorrow, right?" I was tired, monotone. "What time are we meeting, and where do I find you?"

"Oh, yeah." Clay chuckled and turned to face me. "I'm sorry. I'm bushed. I set it up with Mandy, but she and Mary Jane can't wait long or spend much time with us tomorrow morning. They want to be out the door by nine sharp. They'll get Rachel down, too. I told Mandy we'd be there between seven-thirty and eight. That work for you?"

"Yeah, great. And where do I find you, so you don't have to take a cab? Or were you planning to keep our latest luxury automobile?" I asked.

"Shoot, sorry. I am staying with an old friend from Charleston, Miss Emily Ross."

My eyebrows went up like a trial balloon at a fair.

"It's not what you're thinking. We are good friends and she has a two-bedroom apartment, and she's been nice enough to let me use one of them the past couple of weeks."

"Emily? Emily Ross who sings in night clubs around town?" I was devastated. I had a big crush on her, and Morgan here was shacked up with her. At least, that was the conclusion

I jumped to. After what we had been through today, and all the pain in my gut, face, and hands, my body was ready to start collecting Social Security. The wind had been taken out of my sails. I felt dead in the water.

"Yeah, that's the one. Smart as they come, too." Morgan let out some air. "You might as well know. I had an offer from a paper here in town. If I can land the story on Rumsfeld's killer, they'll hire me as a contributing reporter. I was just calling them to let them know I accept their offer. I hope that's all right by you. I know it's your investigation an all, but—"

I slowly got up and waved away his comment. Emily Ross and Clay Morgan. What a cruel blow. Well, there went my love life, or my dreams of one.

I was a mess. My fedora was soaked from sweat and the grease from Anthony's pit. My suit was so stained that I looked more like a clown than a PI, and my shoes had all types of filth, including blood, splattered on them. My head down, I quietly walked to the front door. I had made it all the way to the exit when Maxie stopped me with a yell from across the tavern floor. He motioned that I had a call at the bar. I nearly left anyway, but turned around and trudged back.

When I finally made it to the phone, Maxie was shaking his head. "The way you treat your friends, laddie. Shameful."

I picked up the receiver. "Dugan here."

"Dugan? Is that you, you bastard? What the hell did you do my shop? You still have my pickup? I want it back! Now, ya hear? Now! It better be in good shape, too, like no bullet holes in it, ya hear me?" Man, did he sound angry. I was glad we weren't in the same room. "What the hell are you doing, trying to single-handedly drive me out of business?"

"Anthony?"

159

I left Maxie's feeling bad about what happened to Anthony's. I sure hoped he had insurance. More importantly, I was puzzled about what happened to the pages from Eloise's diary. I needed to kill some time before I dug deeper to find them. It struck me that Yarrow said there was more information for me, so I hailed a cab uptown to Harlem.

Yarrow met me as I walked into the Downbeat, his big hands wrapped around mine with a strong grip as he pointed to a table away from the band and the couples on the dance floor. "What happened to you? You look and smell like you are still in the trenches on that god-forsaken beach."

"I feel like my medipak has come loose and I need a few shots of morphine." I was beat and tired of being reminded of it.

Once again, the smoked-filled place was crowded and enjoying the sounds from a trio doing a jazzed up version of Sinatra's *Fella with an Umbrella*. As soon as we sat, another fella joined us, pulling a chair from an occupied table close to ours. The youngster smiled and doffed his fine chapeau, then readjusted it on his head in a rakish position. He was really spiffed up for the evening, sporting a white suit with thick black lines from the collar to the cuffs. On top of his muted red shirt, a bright yellow tie was held in place by a diamond stickpin.

"This is Norman. Norman works down on the street and hears things. You should have an interestin' talk." Yarrow got up to leave, but Norman put his hand on Yarrow's arm without looking in his direction then let go. "Oh, yeah," Yarrow continued. "Talk is not cheap when it comes to Norman. As I said, he works down on the street." And with that, Yarrow was gone.

By the way Yarrow had introduced him, I was fairly

certain Norman was not this cat's real name. I pulled out my billfold and took out a few twenties. There wasn't much there. I held the DeNato cash in reserve. I had other plans for that. I laid three of them on the table in front of me. "Okay, Norman, you talk and I listen."

"You're still short there, Tex," Norman said.

I peeled another two twenties, put them next to the first three, and looked at Norman. He smiled and reached for the money. I covered all five bills with my hand and said, "You talk and I listen first. Money second. I only pay for quality. And I mean quality."

BY THE TIME I GOT BACK TO MAXIE'S, THE PLACE WAS DARK. When the cabbie let me out he asked, "You sure this is the right address, bub?" I nodded, rounded the corner, and proceeded to the alley. A few minutes later, I stood in front of four garbage cans, all of which seem to be filled. A single light lit the back door entry.

"Four," I said. "Man, I hate doin' this."

I shook my head and grabbed the lid to the can closest to the back door. I thought I might find what I was looking for by traveling back in time through Maxie's garbage, starting with what would have been the last items thrown out.

I don't know about other people, but I hate the stench of garbage, especially when there is half-eaten food mixed with other discarded, smelly stuff. About a third of the way down the first can, I came across a pair of yellow rubber gloves, probably used by the dishwasher to keep their hands from "pruning." They were cute, with little white and green daises printed on them. I shook them, hoping to clean out any seepage that might have gotten into the fingers, and put them on. The left one was just a little squishy, so I searched with my right gloved hand and threw the left glove back into the can. I didn't even want to look to see why it felt wet.

In the first bag of the second can was a lot of bar trash, discarded drink fruit and olive pits. I almost lost my stomach weeding through it then I found what I was looking for. A pain from my rib cage raced to my brain as I stood up too quickly, and my world spun for a few minutes as I grabbed the can's lip. Then I looked at what I had found.

"Well, lookie here," I said aloud and began separating pages of Eloise's diary from the trash. Most of the pages were torn, soaked, or food stained. But there was one or two pages or partial pages that I could sort of read in the dim alley light. I shook those to get the moisture off and then folded them into my pocket. The other pages, or what was left of them, were in such bad shape that I stuffed them back into the bar-bag and packed up the garbage can. "We wouldn't want anyone to think that somebody had gone garbage diving in the alley," I said as I threw the glove I was using into the first can I had gone through. "Good as new." After spending the hundred at Yarrow's club and the small traces from the garbage, I felt I had a better understanding of this case.

I could smell myself coming and going, and it wasn't a pleasant experience. *Homeward for a shower for me and a garbage bag for the suit, preferably outside of my apartment*, I thought. I had serious doubts that any cabbie in his right mind would let me get into his cab. So I began my long walk back to where we had parked the truck, which was about half way home. I felt my piece in the side pocket of my jacket move with every stride I took. It gave me confidence that I had a fighting chance left in this caper.

MONDAY

fter stopping at a Village deli for coffees, one black and
the other with just a dash of cream to change the color,
a dozen assorted donuts, and the morning *Times*, I pulled
Anthony's pickup in front of Miss Ross's apartment building.
She lived about two blocks off Bleeker Street. It was a quarter
to seven, and this part of New York was slowly joining the
hustle and bustle with the rest of Manhattan. At least I knew
the time again. DeNato's watch ran like a charm. In another
fifteen minutes, that alarm in my apartment would go off.
One of the pleasures in life was not being home when the
alarm goes off. It helped to solidify relationships with the
neighbors, just in case there was any doubt how thin the
walls were in that flat. After the beating I took and the lack
of neighborly response, aside from dear Marge, I figured I was
good for at least one day of aggravation with the neighbors.

I decided to trade in my business attire for a more casual
look, since I was running low on suits. I had a green sweater
over a light blue shirt. The shirt was tucked into my cleanest
and last pair of blue jeans. I had washed them just last week
and for me, that's one stop short of new. Completing my
ensemble was an Irish tam a cousin had sent me a few years
back, and my sneakers. My fedora was parked in a trashcan
outside my apartment, along with my shirt, shoes, underwear,
and tie, waiting for the morning garbage pickup. But here I
was, the picture of Sunday in New York, on Monday.

I honked, and the door opened. Morgan skipped down
the steps and Miss Ross stood at the door, dressed in an oriental bathrobe, her long brown hair flowing past her shoulders.
I was jealous. So this is what blond hair and blue eyes gets

you. I was going to get out of the car, but thought better of it. I sat there letting my jaw muscles flex my frustration, staring at the speedometer that was lucky if it ever saw forty-five miles an hour again.

A chipper Morgan climbed into the pick-up. "Morning. What's the matter, no cup of joe?"

I engaged the gears and let the truck take Morgan and me up to 78th. We arrived at the apartment building at seven-twenty and were met and ushered through the front door by the super, who practically escorted us to the unit.

Amanda let us in and led us to the kitchen where we arrayed our donut selection. With a smug grin, Clay dropped the newspaper. On the front page was a half-page photograph of Rocky DeNato followed by an article with a byline credit to Clay Morgan. Mary Jane and Amanda stared at the photo as Clay beamed with pride.

The two women were fully dressed and ready for work. Rachel was curled up on the sofa in the sitting room, looking sleepy. She was probably recovering from a party-filled weekend, just like a normal college kid. Who cared what Dad did to afford room, board, and tuition for college? Well, after this morning, there might be a spark of interest.

Clay had told me he'd filed the story yesterday evening, after composing it in Emily Ross's sitting room and taking a taxi down to the paper to drop off his article in time for the morning's headline. He felt like he was back on his way into the reporting business, and it had been indicated there would be big bucks for him when he submitted the conclusion to the Eloise Rumsfeld murder story. The headlines in the paper read: *DeNato Done In*. It was not a classic.

"Mandy, do you think you could give Rachel a poke so to wake her up? James and I have some questions we would like to ask y'all." Clay was filled with renewed confidence from his story's release. By seven-thirty-five, we were all one big, happy family.

"Yesterday, Rocky DeNato was killed," I started.

Mary Jane broke in. "We know. It's plastered all over the newspaper you brought over."

"Hush, darling," Amanda said.

"He was killed at Anthony's Repair Shop in Brooklyn, where Clay and I took him," I continued. That got a stir from the ladies. "We wanted to ask him some questions, like why he would torch my car. Why send goons to my apartment to give love taps to my kidneys? Who was his employer? Things like that. When the bullets started flying, we thought they were meant for us, but we were wrong. They were meant for all three of us. We guess that Mr. Big, the man behind all of this, whoever he is, wanted to keep Rocky quiet and take us out in the same hail of bullets."

I watched all three of the ladies. Rachel yawned and slumped further into her chair, but I still had her attention. Well, I liked to believe I did. Amanda looked from me to her brother in wide-eyed amazement. Mary Jane fidgeted, her eyes never resting on anyone or anything.

"You all right, Miss Somers?" I asked.

"Yeah, sure. Are you about through? I have to get down to the store and check my inventory."

"Hang around for just a few more minutes, would ya?" I asked. "There was a lot going on the night Eloise Rumsfeld was killed, especially in this apartment." Mary Jane got up and got a glass of water. Amanda watched her, and Rachel appeared more interested. "Mary Jane, you were entertaining Vernon Rumsfeld most of the afternoon, weren't you? At least until Clay here got in row with Vernon."

Mary Jane looked from me to Clay and her roommates but didn't say a thing.

"Tell me, how did you meet Vernon? How is it that you ran into him, literally, in a deli in the financial district, when your job is on 34th? How did you come to travel all the way down to Wall Street for lunch?"

Mary Jane's color changed to a pasty white and she dropped her glass, shattering it on the floor. "I, I…" She looked at Amanda and then at Morgan and finally at me. "I was paid to." Her face was blank, no expression, remorse, or fear. It was like she was in a trance.

The breaking glass spurred Rachel into action. She got up and squatted to collect the bigger shards.

"Let's start with who paid you, and to do what?" It was more of a statement than a question. I stared into Mary Jane's eyes, hoping they would be windows to her soul.

Mary Jane broke into tears and covered her face. "I am so sorry. I didn't think things would turn out like this. I am so sorry." Her shoulders heaved with sobs.

Rachel deposited the glass she had gathered, reached for the box of tissues, and handed it to Mary Jane as Amanda led her to a more comfortable chair. We followed them into the sitting room. Rachel stayed in the kitchen to finish cleaning up Mary Jane's mess.

"I knew Rocky from a ways back. Back when I…had a prior job."

"Doing what?" Rachel called from the kitchen. Her growing anger seemed to come from nowhere, like she knew something and hadn't shared it with us, yet.

Mary Jane turned and nodded to Rachel. "I was a prostitute," she said. "All right? I worked some of the streets between 8th Ave. and Broadway, down around 43rd and 44th. Rocky recruited me. He said he had a job for me and gave me money for an upscale wardrobe with a little left over. He told me he had a friend who could get me honest work. I told him I didn't need that, but Rocky said his job required it. He said it was a 'special' job." Mary Jane's eyes were red from crying and she blew her nose, turning it cherry red, like a blonde, twenty-four-year-old, gorgeous Santa.

"Rocky said that Mr. M.—that's what he called him— Mr. M. got me a job at Macy's in the cosmetics department. I showed up and started working, just like that. About two weeks later, Rocky paid me a visit and told me to move out of my flophouse and respond to an advertisement for a room-mate. He handed me a copy of the ad for this place." Mary Jane kept her gaze on the floor. "When Amanda rented me the room, Rocky upped my pay to cover most of my portion of the rent. He said that what I made at Macy's would cover the rest and then some.

"Once I was all moved, Rocky said I had to meet this guy downtown and get to know him. You know, really get to know him. So I got an extended lunch one day and went down to the deli where Vernon Rumsfeld regularly took his lunch. Rocky had given me a picture of him so there was no mistakin' what he looked like. So I run into him. I really ran into the guy and knocked his tray and lunch on the floor." A chuckle escaped her taut lips.

"Did you take Clay's things and give them to Rocky or his boys? Was that how Morgan's things got into the Rumsfeld brownstone?"

"No, I didn't. But Vernon had time to get them when he was here the day his wife was killed. I left him alone in the apartment when I went back to the room to refresh myself."

"Please go on," I said.

167

"After a few weeks, one of Rocky's hoods stopped at my counter at Macy's and told me to bring Vernon up to the apartment on Wednesday afternoon—the day his wife was killed—and to keep him there 'til after dark. Well, with Amanda's brother comin' in and the ruckus and all, I couldn't stop Vernon from leaving." She broke down again. "I… I couldn't…" And she sobbed again. "When Clay came in, I retreated to my room, and that would have been his opportunity."

"We had left Clay's shoes and cologne on that table, but it was later that afternoon or evening, remember Mary Jane?" Amanda pointed to a hall table next to the front door of the unit while she looked at Somers.

"That's right," Mary Jane responded. "After Vernon left the apartment I found them in the closet in my room. It wasn't 'til after Amanda came home that evening that we decided just to leave them on the table. Amanda said that Clay could come by anytime and pick them up. You never did, did you?" Mary Jane asked turning toward Clay.

Clay just shook his head.

Turning to Mary Jane, Amanda tried to calm her friend, "There, there, sweetie," said Amanda. "Take it easy. This isn't your fault." Amanda had little success, but I wasn't helping things, either.

"What time did Vernon leave, doll?" I asked.

"Right after Clay came in and began shouting at him, around one or two. It was shortly after their argument quieted down, I suspect. I never came out of the room so I don't have a real good handle on the time. I really don't know. I closed the door and just stayed there until it was all quiet for some time. I was afraid."

"What time did you throw Rumsfeld out, Morgan?" I asked.

"Around one or one-thirty. We argued for a bit while he gathered his things. Then he picked up the phone and made a call, like I wasn't there. Just turned around and picked up the phone as nice as you please. I was kind of floored, but I let him make it."

"Who was it to?" I asked.

"Beats me. He never used a name. Just muttered into the receiver and then hung up. He turned to me, smiled, and walked out with his jacket in a bundle." Then in a smaller voice, Clay said, "I never saw the guy again."

"It is strange that you haven't mentioned this before. You've been holdin' out on me." I shot Clay a look.

Something else came to mind. "We need to investigate the possibility that these guys had you booted from your old job, Clay. Whoever this Mr. M. is, it seems he has connections, big connections."

"I had figured Rumsfeld had walked out with my stuff. Now who can I blame?" asked Clay, perplexed over the theft of his shoes.

"I've gotta go," said Mary Jane. She hustled back to her bedroom for a few minutes and returned dressed to attract attention, mascara all cleaned up and clothes looking just so. Mary Jane rushed by us and made for the front door, her purse clutched tightly in her hand. I tried to stop her, but she pushed me aside and fled like Elroy "Crazy Legs" Hirsch.

Amanda looked at her brother and me. "I'm sorry. Really, I am. I had no idea what she'd been up to."

Clay and I stared at her, speechless. "That son-of-a-bitch stole my stuff right out from under my nose and got away with it."

Rachel got up, waved to us, and said, "I'm going back

to bed," then walked out of the apartment and went back upstairs.

Amanda began to get ready for work.

"Now what do we do?" Clay asked.

"I don't know. At least we know how the two met and how your clothes got into the brownstone," I answered.

"Yeah, but who is Mr. M.?" asked Amanda.

"My guess is Rachel's father. Montfort," I answered.

"It's time we have our interview with him," Clay said.

"I'd like to be better prepared before we do that," I replied. "Tomorrow, I'll see Clienfelter again, first thing, and see if we can get a hold of the will." I rubbed my chest. Christ, it hurt like hell. I stretched out on the sofa and tried the remains of my coffee; it was cold. "Do ya think you could brew me a cup of joe?"

Amanda agreed to and left for the kitchen. Clay sank into a chair next to the sofa and looked at me. "What's going on in there?" He pointed toward my head. "Let's go now while we have the momentum. We don't need a will just to talk to the guy."

"Yeah, but I need some recovery time." I gingerly patted my rib cage. "My ribs are killing me. I need to be in better shape than this if we are going to visit Rachel's dad." I saw the anguish on Clay's face. "Maybe I can step up the meet with Bernie later this afternoon. Sort of move things up a little," I thought out loud.

"It's all neatly tied up, isn't it? Think about it. It began as an obvious frame job on you, but why? Why frame you?"

Clay shrugged. "Beats the shit out of me."

"What's that?" Amanda yelled from the kitchen.

"Can she hear us?" I asked Clay.

"Naw, go on," Clay urged.

"Then there's DeNato. One minute he is in this up to his nose and the next he becomes the target. What's with that? He'd just been released from Montfort's employ and apparently took up with some other mystery man or woman."

"I thought you explained that away fairly well," Clay responded.

I brushed his comment aside and stared at the ceiling.

"And about the five grand you took from DeNato on my behalf. I could really use it about now," Clay interjected.

"You must have gotten paid for the story, right?" I asked.

Clay stared at me.

"Okay, here. Sorry about that." I handed him a wad of cash from my pants pocket.

Clay counted the money. "Hey, there's only four G's here."

"Yeah. There have been expenses." I stared at the ceiling again, considering the information. "There's something I'm missing here, Clay."

"My additional grand." He sat there pouting.

I smiled. "You're quibbling over compensation from a gravely mistaken hood who wanted to apologize for his misdeed?"

"No, I'm hearing expenses and not seeing any benefits from them. Where'd you learn such big words? Compensation. That just doesn't sound like you."

Amanda returned from the kitchen with coffee and sat next to me on the sofa, forcing me to sit up again. "What are you boys talking about now? Got the case solved yet?"

"Let's catch up for lunch. I got a few things to go over with ya," I said to Clay.

"Okay. Maxie's?"

"Well, yeah. We can't eat at your place." I looked around the apartment.

171

"Clay, where are you staying these days?" Amanda asked, following my look around her apartment.

I could barely stand the answer.

<hr/>

It was about ten when I returned to my apartment. I thought I needed classier attire to wow the upscale New Yorkers I was going to visit. I opted for a worn brown sport jacket and striped tie over a white shirt and gray slacks and a pair of penny loafers. I needed a new fedora, so I headed to Columbus Avenue. I use a small hat shop in Midtown that carries a brand I love to abuse. By eleven, I was strolling toward Clienfelter's office in my new chocolate brown fedora. Yeah, it was a day earlier than I promised Clay, but I like to surprise people. Especially Bernie Clienfelter.

On my way, I stopped and had a hotdog from one of the street vendors. There's nothing like enjoying a dog while watching all the early eaters come out of their buildings and look for something to go with a two-martini lunch. I was glad that routine was no longer a part of my life. Well, it might have been, in my dreams.

When I got to Bernie's I took the elevator up and approached his office door. It was late enough that the office should have been opened for business with Delores smacking gum at her desk. Maybe they were all out to lunch; in which case, I was prepared to wait again. I hoped I could ask a few questions, get a copy of the will, and get out without Delores having to call the cops. Somehow, I knew Clienfelter was involved in this right up to his caterpillar mustache.

There was no "Out to Lunch" notice on the door. I was in luck, or so I thought.

I pushed open the door, expecting to see Delores's smiling face, but there was no smiling secretary and the waiting area was vacant. My inner alarm went off. When I looked into Clienfelter's office, I could tell things were not okay. I checked my coat for my gun, but found nothing. Did I leave it back at Maxie's? Feeling a little vulnerable, I decided to play mouse and be as quiet as I could, in case there were lingering bad guys. Before I called this in to O'Malley, I thought I'd better take a look, so I could give details over the phone, I told myself. I was feeling altruistic for a change.

In Clienfelter's office, the visitors' chairs were crumpled into kindling, not that they were the sturdiest to begin with. His desk had been pushed into the far corner and his chair was upside down, lying next to the desk. The bookcases were tipped over and their contents lay scattered. It kinda reminded me of my apartment after those goons tried to make riblets out of my chest.

In the small space between the desk and the wall, a leg stretched out amid the clutter. A dark charcoal pant leg, from what looked like a very classy suit, had crept up the calf, exposing pale skin and a black sock under a black lace-up. It looked as though Clienfelter had been put to sleep, permanently. And from my angle, bloodlessly.

I tried stepping over the debris, but it was difficult. There was little in the office that was not broken. Papers were strewn across the floor and the desk, now lying on its side. Talk about needing a maid. I moved the furniture and checked; it was Clienfelter, all right. He was partially covered with papers. Some of the papers were caught in pooled blood just beyond his head. I didn't look to see if it was a gunshot or trauma to the skull from a blunt or sharp instrument. It didn't make much difference. Dead is dead. I'll let the cops and coroner figure it out.

There were a few footprints on some of the paper lying about the floor. Looked like there were two or three of them. Must have been quite a time for Bernie. Now I needed to make sure my shoe prints weren't among the others.

I did a quick scan for the will. I had a feeling that whoever did this was looking for the same thing. I made my way back to the front office and Delores's desk and decided not to call the precinct right away. I wanted some quiet time to explore. I went through Clienfelter's office carefully and then through the small closet, where there was a safe. It was open, but nothing in it was worthwhile. I also went through Delores's desk and then the coat closet in the reception area. I shook my head. It was strange Delores wasn't there. I wondered where she'd been stashed, trashed, or escaped to. I was hoping for the last alternative. I kind of liked her, gum chewing and all. She brought class to the joint.

I was standing with hands on my hips and my fedora perched on the back of my head trying to get my arms around what I was looking at in the outer office when I heard a nearly silent gasp. I turned to see Delores standing in the doorway to the office. She was looking in at whatever mess she could see from her vantage. I walked over to her and put my arm around her, and tried to lead her away from her office, but she resisted my efforts.

"Come on, doll. This is no place for you now. Let's go down the hall and get a cup of joe from the break room. I'll call the cops, and we can wait in the break room for their arrival." I said.

She nodded, and we moved to a quieter place. I seated her at one of the lunch tables and looked at the coffee pot. Ugh, it was going to take some work making fresh coffee.

"Let me go back to your office and call the cops. I'll be right back."

Delores's eyes got big. "Please, don't leave me alone. I… I…" Then she burst into tears. Her shoulders shook in time to her sobs.

"You're fine here. I'll be right back."

I was lucky enough to reach McFarland, who said he'd call in O'Malley. He also warned me not to touch anything. It was a little late for that, but I agreed to leave everything as it was and returned to talk with Delores.

The break room, as it was called, looked just like I had seen it when I was waiting for Clienfelter last week. The coffee pot that had been cooked one or two times too many was still on a lit burner from this morning's hardened brew. The coffee looked like it had already solidified. I tried to clean out the pot with minimal luck. I looked for coffee filters so I could brew a fresh pot.

"They're in the pantry," Delores said. She got up and pulled out some filters and coffee, but left the door open. She stood there, staring at the inside of the pantry, as if mesmerized.

"What's wrong, doll?" I asked.

"The police are on their way, right?"

"Yeah, but if I know O'Malley, he's going to take his sweet time." My voice betrayed my mounting dislike for the sergeant.

I retrieved the filter and coffee from Delores. She turned to me and said, "Hand me a knife, will ya?" She pointed to a set of drawers next to the sink.

"Sure, you got it. One knife coming up." I took out a knife and handed it to her, watching to make sure she didn't plunge it into anything important, like me. Rather, she went back into the pantry and pried open a piece of sheet rock and extracted a file. She handed it to me. "These are our notes on a property transaction. It contains information that I think led to Mr. Clienfelter's death."

I was torn over what to do next, but she made up my mind for me. "We believe these files contain information that implicate Misters Rumsfeld and Montfort in a number of decade-old murders. One of the law enforcement officers on the case apparently turned his back on the evidence and let a suspicious person go with minimal investigation."

"You have names and dates in these notes?" I asked.

"Yeah, sure. You're a PI, right?" she asked, and I nodded. "I am reluctant to let this material fall into the wrong hands, especially since I think Mr. Clienfelter was using it to… leverage, shall I say…a client. And I use the word 'client' in a very broad sense."

"What exactly is in this set of documents?" I asked.

"There's a will and other typed documents in addition to some notes. These documents are not meant for others, least of all the police, except for the will, that is. The officer who was on the old case is still around, and I wouldn't want to leave myself open, if you know what I mean."

"I'll make sure the police get the will. If we ever solve this riddle and nail the dirty cop, I'll bring this to light then. Okay?" I gave her my best serious PI look. Delores nodded and looked away.

"There might be more than one …" Delores kind of mumbled.

For a few seconds there was a lull in our sparkling conversation as I tried to digest what she had just said. Norman had talked of a dirty cop, and now Delores indicating there might be more than just one. *Boy these notes ought to be pretty steamy*, I thought.

"Thanks," I said coming back into our situation. "When

you feel up to it, we can go over the notes in more detail, but just relax right now, okay?" I put my hand on her shoulder to offer comfort. Her tears were gone, replaced by determination in her eyes. She nodded again.

I tucked the folder into the waist of my trousers just over my butt, under my jacket. I watched Delores staring off into some other world, probably one that didn't have her ex-boss lying dead down the hall. The elevators made their familiar noise as they opened and we heard voices of police officers echoing in the hall way as they tried to figure out which way to go. It seemed like a moment of comedy with the bantering in the hall that brought me back to my youth and watching the Keystone Kops films. My smile quickly vanished remembering our situation.

I told Delores to replace the sheetrock and sweep away any dust from her handiwork, making sure that the hiding spot wasn't noticeable. While Delores cleaned up, I went to talk to the police.

Stepping into the hall, I saw the last of the cops enter Clienfelter's office. One was posted on the door like a guardian. He inspected me as I strolled down the hall toward him. I politely nodded and entered the office. He made no attempt to restrain me. *Must know just how important I have become on the case*, I figured.

"'Bout time New York's finest got here. How's business, O'Malley?" I asked.

"Every time I see you, a dead body appears. What's your secret, Dugan?" O'Malley looked a little perturbed. "This is goin' to cause a hell of a lot more paperwork on top of what you've already generated. You're beginning to piss me off. Where you been, anyway?"

"I was down at the break room making sure the coffee

pot was filled up so you guys could have a cup. Hope you brought the donuts."

O'Malley gave me the "don't screw with me" eye and said, "So what do we have here?"

"From what I saw, O'Malley, it appears someone was lookin' for something."

"Do you think they found it?" he asked. I shrugged as he barked orders at one of the patrolmen. "Start looking for anything you think might be missin'."

"Like what, Sarge?"

"I don't know, just look." O'Malley turned back to me, waiting for an answer.

I was turning to leave so I shot back at O'Malley. "My guess would be no, just by lookin' at the corpse over there." I pointed in the general direction of Clienfelter's body.

"Hold on, Dugan," O'Malley called. "Just what were you doin' here?"

I turned back. "Well, the estate owes me money, and I came to collect it. Mr. Clienfelter is, or was, the administrator of the estate, so he had control over the purse strings."

"So you just waltzed in here?" O'Malley asked with some sarcasm.

"No. The door was slightly open and unlocked, like usual." I pointed back to the main door into the office and reception area. "I entered and when I saw what you're looking at, I did what every upstanding citizen is expected to do when they expect foul play. I called the cops. I didn't touch a thing, so your boys can get some prints. Now if there is anything else, I have a place to be and a short time to get there." I stopped and pushed my latest fedora back on my head. "I almost forgot. There's a secretary who works here." I pointed to the desk.

"Oh, yeah? And where is she, Mr. Know-It-All?"

"She's in the break room waiting for you," I responded. "She's a tad upset, so try to go easy on her, for once."

"She see anything or know anything?"

"Not that she told me. Says she was in the ladies' room when the goons came in, and when she heard the ruckus, she made tracks to another office."

"She got a name?"

I leaned over, picked up her nameplate from the front of her desk, and tossed it to O'Malley. "The break room is down the hall on your right, but all those donuts are gone. I checked already. Anything else you need from me, Sarge?"

"Not for the time being, but you still owe me a statement from Saturday, and another for today and another time or two." O'Malley looked perplexed at the whole situation, but well in control of himself. "What do ya think the goons were lookin' for, again?"

"Beats me, probably some legal document that Clienfelter had or knew about. After all, he is a lawyer. Why don't you go with that? After all, I'm only a PI, remember?"

I waved good-bye and headed back to the break room to warn Delores and ask her to swing by Maxie's in a few days for a more in-depth discussion and a review of her notes. It's better to have these conversations once she would have collected herself a little. A cop showed up as I was making my exit and stood outside the entrance to the room. I guess he was there to guard Delores from the vicious criminal elements in the building, or more than likely there to make sure she didn't flee the scene before O'Malley got his *chance* to talk with her.

"Don't worry, doll. They don't bite, but they do bark a lot." At least that got a smile out of Delores.

I made for the elevators. On the way down, I heard

O'Malley calling the lieutenant to report on the next murder victim in the Eloise Rumsfeld trail of bodies.

***

TIME NEVER RESTS. I LOOKED AT MY NEW WATCH. IT WAS ONE-fifteen, and the hot dog was getting lonely for a beer and maybe a tuna sandwich. After a smelly burp and an attack of heartburn, I was convinced of it. I hailed a cab back to Maxie's for a real lunch and an opportunity to go over the new evidence with Morgan. But more importantly, I hadn't checked the track sheet for today's races at Aqueduct and I was beginning to panic.

Maxie's was practically vacant except for a couple of fellas at a table, three guys at the bar, and Maxie. In the corner where the band usually sets up was a new jukebox playing tunes while Maxie stood behind the bar, proud as a peacock. I removed the folder from my waistband and settled in a deserted portion of the bar, avoiding my "office" for some reason. Maxie's just didn't seem the same after my garbage dive.

"What ya think, laddie?" He looked like a proud cow gazing at her new calf.

"Hope you didn't trade in the band for that." I flipped a thumb in the direction of the music.

"Naw, it's for the day customers. Give them a little sound. What'll ya have?"

"How 'bout a Pabst and a tuna on rye. Actually, I'm supposed to meet Morgan for lunch. Let's start with the beer and I can work my way into the sandwich when he arrives." My mouth watered just thinking about the beer.

Maxie pulled a draft for me.

"I had a hot dog a while back, and it's not sittin' right." Right then, an eruption of hot dog gas burst from my mouth, the second sign of a storied New York City hotdog. "Sorry," I said. "The beer should calm it right down. It's kind of an emergency beer, if you wouldn't mind." A not-so-~~gentile~~ genteel after-burp escaped, and I glanced at my old booth.

Using the mirror, I took another quick look around the bar, trying to see who noticed my transgression. The two fellas at the table caught my attention, and I watched them while waiting for my PBR. There was something oddly familiar about them—the way they acted, dressed—something. They were both in their shirtsleeves, with the sleeves rolled up to just below the elbow. Jackets off, ties on, suspenders hanging over their white shirts. Their hats were on the table, nice fedoras, the kind one buys at a real nice men's clothing store, like Saks Fifth Avenue. The suits weren't cheap, either. *Oh, well, that's a puzzle for another day,* I told myself. But it wouldn't let go of me.

Maxie appeared and put down my beer. He noticed me eyeing the two fellas. "Those are the guys that delivered the jukebox. You need to go over there and have a gander at the box, lad. Here's a nickel. Play yourself a tune. It plays 78s. I hear there's one coming out that's going to play 45s, but I didn't want to wait for that."

"Thanks." I grabbed the nickel and stood up. Turning to Maxie, I asked, "Who are those two, really?"

Maxie looked over at them. "I told you. Those are the lads that delivered the box. I guess they work for the fella that runs the vending company. Why?"

"They just seem a little over dressed for deliverymen. Thanks again for the nickel." I walked to the machine, slid the coin in the slot, and moved the metal tabs to find a tune.

"I Can Dream, Can't I?" by the Andrews Sisters and Gordon Jenkins had since fallen from my favorites list; too many memories. Ah, "Rent Party." Now there's a tune I could enjoy hearing again.

The walk to the box also afforded me a better look at the two guys and what they were looking at. It definitely wasn't a racing form. Looked like notes, like the kind you'd pass to your girlfriend during class. They looked up as I walked back to my seat, and I nodded. Their white shirts were a lot fancier than anything I'd ever seen a day-grunt wearing, plus they had cufflink holes in the shirtsleeves. They were out of place. Something to poke my nose into after I healed from the current case.

I got back to my seat about the same time as my sandwich and Clay Morgan.

"Let's sit at the booth," Clay said hurriedly.

"Sure. You patch things up for us with Amanda and her roommates?" I asked, carrying my beer and sandwich to the corner office table.

Clay collapsed into the seat across from me. "Yeah, we're all good there. What a day, huh?"

"You have no idea." I was about to tell Morgan about Clienfelter when Delores appeared.

"You need to stay for this," I said softly to Clay. "We got some things to catch up on."

"Yeah," he said and then caught sight of Delores. "Oh?" He sounded like a spy working a conspiracy.

I turned to Delores and said in a louder voice, "Delores, I didn't know you frequented this tavern."

She spit her chewing gum into a tissue and stuffed it in her purse. "I wanted to come down and see where you work. I thought we could talk about what happened today, but that subject is not appropriate for this atmosphere."

She was still upset, and I couldn't blame her. Matter of fact, I hadn't expected to see her for at least a few more days. She started to leave. Morgan finally recognized the name from our previous conversations. I struggled to get out of the booth, but Morgan's quicker pace put him well in front of me. He met Delores on her way to the door.

"Hi, there, little lady," Morgan said. "My name is Clay Morgan. I'm Mr. Dugan's associate." He paused. "Please join us at our booth. Really, we are harmless." Southern charm always seemed to work on Northern women.

Clay gently guided her back to our booth, and Maxie stopped to see if we wanted anything more to drink. We deferred to Delores with Clay, telling her I would buy whatever she wanted from the bar.

"Coffee. Black, please." Maxie left us, and she turned to me. "Did you get a chance to read the file?"

"Not yet," I said. The file lay on the table next to me, where everyone could see it. "I just got here myself. Didn't the police want to question you?"

"Yeah, that sergeant is a jerk. He didn't have many questions for me beyond trying to figure out what the goons wanted from Mr. Clienfelter."

"What'd you tell them?" I asked.

"Something about a possible foreclosure, probably looking for the papers to delay legal action. Something like that."

"And the sergeant bought it?"

Delores nodded.

"What file?" Clay asked, staring at the manila folder.

"There are more connections in this case than in a telephone operator's switchboard. Delores showed me a file that belonged to Clienfelter. It contains information on a relationship between Montfort, Rumsfeld, and the Baker Building."

Delores stared at me, probably thinking about my oath of confidentiality to her.

"Why didn't you say something about this?" Clay demanded.

"Hush," I said. "I was getting to it. I've been a little tied up since I left your sister's apartment."

Maxie delivered Delores' coffee. Morgan ordered a hamburger and a beer. Delores looked up and thanked Maxie, something strange for folks at this table to do, and then she started rummaging around in her oversized purse.

After Maxie retreated, Delores produced her handwritten notes. "I like to use my notes for reference. I thought Mr. Clienfelter would use the information in the file for no good. I am certain it got him killed. I kept my personal notes, in case the file ended up missing."

"Smart, as long as they didn't discover you or your purse," I said.

"Let's cut to the chase. What's this all about?" Clay said.

Delores looked from Clay to me, and gave a little nod. "You told me you would not share this information with anyone, Mr. Dugan."

"Mr. Morgan is my partner on this case. He's kinda up to his ears in it, if you catch my meaning. But whatever we discuss will not leave the table." I looked at Clay, who nodded enthusiastically.

"Then I have your word, both of you, that you will keep this information between yourselves." We both nodded.

"You two can try to pull the wool over my eyes, but it will take you quite a while to gather what I did in one afternoon." Clay opened his mouth, and Delores shut him down. "Even if you are a hot-shot reporter without a job."

"Okay," I said. "We agree. It will be just between the three of us."

"No secret sharing with the sister, Mr. Morgan," Delores said.

"Okay, okay. No sister sharing," Clay acquiesced. He turned to me and whispered, "How does she know all of this stuff about me?" I shrugged.

Delores looked at both of us and said, "Mr. Clienfelter had me do background checks on both of you after the first visit by Mr. Dugan here. It was interesting." She sat there letting her eyes rest on me for a second. She then began her tale about what she knew about the Baker Building.

Delores' overview included the consortium's purchase of the building and how, one by one, Vernon Rumsfeld's four partners met their demise. Mentioning Clive Montfort's uncle, Delores illustrated how Rumsfeld and Montfort created a history between each other and the ways this history might still be in play.

"I see the connection," I said. "Is this what Clienfelter did with this information? Take it to Montfort and get himself killed, ya think?"

"I think he blackmailed one of the participants, but that is just conjecture, and I wouldn't know which one."

Delores folded her hands in her lap and focused on the table in front of her. She looked tired, as if she'd fought the fight and lost. Delores against the world and the world was landing a lot of solid blows that she no longer had the strength to fight off.

"I don't know which one." Delores repeated as tears welled up in her eyes. "He never gave me that kind of information, thank goodness. But if I had to guess, he was taking aim at Montfort himself. Bernie suspected that this whole thing went beyond these two players. Ya know, he was really a rotten boss, and not a very good person to most of his clients. Mr. Clienfelter knew the law, and he'd exploit loopholes to enrich himself at his clients' expense. His clients expected him to use the law to protect them, but Mr. Clienfelter sometimes turned against clients with or without considerable holdings and set up foreclosures so he could seize property for both himself and his benefactor, Mr. Montfort."

"So why did you work there?" Clay asked.

"That's not playing nicely, Clay. Just listen, OK?" I told Morgan

"No, that's OK. Mr. Clienfelter paid very well and my family needs the money, so ..." Delores just left it there. She looked down at her skirt making sure that it was perfectly smooth over her knees then stared at her coffee cup.

"I think that others involved with his ventures might have had some influence over him." Clay appeared to try to get in Delores' good graces by turning on the charm, but there were gems of wisdom in what he had said.

"Like a brokerage firm with an active acquisition department, looking for property in the city," I said.

"Yeah, like that," she said reaffirming Clay's inferred remark.

"Did Clienfelter ever work directly with Montfort?" I saw more dots beginning to connect. Eloise's diary notes helped to fill in the gaps.

"Yeah, more times than not. Together, they own real estate all over the five boroughs. Come to think of it, Bernie was a minority owner in most of the acquisitions, but not all. And when I say minority, he was a two-bit player in shark infested waters." Delores looked from Clay to me resting her gaze on me while I nodded in response.

"So Montfort became the financier, and Clienfelter created the opportunities. Nice deal." I stared off for a second, wondering if Bernie's killer was his partner and if it was over some fact that Delores and he discovered. That didn't make sense, but it left only one person who would have wanted to murder Bernie Clienfelter, though I doubted he would have gotten his hands dirty doing it. The real question was did this perpetrator do in both Clienfelter and Eloise Rumsfeld? And if so, was it just out of greed or was there something more?

"Whoever Bernie was leveraging, I think he came to make sure that it stopped and all the information he had on hand was destroyed," I said.

"Stop. Wait a minute." Clay looked from me to Delores. "What are you two talking about? Is Clienfelter dead?"

"Yeah, he's dead. It happened sometime this morning, and yours truly discovered the body." I pointed at my chest with my thumb. "After leaving the apartment, I went and bought a new hat. Then I dropped in on Clienfelter, but I found his office ransacked and him—well, I found him in his office. Sorry, Delores. Delores returned shortly after I got there, and she shared the folder with me." I tapped on the manila file under my right arm.

"Delores, why weren't you involved during the attack on your office?" asked Clay.

"I had to use the lady's room. While I was in the hall, I heard shouting from a meeting Bernie was having with unscheduled visitors. They sounded really angry, so I ran down to Clarisse's office to wait it out. Bernie has had those types of meetings before, and they make me very uncomfortable."

"Who is Clarisse?" Morgan asked.

"Clarisse is the receptionist at the CPA firm just down

the hall from us. Clarisse said we should call the police, but her boss said not to. He said if Bernie was getting a tongue-lashing, he probably deserved it. He invited me to stay for as long as I needed. I must have been there for at least forty-five minutes before I returned and found Mr. Dugan standing in the outer office."

I was so entranced with our conversation I missed the departure of the dapper delivery service men sitting across the room from us. Maxie wasn't looking particularly busy, so I signaled another round for the table.

"Delores, was there any other ownership on the deeds that Clienfelter and Montfort shared that consistently reappeared?" I was intrigued with Delores's earlier comment about Bernie taking a minor position on foreclosed properties.

"I think there were a few names and a conglomerate, maybe two. I'm not really sure, but I know there was one that kept popping up."

"Conglomerate?" Clay asked.

"Well, what I consider a conglomerate. Probably a better description would be a consortium of companies operating under a single name for, in this instance, property ownership. Usually for some minority share, nothing really substantial." Delores looked from Clay to me. "Certainly you don't think a consortium of companies wanted to kill Bernie, do you?"

"Delores, why don't you go back to the office and see if anything is missing?" I said. "Mr. Morgan has nothing to do for the rest of the day. I am sure he would be glad to lend a hand."

"What are we looking for?" Clay asked. "And what are you going to be doing?"

"See if you can get a list of the property owners who joined

Montfort and Clienfelter on a usual basis. Let's just see how extensive this ring has gotten in the city."

I looked up at Clay. He was still staring at me, defiance in his eyes. "You're a reporter. You're supposed to be good at this type of thing. I have a meeting to attend."

———◆———

I SUDDENLY HAD A BRAINSTORM, SO I HOPPED A CAB DOWN to the Street—Wall Street, that is—for a pick in today's race. I knew my man had to be located some place with high traffic, where men were likely to gather and chat. There are a lot of buildings, but not that many where the information I was interested in could be over heard. By chance, a block from the Baker Building, in the lobby of a new office building, I spotted his shoeshine stand. Lo and behold, sitting on a stool in front of a brightly polished set of Oxfords, was Norman. There was a vacant seat for the "next in line," so I parked in it and made myself comfortable until the man was ready.

"Yo, man, penny loafers. Who'd figure a tough guy like you runnin' around in penny loafers? Only, you ain't got no pennies for the loafers." Norman moved over to soap up my shoes for the shine.

"Norman—" I was poised to give my latest acquaintance a round of accolades, but he held up his hand.

"Hush yo mouth and sit right there. We ain't in Harlem, Toto. What you want, besides a decent shine on these poor pieces of leather?"

"You said you overhear things, right? You get any good tips on the ponies?" My spirits were high for a change, and my voice carried the hope of days to come.

"Aw, man, you goin to waste my time for a race tip? I thought you were working a real live murder." Oooh. The voice of doubt.

"Yeah, I am, and what you have told me seems to be right on, at least what I have been able to verify. All except the mole on the force, that is. I need a name. I can't verify without one." I prodded Norman. I couldn't go to Matt with just some rumor on the street even though my sources were quite credible and not in collusion.

As Norman thought about the mole, I threw him a question on the real reason I came down to visit, "So how about today at the 'Duct. Say, the fifth race?"

"Yeah. I got that covered, but it ain't coming as cheap as last night's. We goin to split the proceeds." Norman started on the second shoe.

"How much of a split?"

"Fifty-fifty." Norman said without skipping a beat.

"So you're going to pony up fifty percent of the cash for the bet?" I knew he liked his money too much to risk it on some horse race.

"No way. You take the risk, and I'll give you the nags. That's the upfront split and it's in your favor." Norman had made his point.

"Ninety-ten on the results," was my counter offer.

"What?" Norman's voice echoed in the large lobby. "Seventy-five and twenty-five and I get the seventy-five." I like his style of negotiations, just not on me.

"I'll give you seventeen and a half and that's my best offer."

"You make that twenty and you got youself a partner." Norman's last offer sounded acceptable if I can get the mole out of him, so I nodded. "Now here's what I got for the fifth." Norman reached into his pocket and pulled out a slip of paper. He checked the first side then flipped it to the other. "You got a pen?"

"Yeah." And I have another question for you, I thought, as I waited until Norman passed me not one nag's name, but three. "Thanks." I pocketed the info without more inspection.

"Have you ever heard of a third party getting into property ownership in New York, like a consortium, only it's not a consortium?" I asked.

"What you talkin' about, man?" Norman gave me a look, like I was crazy, and then said in a lower voice, "Yeah, I've heard tell of such a thing, but man, you better be careful, very careful, if you're going down that rat hole." He shook his head slowly and finished my shoes.

"That's fifty cents for the shoes and seventeen and a half percent when you get back to me with our winnings." Norman added in a lower voice.

"Any insight on our insider on the force?" I asked in a low voice.

"Maybe. From what I hear, that was some time ago, and the dude is either pretty senior now or dead." Norman kept his voice low and into his box of cloths and polish. I nodded, searching for a tip.

"See me next week," Norman said in a louder voice. Our business was concluded.

I HIGHTAILED IT DOWN TO AQUEDUCT TO PLACE MULTIPLE bets for the fifth race and still had time to walk to the paddock and look over the horses and their riders. The cab ride and subsequent walk did me wonders. I felt good, except for the part where Norman told me again that there really was a mole somewhere in the NYPD and that I had better be very careful with the dirty cop running around. Someone from the other side knew I was nosing around and getting too close. After DeNato, everyone knew I was putting sticks in beehives, searching for answers. I was beginning to believe that there might be a target on my back. That made me a little nervous.

I walked over to the starting gates, holding my three bets tightly in my hand, which was tucked into my pocket. How much more secure could I get? There was our, Norm's and mine, trifecta for the top three finishers, a winner's ticket, and finally, my winner's ticket. I had about $500 in play on the race. The pre-race parade started for the fifth race, and my heart skipped a beat. If the tri came in, I could walk away from all this crap and find something else to do. Yeah, right. I could at least get a new Jag. It was Monday, the start of a new week. All I had to do was pick the top three finishers, in order for the race. After all there were only nine horses running, sounded pretty easy to me. Plus I had Norman's tips.

"Well, well, well. If it ain't Jamie Dugan, PI. What are you doin' hanging around my track? Don't you got nowhere else to go?" A hand gently rested on my shoulder, over my pocketed and tightly clenched tickets in my jacket pocket below.

What's with all this touchie-feelie stuff that everyone is into these days?

"I heard you found the cash to put down on your favorite fifth race. You get an insider tip? Or did you find a way to fix a race?"

"Hey there, horse dick," I said to Brad Kilgore. He was the police department for the track, sanctioned by the State of New York, I guess. "How's it hangin?"

"Got a minute? We gotta talk, but not here. Let's step into my office." His oversized hands shifted from my shoulder down to my arm as he tried to lead me away.

At six feet he was a big boned and portly fella that meant he could muster some pretty effective leverage. His reddish hair was beginning to thin so he kept it covered with a brown hat with a flip-floppy brim. Not real classy but it kept its shape.

"Let's wait until after the race," I pleaded.

"Naw, let's not. I got something to tell ya and it can't wait." Kilgore's tug became more insistent, and I led the way to his office, which was behind the betting windows.

Once inside, Kilgore nestled his big frame in an oversized leather chair behind a really clean desk. You gotta love this type of job. There was a radio blaring in the background; some announcer was describing the horses getting set in the starting gate.

I stood there trying to look cool and disinterested in what the voice was saying, but deep down inside I felt more like a junkie needing a fix. I needed to get back to the finish line and watch the end of the race so I could revel in a long awaited victory. Who says there are not short cuts in making cash at the track?

I looked at Kilgore. "So what's so important you drag me away from my race?"

"One of your three horses was just scratched from the race." The look on my face must have given away the way I felt. I dropped the three tickets in my pocket and held both hands at the ready. He must have really enjoyed this part of our meet.

"What do you mean just scratched?" I said a little louder.

My veins must have been poppin' because Kilgore held up his hands and said, "Whoa, boy. You'll get your money back."

"Which nag was scratched?"

"The number four horse, Victor's Dance. The trainer pulled him at the last minute. Said he had strained something in a lower joint, who knows what. Anyway—"

"That was the odds-on favorite for the win and the leader for the tri. Are the rest running?" I still had one ticket in the race, my pick. It was supposed to be second in the trifecta, but I thought it might be the winner.

"And they're off!" The shout came from the loud speakers and radio in one blast. I couldn't stand it. I stood in Kilgore's office and listened as the jockey on Spoiled Sport, now my only bet in the race, made tactical blunder after tactical blunder and got boxed out of his run for the tape. He came in a dismal fourth. I about cried.

After being reimbursed for the bets, I wandered over to the paddock area to see if I could find my jockey friend, Angel Carbanos. I found him in street clothes, getting ready to make tracks.

"Angel, wait up," I called after him, starting a gentle trot in his direction.

"Hey, man. What's up?" Angel frowned. "Man, you need to work on your form."

"Hey. I need to ask you something about the fifth race. Why was the horse pulled? You know, Victor's Dance."

Angel's faced paled, and he turned and started walking toward the employee parking area.

"Hey, man, come on. What's with this? Just tell me that the horse had a pulled whatever, and I'm outta here."

"Not here, man." Angel took a few steps and then said in a low voice, "Meet me at Yarrow's."

"The Downbeat? What's a solid Latino doing traipsing around in Harlem?" I asked.

"Just do it," was all he said and he was gone.

"Hey, can we share a ride? I got here by cab." I was shouting at the diminishing figure as Angel got into his car and drove off.

I spun around to see what Angel was so upset about, but there was no one there.

It took me a while to get all the way up to Harlem from the 'Duct. When I got there, a line had formed, and one of Yarrow's boys was out front. I asked if Angel had dropped by yet. The guard at the door just nodded and let me in. It was the same stale smoke and booze that gave the place its class—that and the music. There was a guy pulling on his guitar strings with a standup bass, piano, and drums on stage. They were cutting the riffs, making the house sway to a lost tune but ride along the music's improv.

Yarrow saw me standing there like a deer about to be plowed over by the sound and led me to a small table away from the door, tucked back by the bar, a table I'd never seen before. That's where Angel and Norman sat, waiting for me to arrive.

"We got set up, man," Norman said as I slid into my chair. "Somebody did that on purpose, just to piss you off."

"Who was it, Angel?" I asked. I figured he knew what was going on.

"I don't know, man, but whoever it was has got some serious pull. That scratch could cost somebody jail time unless all the skids are greased."

195

"Who do ya think could have done this and had enough connections to get away with it?" I was getting a little concerned.

Yarrow came back to our table, pulled up the fourth chair, and sat down. Norman filled him in.

"You guys ever hear of Mr. M?" I asked.

"That's it? M?" Norman uttered.

I nodded. "That's it."

Yarrow slowly shook his head. "There's a Monsignor down in the financial district that I've heard people call M, but that's it."

"Well, that appears to be a dead end," I muttered.

"Maybe not," Norman said. His eyes stared unblinkingly at a place on the wall behind me.

"How did they know you would be down for the fifth race?" Yarrow interjected.

I took my gaze from Norman and looked over at Yarrow. "I'm always somewhere for the fifth race, and this time of year, it is the 'Duct. A lot of folks know that's just what I do. That suspect list would be too big to manage."

"Okay, we'll keep our ears to the ground and see what we can find out. But one thing does come to mind, and it is not any type of consortium like you talked about. It is just an individual, Clive Montfort. That would also fit the Mr. M description." Yarrow looked proudly at me, like he'd just thought of Montfort mid-sentence, which I believe he did.

"Does he have enough juice to pull off that race stunt?" I asked Yarrow. He just shook his head, raised and lowered his shoulders in response.

I looked back at Norman. "What do you mean, 'maybe not'?" He had peaked my interest.

piqued

196

Norman came back from his "other world" and looked over at me. "Monsignor might be the same guy that it's rumored has pull in this 'consortium' we keep dancing around." Norman had a serious look on his face. "But I hear the dude is really bad news."

Yarrow added, "Sort of like when we were finishing the clean up on Tarawa and realized that there was a freeway to Jap army headquarters and the road was open, both ways."

"Meaning?" I asked.

"You remember when we had cleared out enough Japs that we could practically see the other side of the island? The captain thought we had a road to divide the remaining enemy troops and was really pumped. As it turned out, it was a trap where we lost more good marines in a hail of enemy fire. You be careful of what you ask for." Yarrow's brow knitted and he looked a little sad as we recalled what we lived through. This was also like posting a warning flag in the face of an oncoming storm to both of us.

"I know nothing about this man. What else do you have?" I asked cautiously.

"He is just shadows," Angel added. "I hear whisperings of his activities, but just that—whisperings." Angel looked around the table. "I hear he has ears everywhere and a broad reach. He might have slammed your horse today."

"Why the title Monsignor?" I asked the table.

"I never got a name, just the title," said Norman.

"Maybe he's some kind of Catholic priest," added Angel.

"Naw," Yarrow said looking in Angel's direction. "Why would a priest go and do all of that?"

"Greed," was my answer. "Maybe he lives two lives. Priest by day and greedy bastard at night."

Norman just looked at me, eyes wide-open, mouth firmly

shut. He knew something more, but I couldn't seem to get it out of him.

There was nothing more from the guys around the table, so with that, I left. All of us were about at the same spot in the case: Suspicions, whispers, and conjectures. *But that was way ahead of Dingle and Morgan. O'Malley? I wonder... could he be the mole, or at least one of them?*

TUESDAY MORNING

Tuesday looked like it might be the start of a really good day. The sun was out, and temps were settling in to a comfortable level. After the news yesterday, I thought Morgan's head would be spinning with new information, so I wanted to give him a call. Maybe we could compare notes or something.

There's a small Italian deli across the street from my apartment with a phone just out front of the place, you know, like a public phone. While I was at it, I could get a coffee and a cannoli, which I did before making my call.

I tried Morgan's one or two newspaper friends that I knew. That was all the phone numbers I could remember, and I was running out of luck. In desperation, I called Maxie, even though he probably wasn't open yet. Much to my surprise, he picked up, and when I got a "Ain't seen him, laddie," I asked for Emily Ross's phone number. I hoped she was working out of her home and might shed some light on where the bum might be. After a few rings, I got a female voice. Well, at least it wasn't his voice with her in the background.

"Hey, doll," I began, between bites of cannoli and sips of coffee.

"Jamie?"

"Yeah." I had a knack for seducing women with words.

"Clay called here, looking for you. Did he reach you?" Emily's voice was a little edgy, not the usual smooth and sweet-as-honey tone that would have me tied up in knots for an hour after I hung up. This was more like *I've had too much coffee, and by the way, there is a burglar in the house.*

"No, doll." was my response. I wanted to say *you mean your housemate?* But I refrained.

"He wanted to leave you a message in case you called here." Emily went on.

"Oh," I said a little off handed.

"You're not jealous now, are you?" Emily responded, apparently getting my dig.

"Naw," I said, oozing jealousy out of every pore in my body.

"I know it doesn't look good, but Clay and I are just friends," Emily said. "We went to college together. He had a slight set back, and I thought I would help him out while he recovered. There are not many people around town who know where he hangs his hat for the time being, and we'd like to keep it that way."

She sure was a sweetheart, the kind that makes me grind my teeth at night. It made me wish I had been thrown out of my apartment. That sounded like a pretty good idea, given what I had just gone through. Either that, or there was something deeper there between the two roommates. Makes a guy wonder, don't ya know.

As I stood there in the phone booth, my aches and pains began to remind me that I had not recovered. I rocked and twisted a little, trying to stretch my back and ribs into a more comfortable position. That was about all the mobility I had this morning, but at least I had mobility.

"Do you know where he went?" I asked.

"Yeah, sure. I know where he is. He got a call from his sister and ran out of the building heading uptown. There's some sort of problem up there. He left word if you called to have you call the flat or join them. You want the number?"

I jotted the number on the back of the Rents Estimate sheet I'd been carrying around.

"Is everything all right, Jamie?" Her voice showed the

rising concern she had for her housemate. I wished it was concern for me, rather than Morgan, and I realized what a dope I was for thinking a dame like Emily could be interested in a lug like me.

"Yeah, everything is just fine. We were supposed to meet up again around now, and I was just checking on where he was. This explains it. Thanks for the info."

"Ah, Jamie? I'm going to be singing over at the Oynx this Friday night. Do you think you could make it? I sure could use a friendly face in the audience." She sounded so innocent and sexy I had to say yes. It was sort of like a date, I guess. I think I must have blushed a little because my ears were burning.

"Sure, doll, do you need a ride?" I asked, forgetting that my Jag was garbage stored in a burnt out auto repair shop whose the owner was convinced I was out to destroy his business.

"No, that's all right. I'll take a cab. I don't know when I'll be finished with the story I'm working on. Wait, isn't your car in the shop?"

So my plight had reached the masses. My sunny day grew overcast. We settled on a time, and I rang off.

As soon as Emily disconnected, I slid another dime into the slot and called Amanda's apartment. I got a busy signal. Yup, it was getting cloudier and cloudier.

I hailed a cab from in front of the deli and headed back to 78th. I was beginning to wear a rut in the road on the route from midtown to 78th. It took the cabbie twenty minutes, and that was with running two red lights and a whole lot of horn honking. He got a nice tip for trying.

As I walked up the stairs to the front door of the building, I noticed the super working in one of two small flowerbeds next to the curb. He looked like he was still wearing the same jeans and sweaty T-shirt from the first day we met; either that, or his whole wardrobe was filled with dirty jeans and stained T's. I wondered who did his wash. The super nodded as sweat dripped off his chin. I guess he needed the twenty dollars I gave him. I waved, smiled, and buzzed Amanda's apartment all in one motion. We were pals now.

"Yes?" It was Clay.

"Clay, it's Jamie. Let me in, will ya?"

"Where the hell have you been?" Then the buzzer sounded and I entered.

When I got inside the apartment, I found Rachel and Amanda sitting in the lounge. Rachel was in her bathrobe, as if she had just rolled out of the sack and down the stairs. *Damn,* I thought. *When is this girl not sleeping?*

Amanda, on the other hand, was dressed for work in a very stylish tan tweed suit. Damn, she looked finer every time I came up here. I needed to take my mind off women and get back on the case. I was sure they would be the death of me. What was that old saying? "Women, can't live with them, can't live without them," or some such crap.

Clay was not looking dapper. He had bed-head and looked like he, too, had just rolled out of bed. His tie hung loosely from his neck and his jacket was tossed over a chair. Worst of all, he needed a shave. I scratched my chin looking at him realizing that no blade had touched my face in some time either.

"Mary Jane is missing. Nobody has seen her since Sunday morning." Amanda said to me.

Clay said, "About an hour ago, Macy's called looking for her. Apparently, she didn"t show up for work this morning, which sent up red flags for Mandy, so she called me."

"Must have got you out of bed, I suspect," I said, with enough sarcasm to make me wish I had kept my mouth shut.

Apparently, Rachel ended up on the sofa after she wandered down the stairs looking for coffee after a long night of God knows what. She never made it to Amanda's kitchen or got that cup of coffee. She did get to the sofa, and there she lay, all curled up like a homeless dog.

"Do you know whether she stayed here last night?"

"I'm not sure," Amanda said. "It was a long day, and by nine, I was asleep. I checked her bed, and it looks like it hasn't been slept in for a while, but maybe she came back, stayed here, and then left before I got up. She's pretty good at keeping her room tidy. You know, bed made and all." She sighed loudly and looked around the room. "Hell, I don't know. It's not as if she moved out." Amanda's exasperated voice reflected her concern for a friend.

"And you?" I looked over at Rachel and kicked the sofa to wake her.

"What? Oh, nope. I haven't seen her, but I rarely do, anyway." Rachel looked at me and then Clay. She had a lost-puppy look that begged us to leave her alone so sleep might come again.

"Has anyone else checked her room? Clay? Does it look like she moved out?"

"Yeah, I checked it," Clay responded. "It's just like Mandy said, it looks like she anticipated coming back here and no, I don't think she was fixin' to move out."

I dropped my fedora on the coffee table and stood there for a second. "Well, this is turning out to be some day. Is Macy's expecting a call back from anyone?" They all shook their heads. "Well, she's an adult and knows her way about town. Maybe we shouldn't worry so much." I tried a weak smile, but didn't have it in me to pull it off. I gazed around at a lot of long faces in the apartment.

I turned around to survey where I could sit and then launched myself into an oversized chair. It took me a few seconds to recover from my landing, then Clay and I caught them up on the latest regarding Clienfelter and Delores, but carefully omitted the parts about the corrupt police officer and the juicier parts of the relationship between Vernon and Rachel's father. I also avoided discussion of a possible third party pulling strings, manipulating the players, so to speak. Right now, that was for internal consumption only, and God knows I didn't want the press putting stuff like that in the hands of the public, let alone starting rumors with our merry band.

After we finished up, the four of us sat in silence for a minute or two. I dropped the Clienfelter file on the coffee table in front of me and tried to find a more comfortable position.

"What ya got there?" Clay asked with keen interest.

"This? Oh, this is the Eloise Rumsfeld will. I sort of borrowed it."

"Well," said Clay. "Aren't you going to read it? There's been a lot of blood shed over this so far."

There were papers stuffed in with the will and they drifted to the floor as I opened the double-creased legal document. Two pages of handwritten text glided to a stop in front of Amanda. I reached down, but my perch on the chair was tenuous at best, and Amanda beat me to them. She picked them up and read aloud:

> *To whom it may concern:*
>
> *As part of the divorce agreement between Eloise D.*

Ziomek, the former Eloise Z. Montfort, and Clive B. Montfort, it is mutually agreed upon that the Property and structures therein, which includes the Baker Building, of and on Pine Street, in New York City, New York, USA, is hereby transferred to Ms. Eloise Ziomek. Should Ms. Ziomek become deceased before Mr. Montfort, the property will revert back to Mr. Montfort. However, if Ms. Ziomek should die under questionable circumstances, the property will not revert back to Mr. Montfort, but remain as part of Ms. Ziomek's estate. If for any reason, Mr. Montfort dies first, the property will remain under the care, custody, and control of Ms. Ziomek and her executors and heirs.

In return of receipt of right to the aforementioned property transfer, Ms. Ziomek will drop all claims and/or interest in or for any other property under the ownership or partial ownership of Mr. Montfort and will consent to sole custody of the couple's daughter, Rachel Bertrade Montfort by Mr. Clive Montfort.

Signed and dated on December 26, 1931.

Eloise Ziomek Montfort

Clive Bertrade Montfort

I SCANNED THE WILL, MUMBLING TO MYSELF AS THE OTHERS looked on. After fifteen minutes or so, I finally looked up and tried to summarize what I thought I'd read and work it in with the agreement that Amanda had just finished reading.

"Well, the property, the Baker Building, reverts to Clive Montfort unless she, Eloise, dies under suspicious circumstances. In that case, it goes back to Vernon," I stopped there and looked at the people in the room. "That sounds a little strange." I turned back to the will and continued. "… and the house also goes to Vernon." I stopped and muttered, "Humpf." Continuing, I said, "Along with an annual stipend to pay for taxes and upkeep. From what I understand, there was also a codicil drawn up by your mother, but I never saw it. Clienfelter said it would have changed the will, but since it was not witnessed, it was non-binding." The four of us tried to digest the paper's implications in the Rumsfeld murder.

"The rest of the estate goes to Vernon as well," I said. "The property Vernon now owns generates a great deal of money in rents, especially since it looks like he just locked in a sizable client to occupy at least one floor of the Baker Building."

"If he has a typical mortgage rate for commercial property," said Amanda. "He could be a wealthy man, projecting potential earnings and what all." Her legal, serious tone was so unlike Clay, it made me stop and wonder who was the adopted sibling.

"I wonder if he'll let me stay in the house," Rachel said to no one in particular. "There is plenty of room for both of us." There was a moment of silence as the rest of us sat there staring at Rachel. She was so self consumed she didn't notice the silence or the stares but continued. "Do I call him Uncle Vernon?"

"Well, that was interesting," Clay said. Turning directly to Rachel, Clay asked, "That's some middle name you and your daddy have. Where does 'Bertrade' come from, Rachel?" Clay asked.

"Daddy thinks we're descendants from Madame Bertrade de Montfort, Queen of France. He dug her up in some history book before I was born. Apparently, she was in power back in 1059 or some such time. Our relationship is probably bogus." Rachel said with a disinterested shrug. "Daddy got his name changed about twenty-five or six years ago to incorporate

'Bertrade.' We also had an uncle named Bertrade."

"Yeah," I said. "Your uncle Bertrade was one of the owners of the Baker Building. Delores found information on him. We have reason to believe his death was not accidental." It was all I could do to keep from telling Rachel that her ole Uncle Vern was probably the culprit in bumping off her uncle.

Amanda looked at her brother. "What about the Mr. M we talked about the last time we got together? Do you think he might be...?" Amanda hesitated.

"Clive B. Montfort?" Rachel said. We were all beginning to realize that the two men were linked, and possibly one was Eloise Rumsfeld's killer. Rachel had a silent and captive audience. "Yeah. I think it's my father. Matter of fact, with all the evidence you have dug up, I'm almost positive." Funny how Rachel's reference to her father went from "daddy" to "father."

"Now, Rachel," I said. "Don't jump to conclusions. They may both be innocent bystanders, like Clay here." But Rachel was on a roll and couldn't help adding more kindling to the fire.

"I recognized DeNato's face when I saw him in the Sunday paper. He'd been in my father's office on more than one occasion. I know it sounds crazy, but I believe my father is at the bottom of all this."

"Where's the love of a daughter for her father?" I asked. "How can you talk about him as a murderer and swindler? Aren't you even a little blinded by love for the man? Sorry, 'blinded' might not be the right word."

Rachel looked at me, doing a slow burn in reaction to my sarcasm. Her jaw muscles worked and her eyes narrowed. I was glad she didn't have a weapon.

"I had heard DeNato no longer worked for your father," I said. "His services had been terminated and he was working for someone else." There were deep implications there. I shut my mouth.

"I'd overheard harsh words between my father and DeNato. I think it was two or three weeks ago, but I'm not so sure my father fired him. He said he did, but he's said a lot of things that have not necessarily been accurate. I guess that's the nice way to put it." She looked at Amanda and Clay. I guess I made her "shit list."

"Why haven't you told us this before?" I asked. Rachel ignored me.

Amanda turned to me. "Where did you hear DeNato had left the employ of Rachel's father?"

I wanted to shrug it off. "Give me a second to see if I can remember where I heard that," I said, stalling for time and an out.

"I told him," said Clay. "I had a conversation with some of the boys who do the city beat for one of the papers, and they keep close tabs on guys like DeNato. They said the word was out that he was looking for a new connection and that there was bad blood between him and Montfort. They said he had hired on with a new 'thug.' Nobody knew who that was."

"That doesn't put the blame on him," I said. "The wording of the will makes Rumsfeld look like the suspect. All this does is raise more questions." I looked around the room. "Montfort gains nothing if someone murders his ex-wife. Matter of fact, it ensures that the property goes to Rumsfeld and not him."

I scratched my chin and looked at Clay. "Maybe it's time we pay Montfort a visit, Clay." It was more of a statement than a question. "I'm sure he can clear up matters for us, real quick-like." I couldn't help grunting and groaning, trying to get out of the chair. I felt like it had grabbed me and sucked me into its bowels and with my ribs still aching, it was a real pain trying to find the right leverage.

"Yeah, but it might not help our longevity. How're your kidneys?" Clay asked, but question went unanswered.

"If you are going to see my father, I'm coming with you," said Rachel, already standing and heading for her apartment to dress.

"That is a really bad idea," I said. "Someone is trying to cover their tracks and the further we go, the more people are hurt. You're going to be next if you're not careful. Stay here."

"I don't think y'all are invited," said Clay as he rose from the sofa. "Why don't you stay here and do your homework?"

Now I know a little about "coming of age" women, but my money was on Rachel getting her way. *Do your homework? Really?* That's like declaring war. Amanda watched us, trying to decide if she should take a sick day and watch out for Rachel or go into work and let us all get killed. I was hoping she would go to work and stay out of harm's way.

"You wait there. I'll be right down. Besides, you won't be able to get into our house. He has guards, and they have guns," Rachel yelled indignantly as she closed the front door on her way to her apartment.

"Time to leave," I said to Clay. "We're going to be late for the next act." I grabbed Morgan by the sleeve and pulled him toward the door.

WE DASHED FROM THE APARTMENT, RAN ACROSS THE STREET, and climbed into Anthony's pickup truck. I turned the ignition key. Nothing. I tried it again, praying that the damn thing would catch, and all I received for my kind words to the deity was a choking sound from the engine. I was about to try for a third time when Morgan looked back toward the apartment entry and pointed.

"Oh, shit. Here they come. Get this crate started, James."

They? I looked up again and stopped trying to turn over the ignition. Rachel was making a mad dash up the street, Amanda right behind her. I leaned over and tried to start the engine. It began to spit and sputter. I pumped the gas like mad, hoping it wouldn't flood the engine.

"Come on, man!" Clay cried.

"C'mon, you son-of-a-bitch, start," I shouted.

Finally, the engine roared to life. Billows of black smoke streamed from the tailpipe and covered the car behind us. The auspicious start was followed by the engine revving and the truck backfiring. I carefully put the truck in gear and eased it into traffic.

"We're off!" Clay shouted with excitement.

Our forward movement lasted for about one hundred and fifty feet before the engine died with another backfire and more smoke. This time, the truck died for good.

"Shit, shit, shit!" I banged on the steering wheel a few times and tried the key once again, and all I got for my effort was a cough and a sputter.

"There's a cab." Clay leapt out of the pickup and flailed his arms to attract the cab driver.

I got out and tried to push the truck out of the flow of traffic toward an open space, paying no attention to where it came to rest or the fact that I'd left the keys in the ignition.

"James, come on." Morgan was in the back seat of the cab. "Where does Montfort live?" Morgan gave me beckoning hands, like he was trying to physically coax Montfort's address out of me as I settled into the back seat of the cab.

"You did the research. Don't you have the address?" I asked. The cab driver looked at us with a crooked grin.

"Oh, yeah." Morgan went through his pockets, pulled a sheet of paper out of his breast pocket, and read an address to the driver, ending with "and step on it."

I closed my door when the cabbie took off, and we began one of the most harrowing cab rides I've ever taken through the streets of New York City.

The cab was heading east on 78th when we hailed it, and after running about two blocks, it turned north and headed toward Harlem. I had been to Harlem enough this week and had no desire to return. As the cab swung up Second Avenue, Morgan and I were thrown against the passenger-side door and Morgan let out an "Ugh."

"Where the hell are you going?" I said. "East 67th is the other direction. Hey! Mack, are you listening to me?"

I looked in the rear-view mirror and saw the driver gazing into the back seat. His crooked grin had become sinister and his two cold, hard, black eyes were fixed. The cabbie closed the little plastic window between the front and back seats. The hack surged up Second and began to pick up speed. Morgan and I grabbed the cab's straps above the windows. It was Tuesday morning, and the traffic was fairly thin for that time of day, just not thin enough.

As we sped along, I turned to Morgan. "Don't you check the drivers before you get in these things?"

We surged across 87th Street after running a red light and swerved to miss crossing traffic. The speedometer was beyond the 50s and had just nudged into the 60s when Morgan reached over the seat, reopened the little window, and grabbed the cabbie by the arm, then the head.

211

"What the hell are you doin? Trying to get us all killed?" I yelled.

"Trying to slow the bastard down," Clay replied. He turned his attention back to the cabbie and the oncoming traffic. "Look out, you idiot!"

The cab swerved to miss a coupe turning onto Second and the taxi was thrown into a slow circular skid. Maybe I was watching my life pass in front of me. Morgan let go of the driver and ducked next to me as the cab rocked from side to side. It clipped a trailer sticking out about a foot beyond the parking lines. The cab went into a faster spin, still heading north toward 88th. It was worse than any carnival ride I had taken, and I hate carnival rides. We spun for what seemed like an eternity. Finally, the front left side of the cab jumped the curb, propelled into a furniture store's barred-up picture window. One of the bars pierced the windshield, impaling our driver through the chest and nailing him to his seat. The spear penetrated the back of the seat and stopped inches from Morgan's stomach. The car shuddered to a halt. Smoke plumed, and an odor of gasoline filled the taxi.

Clay and I sat there, looking at the bloody rod. "You all right, Clay?"

All I got was a nod as Clay loosened his tie and let out a long slow breath while touching the rod's point poised for more penetration.

I peeled my hands from the roof strap, which I'd been holding onto for dear life. Warmth flowed from my forehead. I was bleeding, again, and my fedora was gone. I looked around the cab, but didn't find my hat. Damn, there went another. This one hadn't even lasted a full day.

"We gotta exit the cab over here." I pointed at my passenger door. "Your door is smashed up against the side of the building. It could be in the building, for all I can tell."

I inspected myself and found no broken bones or bleeding lacerations, just the bloodied bump on my head. The aroma of gasoline got stronger and gave me extra incentive to open the passenger door, to no avail. The window was smashed from our untimely and precarious arrival at the furniture store, so I exited through the space that used to be the passenger window. Broken glass sliced my hand as I rested my palms on the doorframe. I reached up, grabbed the torn front seat cover, and wrapped it around my hands. I heard Clay trying to get around the bloody bar that held our driver in place in the front seat.

After crawling through the window, I stood on the street. I wanted to make sure no one in the immediate area was out to get rid of us. Looking up and down the street, I checked my pants belt at the small of my back to see if my gun was there; it wasn't. I turned to see Morgan still struggling, his shirt snagged on the bar.

"What the hell's wrong with you, Clay? I smell gas. Get out of the fucking cab!"

"I just can't seem to get around this damn metal rod," he said. "Screw it." He ripped his shirt and wriggled around the bar, then looked up at me triumphantly.

"How about the driver?" Morgan asked while climbing out the window.

"He's not looking too good right now. We better just let him be so he can think about improving his driving habits." I looked at my wrapped hands and then at Clay's hands. No blood. I must have taken one for the team there.

We heard sirens in the distance and looked at each other. It would be a bad idea to run, but we wouldn't be making it to Montfort's at all if we stayed. What's the worst that Dingle and company would do to us if we did flee the scene?

"James, I can't run. I smashed my leg pretty bad in the collision. All I can do is hobble. You go on. I'll stay here and delay 'em." His face was pathetic. There was a red bruise on his cheek, and blood seeped down the sleeve of his left arm. Hair fell over his forehead determined to stay there regardless of how often he tried to push it back. He looked like he was prepared for some kind of horror show, where he was the mass murderer.

I draped his right arm over my shoulder and pointed across the street at the subway station. "You can make that. Come on." We moved toward to the station, Clay dragging his leg. Just before going down the steps into the subway, there was a loud whomp. We turned to see the cab go up in flames, along with the storefront. In the distance, the sirens got louder.

"Some ride," I said. "So glad you got us a cab." And down the steps we went.

TUESDAY AFTERNOON

All the good Samaritans who'd gone out of their way to stare at the cab that had hurtled into the storefront were now fleeing for their lives. The subway station became a safe haven. Survivors pushed and shoved as they tried to get down the stairs and away from the flames devouring the building and cab.

Supporting Clay, I stood in line to get two tokens downtown. Moving like wounded grasshoppers, we crawled through the turnstiles and walked to the platform for the downtown subway. The crowd had inched back up the stairs, curious about the fire and wanting to see if the fire department had arrived yet, leaving the platforms vacant except for us. Our timing was right on schedule, as the next set of cars pulled up to the platform almost immediately. We were grateful. Standing had become a chore.

Once on the subway, Morgan sank into the seat and moaned. I looked at my friend and noticed blood beneath him on the subway floor. There was a trail from the door to his seat. I rolled up his pant leg and found a four-inch gash on the back of his calf, ending a couple of inches above his Achilles tendon.

"You have a handkerchief, Clay?" I asked.

He produced a nicely pressed white hankie as onlookers stared at the bloody mess, offering silent encouragement and thanks that it wasn't them. I eased off his ratty shoes and blood soaked socks, and thought about throwing them under the seat. I dropped them on the floor.

"This looks almost too good for what I have in mind," I said, referring to the handkerchief. "What do you use these for?" I wrapped the hanky around his wound. "It looks sanitary enough to use in an operating room, don't ya think?" I gently smoothed the starched handkerchief over the wound and watched the blood seep into the white cloth.

"You need some clean socks?" a fella in his mid-twenties asked. He offered me a pair of white athletic socks from a shopping bag. Large eyes surveyed our scene in particular Clay's suffering. *What was I saying about good Samaritans?* He wore a black leather jacket zippered to the neck and blue jeans.

"You are most kind," Clay said, reaching for them. "Y'all just buy these?"

"Yeah, take them. You need them more than I do." It was easy to detect the New York / Italian accent in his voice.

I nodded and took the socks.

Having bound the leg with the handkerchief, I pulled the laces from Clay's shoe and secured the hanky. I covered the hanky and shoelace with the newly acquired socks, keeping the pressure on the wound and the lace. After cleaning the shoe with his bloody sock, I eased his foot back into his shoe and tossed the bloodied sock under the subway seat. I couldn't resist.

Clay looked at me and nodded.

"That should hold for a little bit," I said.

"James, where did that cab come from? What was it, a cab from hell?"

"Yeah, or mob elements," I answered. "I've been talking with some new friends in Harlem, and they seem to think there is a lot of corruption involved here. Sort of like we have scratched the surface of a horrible iceberg."

"What ya talking about?" asked Clay.

"Vernon has not been a very nice person. Apparently, he murdered his partners in order to acquire the Baker Building."

"Right," said Morgan.

"One of whom was Clive Montfort's uncle."

"Yeah," Clay said weakly, like he was thinking more than talking. "We already knew that, right?" *See, Clay had really been awake and listening all the time, wow.*

"I learned it from another source before going over it in the apartment and piecing it together from the diary pages that remained for the crowd."

"So he has a motive then?"

"Seems that we have stumbled across more than a murder here. The real kicker is that there is a turn-coat in the NYPD."

"What?" His response was loud enough to be heard throughout the subway car and probably at the passing stop. I think he was on overload.

I sat there until the doors to our car closed and the subway started to roll again. "Hush. Let's not involve the passengers in all of this. Christ. And for God's sake, don't go publishing that dope in any story you write. Especially if you value Matt's life as well as your own."

"Sorry. Don't worry, I won't." he said in a hushed tone. "Who is it?"

"We have no idea, but I'm working on it. Apparently, he's been there for some time, and is deeply buried. Keep it under your hat."

Clay leaned back in his seat taking a deep breath pushing back another errant hair from his forehead and closed his eyes. "Ain't life a bitch," he uttered.

WE CAME TO OUR STOP AND EXITED ONTO THE 68TH STREET platform with the surge of the crowd. His arm around my shoulder, Clay and I limped up the stairs looking for sunlight and street signs while trying to catch our collective breaths.

Clay and I surfaced about two blocks from Madison and 67th. I hailed a cab and poured Morgan into the backseat. It didn't take long to arrive at Montfort's front door step, right across from Central Park.

The mansion was gray masonry with double front doors. The shutters were black, and thick curtains were drawn over the windows across the front of the house. A broad set of steps led up to the front door. The mansion was three stories with an attic, or at least, what I thought was an attic. It was either that or where the bodies were stashed after Montfort got through with them. Spires jutted from the side of the house, like guard stations on old castles. It did not look like a home. It looked like a fortress designed to keep out ne'er-do-wells, like us. The architecture was a cross between early gothic and late creepy.

Rachel's car was parked on the street near the front of the house in a space marked Loading Zone. Clay and I exchanged glances as we exited the cab and stared at the front door.

"You ready for more climbing?" I asked Morgan, and we proceeded up the stairs to the front door. I was beginning to think that we could tackle mountain climbing if it weren't for the gash on Morgan's leg and me struggling to catch my breath. After all, it was a hike up the eight stairs, but not as bad as the stairs in either subway station.

"This guy knows how to live," I said. Morgan grunted as we limped up the final steps.

I decided not to ring the doorbell. I figured the house staff would be armed and dangerous. I twisted the doorknob with my still-wrapped hands, and much to our surprise, it opened. So we entered the vestibule.

With the front doors closed, Clay and I were caught in what felt like a fish bowl. A set of glass French doors lead into a sitting room. Our view into the house must not have been as curious as the view from within—the two of us standing there like bums looking for a bite of bread or piece of fruit to tide us over until our next drink.

Clay's jacket was stained and torn, the breast pocket hanging by a thread. His tie had been discarded somewhere during our subway ride from hell. His pant leg was torn, and the handkerchief, white socks, and shoelaces were visible to any fascinated on-looker. I could only imagine what I looked like. I certainly didn't feel much better.

As Morgan closed the door quietly behind us, one of the day-guards opened the French doors. He held up one hand, as if to stop us; the other mitt was still on the door. He began to speak as the hand on the door moved to his hip, his foot propping the door open. I guess he didn't like the way we were dressed and was protesting our entry. Not a smart thing to do, as we were both having a bad day.

"No, no, no. Stop right there. Mr. Montfort is not seeing anyone today. I said, stop right—" That was as far as the receptionist got before I broke his nose with a perfectly delivered right cross. I grabbed Clay, who was about to topple without my support. And here I thought Morgan was getting his strength back.

"Not much style, ya know, but it gets the job done," I told Morgan as I shook my hand. Thank goodness for the wraps. "That's gotta hurt. Sure enough hurt me."

"I'll let it go this time, but you didn't even give him a chance to finish his greeting. You New Yorkers aren't all that polite, are ya?"

"Yeah. Let's make sure Rachel and Amanda are all right

before Montfort extends his silent treatment, if you know what I mean." Morgan nodded. We stepped over our greeter and entered Clive Montfort's New York mansion.

From the entry lounge, three exits opened into the further reaches of the house. To the right, a sliding wood panel door was slightly ajar. It looked like it went into a den. Straight ahead, a grand staircase led to the second floor and a short hallway on the main floor led to the back of the house. At least two doors led off the hall, past the staircase. To the left of the lounge was another set of French doors with etched glass center panels providing a partially obscured view into a dining room. The table in the dining room looked like it had just been polished, allowing the sun's reflection to sparkle back at us through the etched glass.

We edged closer to the den then heard a toilet flush down the hall. I pointed toward the bathroom and let Clay stand on his own while I picked up a small Venus di Milo granite statue from an end table, on the way to the bathroom door. We moved quickly and quietly, at least for us, crowding the door. Morgan took up a position on the far side of the door while I stood next to the door handle. The handle turned, and a thug stepped out, turning to ensure that the bathroom light was off. He exposed the back of his head to me, and it was just enough of a distraction for me to put his lights out with the statue. There was a notable "thud" as he crumpled to the wood flooring. I frisked him for a gun, but there was none.

Clay asked, "Aren't you going to turn off the lights?"

To get back to the den, we navigated around and between an overstuffed chair and round-drum table that held an oriental vase that had been re-engineered into a lamp. On the other side of the chair was a pole lamp apparently used for reading, sewing, needlepoint, or whatever these people did in their spare time. A bag of yarn leaned against the chair. Two long needles protruded from the bag. Clay leaned down, using me as support, and grabbed one of the needles from the basket.

He turned and smiled. "Protection," he said. I shook my head and we moved forward, Clay armed with his dangerous knitting needle and me with a statue.

"We're here to ask questions. From everything I've heard, the guy is not who we're looking for. No motive." I put my finger to my lips and faced the den.

As we passed the table, Morgan nodded at the vase lamp and whispered, "Love it. I gotta get myself one of those."

"If you ask real nice-like, maybe he'll give it to you," I whispered back. "Now, hush."

We heard voices from the other side of the sliding door, confirming the location of our party.

Morgan looked at me and asked, "Father and daughter?" I nodded and put a finger over my lips again. He nodded.

Through the door we heard, "That's a wild story, Rachel. I would never endanger anyone's life for a building. You of all people should know that." Montfort sounded agitated.

"DeNato worked for you. I saw him here at the house and downtown. You can't deny that."

"That's right," the shaky voice said.

"Must be Mary Jane," I surmised. Clay's eyebrows rose.

Somers continued, "DeNato hired me and asked that I get real close to that Rumsfeld fella. Said an "MM" would get me a legit job and help pay my rent at the apartment in order to make it all look okay. It was you, wasn't it? You told one of DeNato's hoods to get me to lure Rumsfeld up to the apartment the day Mrs. Rumsfeld was killed." Mary Jane began to sob quietly.

"We know you're MM, Dad," Rachel said. "I just can't

understand why you would go through all this. Why kill Mom? Certainly not over one building."

"MM? What the hell does that mean? You don't think that refers to me? There are a lot of folks in this town with that initial. Hell, you don't know if it's for a first or last name, and my initials are not MM, they are CM. Now, shut up, the both of you," Montfort ordered. "Jimmy? Jimmy! Where is that little bastard? Jimmy! Get in here."

Montfort moderated his tone and spoke to his daughter. "I loved your mother, really. When we first got married, it was all hearts and flowers. The opportunities began to appear as the world's financial systems began to fall apart. But I didn't kill your mother. That you have to believe." We heard footsteps within the den. "I canned DeNato about a month ago. His methods were a little too rough for my taste, so whatever you are doing to connect me and that DeNato bum is wrong. It did not happen."

"Then, tell me, Daddy..." We heard the sarcasm dripping from Rachel's voice. "Why did you give Mom the Pine Street property? Huh? It looks like you want it back badly?"

"When we divorced, I didn't want her to starve. I wanted her to have an asset that she could use for income to get her through the tough times ahead. Okay, so I came by the building in a less than up-and-up fashion. Let's say it was retribution. But it was still legally mine. Clienfelter made sure of that."

"But why do you want it back, and why the formal agreement to cede it back to you should she die first?" Rachel pushed.

"That was purely a financial arrangement, Rachel. She could have sold the property and kept the money, and I would not have received a thing."

We heard what sounded like a drawer opening. I looked at Clay. "Desk drawer? Gun?" Clay's face turned serious. He shed my support and stood on his own. He grabbed hold of the lower portion of his jacket and pulled it downward as if he was getting ready to mount a podium for a speech. Straightening with a grimace, he reached for the door. I put out an arm and held him back.

"And sole custody? How could you do that to me and Mom, Dad?"

"It seemed like a good idea at the time. Why would I want a poor, needy ex-wife raising my daughter when I could give her everything she could possibly want? Plus, I didn't need her snoopin' around in my affairs anymore. I caught her eavesdropping on more than one of my meetings." Montfort stopped for a second and then called out again, "Jimmy?" Montfort's call sounded more urgent.

"Sounds like he's about to take matters into his own hands," I whispered to Clay.

Morgan nodded, prepared to open the door to the den and make his debut. Solo. He might have changed his mind if he'd realized Montfort had his pistol raised and ready to protect himself. I wasn't quite committed yet.

With a loud bang, the sliding doors rammed back into their pockets and Clay Morgan entered, bloodied and hurting.

"Sorry, sir, but Jimmy has been detained. He is out like a light." Clay limped into the den with a grin on his face and the knitting needle in his hand. There was blood caked around one eye and just below his ear. He must have been some sight. "Thought you could stop us from paying a visit, did you? Your taxi driver is also out, but for the rest of his life. How many more are you planning to send our way, Montfort?" Apparently, Clay was convinced that Clive Montfort was MM.

Montfort looked at Clay with amazement, not believing his eyes. Then he raised his revolver. "Who the hell are you?" Montfort asked.

I tried to blend in with the wall just outside the den, safely out of sight. "How you doin' this fine day? My name is Clay Morgan. I'm doing some investigative reportin."

I could just picture Clay smiling his warm southern smile at the crowd in the den, then looking around for me, his trusted sidekick. I was still trying to make up my mind what to do next.

"I know why you might have had it in for your ex-wife." Morgan looked at Mary Jane, and his eyes softened and lingered.

"Yeah?" Montfort said. "What's your story?"

"I know your uncle and Vernon had a run-in. Must have been ironic that your one true love up and married the man you had tried to destroy. Must have seemed like he got new life breathed into him. He was going to rise again, and your uncle would go unavenged."

"Okay. Why kill my ex-wife?"

"The way I figure it, you tried to talk her out of leaving the property to Vernon, and when she said no, you offed her out of rage."

Don't say it, Morgan. Keep your mouth shut, or Montfort will shut it for you.

I was still trying to decide if I wanted to join the meeting or stay where it was safe. I still didn't have my gun, so I crept back to the vestibule to steal our friend's. He was beginning to stir, so I slammed his head against the entry's marble and the light went out again in his little house. I patted him down, found his gun, and headed back toward the den, taking the wraps off my hands. The bleeding had stopped, but boy, my palms looked angry. The rod didn't fit comfortably in these sore hands, either.

About three steps from the den, I heard the report from a firearm. I didn't even check to see if the rod in my hand was loaded. I leapt into the den, gun drawn and aimed where I thought Montfort would be, but found Rachel in my sights. She was clutching her purse, anger in her eyes and posture. Montfort stood in the center of the room, the desk between him and Rachel. Morgan was directly in front of me holding his knitting needle like a sawed-off epee. Mary Jane and Amanda were to the left of the fireplace. Mary Jane was in a tan chair. Amanda was tending to her. A bloodstain was spreading across her white blouse, and she grasped her stomach. A cute, lady-like pistol lay on the floor about two feet from where she sat.

There was an end table next to the chair where Mary Jane sat. Its contents, what must have been delicate porcelain figurines, were in shards beneath and to one side of it. Mary Jane must have been struck by the bullet and fallen backwards over the table into the chair.

Montfort turned and leveled the gun at Morgan and me.

"What the hell is this, open house?" Montfort exclaimed as he pointed the pistol at my chest. "Don't move, whoever you are." He took a step and aimed at Clay. "Drop the gun. I'm not afraid to use this. I don't want to have to kill the reporter here."

I slowly lowered the pistol to the rug in front of me and stood up. Montfort took a step to his left to keep an eye on me and turned his back to Rachel. Given the look in her eyes, that was not something I would have done.

Montfort was dressed in steel grey slacks and brown bedroom slippers. His smoking jacket didn't hide the suspenders over a white shirt and tie. It looked like he was running late for work. His dark hair was mussed, as if he hadn't yet combed it after his shower. There was a lot of it, too. Greying at the temples gave Montfort a look of distinction. He was handsome, even in his late 50s, a couple of inches shorter than me, but well built. His gun looked like an old German luger. He was calm, but his eyes gave away his confusion.

"Where the hell did you come from?" asked Montfort.

I was about to answer with something really witty, but Montfort turned his attention back to Mary Jane.

"And you. Why the hell did you pull that gun on me?"

"You bastard," Mary Jane gasped. "You used me, and you can't deny it. I'd do it again if I had the chance."

"I did nothing to you," Montfort said. "I had no part in contracting you to…to seduce Rumsfeld. If DeNato got to you, he did it on his own, without my knowledge."

Mary Jane moaned and tried to curl into a ball in the over-stuffed chair. The sleeves of her blouse were stained red where they hugged her wound. She looked at Montfort. "You'd use any means to get to Rumsfeld. You bastard."

"Rumsfeld is a blood-sucking son of a bitch, and if anyone had a motive to kill Eloise, it would be him." Montfort's eyes flashed with hate.

"Can you give me something to help stop the bleeding?" Amanda asked. "A compress? Something?"

Montfort waved his gun at Mary Jane and Amanda. "If you are lucky, my aim was off and the bullet didn't penetrate any vital organs."

We were all looking at Mary Jane when a shot exploded in the den. Clay and I jumped, and Montfort staggered. He faced his daughter, who stood there with a pistol in her hand. Agony and disbelief crossed his face.

Rachel kept the pistol fixed on her father. Two more shots rang out from Rachel's weapon. Montfort fell backwards, bounced off his desk, and landed with a thud on an oriental rug. He lay silently, no longer confused why so many people were in his den, accusing him of killing his ex-wife.

We were all in shock. Well, at least, I was shocked. I never thought Rachel would pull the trigger on her old man. I waited a few seconds to let the ringing stop while I tried to digest what I'd just witnessed; Montfort's collapse replayed in slow motion, like a loop in a movie reel.

I picked up the pistol at my feet and slowly walked toward Rachel, kicking Montfort's pistol away from his body on my way. "Rachel, let me have that gun, will ya? That's it."

She let me take it from her hand while she stared at her father. Tears began to stream down her cheeks. She collapsed into the leather chair behind her, hands over her face and sobbing.

"What the hell is this?" Clay asked. "Everybody has a gun but me."

"Yeah, but you have a knitting needle. Quit complaining and call the police, and get an ambulance over here pronto for Mary Jane." I went into command mode as I approached Montfort. I couldn't tell if he was alive or dead. I checked for a pulse. Nothing.

"That won't be necessary, Morgan," said a voice. "The ambulance is on the way. I'll take those peashooters, Dugan." It was O'Malley.

O'Malley turned to one of the other cops with him. "Bag the gun on the floor." "You guys got any more weapons I need to confiscate?"

"Yeah," said Morgan. "You want my knitting needle?" Morgan extended the needle to the sergeant.

"Give me that," O'Malley said, grabbing the needle.

"How the hell did you get here so fast?" I asked. I got no reply, just a toothy grin.

CLAY AND I LEANED UP AGAINST A RED LEATHER CHAIR AS THE EMTs carried Mary Jane from the den on a gurney, Amanda in tow. The police led Rachel out of the brownstone in cuffs. One of the EMTs eventually came over to Clay, got him to sit in the chair, and gave him first aid. The coroner inspected Montfort's body, which was splayed on the bloodstained Oriental rug. After a few minutes, he signaled to have Montfort wheeled away. I guess he came to the same conclusion that I had. Clive Montfort was dead. With him went important answers to questions I still had.

Dingle had shown up about ten minutes after the sergeant. He was getting updates on the shootings from O'Malley. I couldn't hear, nor did I really want to. I just got uneasy whenever O'Malley pointed at Morgan and me. O'Malley was starting to get on my nerves. The impact of the day was beginning to take its toll, and I collapsed into a chair I'd pulled over from in front of the desk.

Morgan looked at me as I sat down. "You know what I could really go for right now?"

"Unless it is a double scotch and winning the trifecta at Aqueduct, I wouldn't even want to hazard a guess."

"Yeah. I thought you were going to the track yesterday. You pick a winner?"

"It was an education," I said, a forced smile on my face.

Amanda reappeared with two pieces of paper, one in each hand, heading for Clay and me. A woman on a mission, I thought. Time to be afraid.

"Montfort is not Mr. Big. Do you hear me?" she said, waving the papers. She looked to be on heavy dose of caffeine and adrenalin. "After the ambulance took Mary Jane away, I realized I still had these documents. I re-read them, and Mr. Big, MM, is not Clive Montfort."

"I have been trying to tell you people that for what seems like forever," I said. "Why you decided to come here is beyond me and probably the reason Montfort is dead." I was exhausted and exasperated, and it showed.

The conversation attracted Dingle and O'Malley.

"What on earth are you talking about, young lady?" Dingle asked.

"I worried about Rachel getting angry over all this talk about her father. She only heard the stuff she wanted to. She took what you had come up with and reached her own conclusions, but she is young and easily influenced." Amanda waved the papers again.

"What did we tell her to make her believe her dad was the killer?" Clay asked.

"What didn't you tell her?" Amanda retorted.

I held up a hand to stop the conversation and turned to Matt Dingle. "Amanda Morgan, this is Lieutenant Matt Dingle of New York's finest, and this is Sargent Seamus O'Malley. Gentlemen, this is Amanda Morgan, Clay's sister. Let's take a breath and relax." If there was a storm coming, I didn't want to be caught in front of it.

Amanda looked around the den, as though reliving what had taken place. She looked more closely at her brother. "Are you all right? What happened to you?" It was as though she'd just noticed Clay's deplorable state.

"Oh, he's all right, Miss. He's just a little shaken up,"

O'Malley said. "I don't think he's any worse for wear."

Clay looked up from his seat, raised one hand, and offered a halfhearted wave.

"Let's start again," I said to Amanda. "What are you talking about?"

"You know the papers that fell out of Mrs. Rumsfeld's will? There were two. This one, which I read in the apartment, and this one, which I'd overlooked until a few minutes ago."

I checked my jacket and felt another few pages of paper and what I hoped was the will. I was relieved, feeling the crumpled wad in my jacket. It left me wondering what else I'd missed in the Clienfelter file. I resisted taking out what was in my pocket and turned my attention back to Amanda.

Amanda looked at me strangely. "And what happened to you?"

"That is a long story," I said. "But basically the same thing that happened to him." I jabbed a thumb in her brother's direction. Amanda's face softened and my insides got all gooey warm like after down a shot of scotch in one gulp. But only the best scotch.

"What's this about a will?" asked Dingle. "Where is it, and how did you get it?"

"It's all right. I have it right here." I pulled the Last Will and Testament of Eloise Rumsfeld out of my jacket pocket. It was crumpled with one or two bloodstains from the taxi accident, so I smoothed it out on the coffee table beside our chairs. "Don't worry," I looked at Matt, "The blood is probably mine."

"Let me have that," O'Malley said. He pulled it away from me, slightly tearing the first couple of pages. For a second, I thought he might pocket the will for himself, but after looking it over, he reluctantly deposited it in the lieutenant's out-stretched hand.

"This paper is the agreement between Eloise and Clive Montfort on the day before their divorce," said Amanda, "stipulating the transfer of property to Eloise from Montfort." Amanda waved the paper over her head while Dingle tried to snag it. She held the paper to her side and Dingle finally secured it. "But this paper," she waved the other sheet over her head, "which Bernie Clienfelter wrote just before he was killed, shows that Montfort had no desire to murder his ex-wife and no interest in the property. Mr. Clienfelter believed that someone else murdered Mrs. Rumsfeld. He fingers a third party as the triggerman, but..." Amanda turned her attention back to the paper and read:

> *I have worked with Montfort for some time and find that there is evidence to support his involvement in Mrs. Rumsfeld's murder, but I do not believe he committed the act. His significant property holdings help to substantiate this.*

"What the hell does that mean?" O'Malley shouted. Dingle and I turned to the sergeant, surprised at his outburst. He held up his hands and backed away.

"It doesn't say." Amanda lowered her hand, and Dingle took the second sheet from her. "It's like he was interrupted mid-thought."

"Dugan, you're coming with me to do some explaining." Dingle turned to his sergeant. "O'Malley, wrap things up here and bring the Morgans with you. I got some questions for them, too." Dingle moved to really pissed in record time. When he set his jaw, as he was doing now, it meant, "I'm gonna get some answers, and I'm gonna get them quick."

Before I got out of the chair to join the lieutenant, I

heard Amanda ask Clay, "Was that all the information you had when you were explaining why Montfort had probable cause for murdering Eloise Rumsfeld? Did it really implicate him or were you making things up again, Clay?"

"Not now. I'll tell you later," he said.

Dingle waited for me at the front door while I limped along, making him even more impatient. After climbing into his squad car, we rode together in silence from Montfort's estate to the precinct.

"Where's his wife?" I asked as Dingle was about to park.

"Huh? Whose wife?"

"Montfort's. Where is Montfort's wife?"

"How the hell do I know?"

I DON'T VISIT THE OLD PRECINCT VERY OFTEN, BUT THIS MADE twice in seven days. Not only that, the atmosphere was different. When I strode these hallowed halls in the past, I had the upper hand, but this time, I felt like I was in trouble and there was no big brother to help me out. Big brother was after my hide.

We got to the second floor and I hobbled through the sea of desks I associated with the precinct. Desks used by the on-duty officers crowded with the hustle and bustle of the days activities, both cops and criminal until we found ourselves at Dingle's desk. He had an office. I was impressed. It was nice, decorated in early WWI battleship grey—desk, chairs with faux leather, metal tables, and a lamp. It looked like someone had sneaked into his office when he wasn't there and spray-painted everything grey. There were no blinds to shut out prying eyes, and it seemed set off by itself, as if it didn't like the other desks. I was wondering if it was a step up from a few years ago when we shared facing desks in the bullpen, or if Dingle was trying to avoid others. Maybe it was a reward for not being able to solve this Rumsfeld thing. I had to stop and think about that for a second.

"Sit down, Dugan," Matt said in a low voice. I limped to an uncomfortable looking faux leather seat to one side of his desk. Dingle was meticulous and kept his desk cleaner than did most men in the precinct. He had come a long way since our days together. He'd passed the lieutenant's exam and was now a homicide lieutenant in one of the busiest precincts in New York. Think of Grand Central Station active, jacked up on a double shot of espresso kind of busy. I figured he was on the hunt for something bigger, and if he wasn't careful, he just might get it.

Matt threw his hat onto a coatrack near the door into his office, then eased into his well-traveled chair, pulling himself closer to his desk. He hadn't bothered to take off his jacket, rather rifled through his pockets until he found what he was looking for while he maintained his seat. It was a moment of amusement. He took out the Rumsfeld will and the two papers he'd taken from Amanda, then spread them on the desk beside a notebook, which he leafed through for a blank page. See? Neat, just as I told you.

Dingle looked at me. "Let's begin," he said. He raised his hand as I began to speak and added, "I'll ask the questions, and you answer them yes or no. If I want further explanation, I will ask for it. Got it?"

I've seen Matt get like this maybe once or twice. When he does, it's best just to go along with him to avoid bodily harm. On the outside, he appears calm and collected, but that's a ruse, like he's trying to bait you so he can release his anger.

Inside, he was a raging torrent of pent-up aggression. I used to think it would be better for him to get it out of his system, but after seeing him lose his cool and let the monster out, I figured that control was far better for everybody. I nodded and sat back, hoping it would pass.

"Let's see if we can organize the facts as we know them. Then we'll get into the details, okay?"

I reached up to remove my fedora, forgetting it was lost in the cab ride. "Sure," I said. "Do you think I could get a cup of joe?"

"Maybe, if I get all the answers I want. Let's start. Eloise Rumsfeld hired you to spy on her husband. True?"

I nodded. "How about some water?"

Dingle ignored my request. "She thought he was cheating on her. True?"

I nodded and tried to elaborate, but Dingle held up his hand.

"How about a nice cup of tea?" I asked.

Matt looked at me suffering from a slow boil. He paused to contain himself and then said, "You tailed Vernon Rumsfeld for a few days and ended up at an apartment building on 78th Street and took some pretty revealing photos of Mr. Rumsfeld and a woman, which in turn validated Eloise Rumsfeld's concern. True?"

"Mary Jane Somers," I said.

Dingle looked at me. "What?"

"Mary Jane Somers. The broad Vernon was shacked up with is named Mary Jane Somers. You know, the woman that was presumably shot by Montfort."

"Hold that thought. We'll get to that. Now—"

"Can we cut to the chase? Yeah, I did the snoop job and visited Clienfelter. I nosed around a little, got my car torched, got beat up in my apartment, got even with the thugs that did the tap-dance on my kidneys, and gave DeNato a ride to Brooklyn, where some thugs shot up Anthony's joint as Clay and I were asking him questions. Sure, he got hit a few times, but it couldn't've happened to a nicer guy.

"I also learned that Eloise Rumsfeld had a daughter, who gave me her mother's diary, which you now have, by the way, or at least some semblance thereof, thank you very much. I also found Mrs. Rumsfeld's will and those two other documents." I pointed to Dingle's desk. "But not in Clienfelter's office. I found Bernie Clienfelter dead in his office.

"I've been on a high-speed ride through upper Manhattan ending in a furniture store's window. Clay and I then visited Clive Montfort's palatial estate. Apparently, not all roads lead to the killer, as Montfort denied any participation in his ex-wife's death. Something I believe, by the way." After finishing the recap, I stared at Dingle. "Did you want to discuss any of this? If not, there's more, but it will have to wait. You have to go A, B, C or 1, 2, 3, so you can get your facts straight."

Dingle looked at me for what seemed like an eternity and finally leaned over and picked up his phone. "Yeah, Joyce. Can I get two cups of coffee, please? One black and the other with a dash of milk, just enough to change the color. Thanks." He hung up the phone and cast his eyes back on me, shaking his head. He picked up his phone again. "Joyce, see if you can get a doctor or nurse up here to tend to some wounds." Dingle nodded a few times and said, "Yeah, he looks worse than he is, but he's bleedin' on my furniture. Thanks." Matt put down the phone and then looked at me again. "How you remain alive is beyond me, Dugan. There is no reasonable explanation. Why did you kidnap DeNato?"

"It seemed like the thing to do at the time. He'd torched

my car and two of his thugs roughed me up. I just wanted some answers." I thought I was a pretty reasonable guy.

"Yeah, but kidnapping? That is pretty aggressive, don't ya think?"

"For DeNato? It was right up his alley. I bet if he didn't get offed, he'd have told us who his employer was and if he was the killer. I have this theory—"

"Dugan, you always have 'this theory,' but not now, not here. Let's deal with facts, first. No short cuts. Okay?"

"Yeah, sure," I agreed as a patrolman broke into our meeting.

"Lieutenant, I'm sorry to interrupt, but there's a development that needs your attention." The patrolman's head was just inside the door; the rest of him was safely tucked away in the hall, ready to run.

"What's the problem, Mac?" McFarland was fairly new to the force. I didn't know him other than when I reached him on the phone. It was refreshing to put a name with a face. He seemed like a nice kid. Sort of like Matt when he joined the force, and probably why he took a liking to him.

"It's Mrs. Montfort, sir. She's been involved in a hit-and-run. The truck that hit her was from Anthony's Repair Shop, over in Brooklyn. You know, the one Mr. Dugan got as a loaner. Mrs. Montfort's been taken to Roosevelt Hospital."

Dingle turned back to me. "What do you make of that?"

"Well, I did sort of warn you. Remember when I asked—"

"Yeah, yeah, yeah. You asked where she was. Are you some kind of harbinger of bad things?"

I shrugged. "Let's go find out."

As we got up, Dingle cautioned, "This debrief isn't over, Dugan. You owe me a lot more."

I looked at the desk, searching for my hat, and then I remembered that I still needed to get another. "We are running out of suspects," I said.

"Yeah." Dingle said grabbing his hat.

"I guess my doctor will have to wait, huh?" I muttered painfully and I hobbled toward the precinct stairs.

THE ACCIDENT OCCURRED NOT TOO FAR FROM MONTFORT'S home, just above 68th. The latest Mrs. Montfort had been broadsided by the same pickup truck I'd left for dead on 78th. I recognized it right away from the bullet holes in the paneling. The hood of the pickup was buried halfway into Mrs. M's Packard. Luckily, Judith Montfort was still alive. Sawhorses were everywhere. New York likes to dress up for its accidents and what better way than sawhorses? The beat cops were out canvassing possible witnesses, and a detective was poking through the car. Another was in the pickup. The detectives failed to see the lieutenant and me show up. They were buried in their work. The nearest officer conducted his inspection of the truck with his head firmly inside the driving compartment and his tail sticking out as if a massive python was swallowing him up but hadn't quite finished the job. I was afraid we might surprise the poor lad if we made a lot of noise, but Matt wanted answers, with or without manners.

"Detective? Yo. You got a name so I can get your attention?"

The detective's head popped up, knocking against the pickup's doorframe. He looked at Dingle and recognized him. "Yes, Lieutenant, it's Detective Morreau. I was just digging something out of the carpet. Sorry." He backed out of the pickup and faced us. *He looked like we must have eight or ten years ago—young. What's with all the young guys on the force?*

"What did you find, Detective?" Dingle asked.

"Looks like a stain of some sort. I thought I'd bag it and see if the lab could identify it." The detective held up an evidence bag with a bit of carpeting in it, happy as a hunter who'd taken down a charging lion. I was so proud of him.

"What else did you find, Morreau?" I asked.

"Other than this, nothing much. No prints on the steering wheel, but there was the lever from the jack on the floor on the driver's side," he said nonchalantly.

"That explains quite a bit. Looks like our guy, or lady, used the lever to press the gas and used the truck like a torpedo," I observed. "How do you think they managed to get the truck started? I mean, earlier today, it wouldn't move more than twenty feet. Now, it's a rocket, for Christ's sake."

"There's more to this crime than I first thought," Dingle said. "A lot more. I gotta check a few things. How about we meet up at Maxie's in a few hours?"

"Sounds good to me. You going to let Clay loose from the clutches of your police sergeant so we can compare notes?"

"Yeah, sure." Dingle raised a finger in my direction. "No more kidnappings or killings, you got it?" Dingle turned to the detective and said, "Impound this truck and get it down where a mechanic can go over it with a fine-toothed comb."

With that, I left the scene and headed toward the library.

NEW YORK HAS SOME OF THE GREATEST LIBRARIES IN THE country, or so I've been told by a few librarians I've gotten to know, so I went to the New York Public Library, at the intersection of 5th and 42nd. It is the main branch of the city's public library system, and it is chock full of reference materials.

Out front of the main entrance were two lions made of Tennessee marble. They acted as guards. The lions were nicknamed "Patience" and "Fortitude" by Mayor LaGuardia in the 1930s. They reflected my mantra for this case, and I was running low on both.

The main branch's reading room measures seventy-eight feet wide and two hundred and ninety-five feet long, with ceilings that rise to fifty-two feet. It's called the Rose Main Reading Room. It's lined with thousands of reference works on open shelves at floor level and on the balcony. It's lit by massive windows and grand chandeliers and furnished with sturdy wood tables, relatively comfortable chairs, and brass lamps. Right then, I needed comfortable and well lit. This was the cathedral of reference and light and comfort would come better with a beer and bar lighting.

Libraries house all kinds of information, like newspaper clippings of who married whom, on what date, and who the bride and groom's relatives were. I settled into one of the comfortable chairs with a stack of newspapers dating back to the wedding of Clive Montfort and Eloise Ziomek and started browsing the society pages. With Montfort running in the financial circles that he did, it was a sure bet the wedding would be listed there. I was looking for an elusive missing person to this sordid affair, someone undetected, someone I needed to find and unmask.

I found Eloise and Clive Montfort's wedding and then their divorce. Setting those issues aside, I then moved to Judith and Clive Montfort's wedding. Guess who wrote the article. Emily Ross. I shook my head slowly over the flowery prose as I moved through the paragraphs trying find my nuggets of solution in the lines. I read the write-ups on all three events again, relishing the one by Emily, and smiled as I jotted down the information onto notepaper provided by the library. *You just gotta love the library. So thoughtful.*

The library began to close, so after double-checking my information, I made tracks back to Maxie's to wait for Clay and Matt to drop by.

As I walked along, I thought to myself that I knew how most of this thing worked, who was guilty of murder, and the roles of most of the other players. At least, I thought I did. Maybe there was an angle or two that I hadn't figured yet, but it would come together, I hoped. A few things still nagged me, like how O'Malley seemed to be at the right place at the right time and the feeling that there was some overlord moving people around like chess pieces. And of course, the mole in the police force. I wondered if my problems could be wrapped up into one answer. Naw, too easy.

It was seven-thirty by the time I walked into Maxie's. The joint was jumping and my office was occupied, again. Maxie met me about three feet in and pulled me aside. He had my briefcase. At least I thought it was, but it was all shiny and new, definitely not the one Dingle pulled out of Anthony's garage.

"Laddie, I was feeling sorry for ya, so I arranged for an office for ya for a couple of weeks." He handed me a set of keys and my briefcase. "You can conduct your business there. The brief case is on the house."

"Thanks, but I like it here just swell," I responded

"No, laddie, this is not the spot for you anymore. I'm askin ya nicely to take these keys and your briefcase and set up shop in a real office." He jangled the keys in my face. "This one's close enough. It's three doors down and a third-story walk-up. It rents cheap, and the first month is on me. I think it will be better for both our businesses. Maybe more mine than yours." He handed me the keys and briefcase with a wry smile.

I took the keys and pocketed them. I must have looked like a wounded hound, 'cause Maxie put his arm around me and asked, "Have ya eaten in a while? Let me have the cook fry ya up a hamburger and some fries. Come sit at the bar while ya wait."

I looked over at my used-to-be office. There was a young couple sitting on one side of the booth, sitting so close it looked like the merger of man and woman. I frowned. I guess it was for the best. There are just so many hormones one can deal with in one evening.

After five or six beers and a hamburger, with no friends apparently coming or a-calling, I climbed off the bar stool and weaved for the door. I was a mess of rejection and depression. The booze helped tone down the hurt from all the injuries I had sustained, but the ego was in bad shape. I felt like I had been deserted by every friend I had, except for Maxie, and he was acting out of pity, I was sure of that.

I waved at Maxie. "I'll be in my other office if Clay or Matt stop by lookin' for me." That made the divorce official.

I wandered out the door and into the fresh evening air. The city smelled particularly rancid tonight, as if my manhood had been taken away and replaced by a smack on the fanny. I started down the block the wrong way, turned around, and headed toward my new office building, I hoped.

241

There was a double set of doors into the building. The outer door was unlocked, but the inner door wasn't. Next to the second door was a list of businesses with intercom buttons next to each name. *Mine must be the one with no name next to its button*, I thought. *Is this going to hurt my walk-in business?* Then I remembered I don't have any.

Along the right wall were mailboxes for incoming correspondence and a sizable letter slot for outgoing mail. I let myself through the inner door after trying both keys in the lock. Directly across from the door was a grand staircase. There was no elevator, so I began my walk. Three floors is a long haul for someone who was in pain. On top of that, I had just finished six beers and a hamburger. When I reached the third floor, the staircase continued up for at least two more floors. Lucky for me, there was a number on the key—32. I found my door, and with little to-do, I unlocked the door to my new office and turned on the lights. A single overhead light went on in the outer office. As the door closed, it automatically relocked. Strange feature. Maybe it was the neighborhood or past clientele. The door was a thin, wooden piece of crap that made the self-locking feature a ridiculous joke.

The suite reminded me of Clienfelter's office, only a tad larger. There was an outer office and an inner office. That's where the comparison ended. There was no furniture in the reception space or a closet. Papers left behind by the previous tenant were scattered across the floors of both rooms, along with other trash. I guess the maid never came to this joint.

There were two wooden chairs in what was to become my office. I had to admit, a smile was creeping across my lips. Maybe it was the beers, or maybe there was a warm glow in my chest. My office, on the third floor with no elevator. No wonder it rents cheap. *I wondered what an office went for on the upper floors.*

The inner office had no desk, no light—just the flickering of the neon from across the street shining in the two windows. It did have Venetian blinds on each window, but they were useless bent aluminum. The blind on the right window hung half way down at an angle, and the blind on the left was pulled almost to the top, but bent and abused.

I hung my jacket on one of the two chairs and stared down at the street below. It had started to rain, and the water was cleaning the sidewalk, moving the grit and dirt to the sewage system beneath the city. I walked over to one of the many vacant walls and slid my back down the drywall to the floor. I was afraid that if I fell asleep in a chair, which seemed likely, I would fall off and hurt myself. The room spun as I tried to recall how I got to this point in the case. I didn't last long. I curled up in a sleepy bundle of pain, washed in the sedative of beer and exhaustion.

It had been a long day. It felt as real as being alive. It couldn't be a dream and yet I was reliving my hell. You only experience those horrific events once in your life. I just kept reliving them.

I could see myself lying in the middle of a sandy crater created by an exploded artillery shell. There were two other fellas in the crater with me, neither one was alive. How could I tell? They were both Japs and their bodies were twisted and misshapen; no one could hold those positions for more than 2 seconds. Sporadic gunfire could be heard not too far off, but at least not advancing in my direction. I had no idea where

I was. I was helmetless but a newly acquired rifle lay beside me. It was some kind of British rifle. It was pretty well worn with a few rounds left in the magazine. Looked like the butt of the gun had been used as a battering ram of some kind. I wondered what I did last night?

I took inventory of my situation. I remembered swimming ashore during our landing on Tarawa Island, as part of the Marines first step in taking this island. My uniform had dried from yesterday's swim, but there was the tale -tell sign of blood on my sleeves and legs along with some caked on sand and dried salt from the ocean. One of my pants legs was badly torn below the knee where I sported a minor cut that was oozing a little. A bullet hole was located in my jacket sleeve just above my elbow. Apparently the bullet missed my arm except for a small scratch, sort of a passing kiss of good luck.

My whole body ached as I fought to get to a kneeling position and take a look around me. First checking from where I heard gunfire. There was a GI standing over two others. One on his knees was attending to the third who was lying down on his back and looking hurt really bad. They were situated near a burned out pillbox. It looked like they had dragged their buddy to the pillbox to avoid fire from somewhere, but I had no idea where. Next I checked the perimeter around where I was currently hiding but saw nothing. There was little to no enemy fire anywhere close to where we were and certainly no movement. I made a mad dash over to where the three GIs were.

As I ran toward the box, one fella raised his rifle in my direction and I thought, *well this is it, killed by my own GI's.* But the second man put his hand on the rifle and pushed the muzzle toward the ground. The two just stared at me, one with really enlarged pupils, almost bug-eyed, the other showing a calm demeanor, at least on the outside.

Panting, I dove to the safety of the pillbox, hearing the wounded soldier moan. I could see why. He had taken a bullet or shrapnel to his stomach. His clothes were red and gooey over his soaked hands. Eyes firmly shut trying to ward off the pain he was going through, he was as pale as any black man I had ever seen. It was obvious he had lost a lot of blood. I turned to the other two and shook my head.

"He's not going to last very long," I said in a hushed voice. "Where's the rest of your unit?"

"There ain't no more, they all dead," said the bug-eyed soldier.

"Take it easy, Ned," the second one said. "We just got separated from them." Then he turned to me, "Name's Yarrow. You've seen much action?" And he held out his hand.

"A little," I shook it warmly. "Glad to finally meet someone friendly. What happened here?"

"Took some enemy fire from this here pillbox and after we cooked them up good, a sniper got Jasper here. That was about 15 minutes ago. Surprised he didn't take a shot at you when you ran from your foxhole."

About then I heard the ping from a bullet as it nicked Ned's helmet. I quickly hugged the wall of the pillbox. Ned went a little bonkers, stood up and pointed this Tommie gun into the trees and pulled the trigger. Palm fronds and branches flew everywhere as Ned's weapon brought down hell on the closer three or four palm trees. Yarrow grabbed him and pulled him back against the wall. Two splashes lit up the sand not far from where Ned was standing.

I turned to Yarrow, "At least we know where this guy isn't."

Ned looked at the two of us and said, "Well I know where I'm not going to be." He started to take a step and I tripped

245

him. Yarrow grabbed him and brought him back against the wall. We watched more sand get kicked up from the sniper fire.

"You stay here," I said to Ned and began to sneak around the back side of the box to get a better view of where our sniper might be. It didn't take me long to see a glint from the steel of this rifle reflect sunrays, dull reflection, but still a reflection. He's just hiding in a vulnerable spot I quietly mumbled. Yarrow crawled up next to me and I pointed to the treetop. He nodded and the two of us unloaded our clips into the nest. Not one, but two birds fell out of their nest and on to the sand below.

"Cover me," I said to Yarrow, rose and slowly trotted to the two bodies now on the ground. Just for safety sake I put an extra bullet into the head of each one and then went through their weapons to see if I could up grade from my British knock-off of a Czech rifle I had found earlier. I settled on the Jap sniper's rifle with a scope and four clips of ammo. *Man, my sergeant would have a field day with me. Constantly after me about keeping up with my weapon, keeping it clean and all that crap. This was more like 'let's make a swap.'*

Yarrow and I went to join back up with Ned and Jasper, our wounded comrade. When we got there, there was no Ned and Jasper was dead. We put his helmet over his face; burial would have to wait until we returned, if we returned.

Yarrow looked at me and said, "You want the flame thrower?"

"Naw, you can have it. I've upgraded to this here sniper rifle and want to give it a chance before I go whole hog with a flamer."

We heard some shouting and turned to see Ned running back through the woods yelling, "Japs, Japs, Japs." Then there was a burst of bullets and Ned crumbled to the ground. I turned, flopped on the ground and open fired, one shot at a time into the squad of Jap soldiers. Yarrow stood his ground and covered them with a pretty orange spray of flame.

"Vengeance is mine," Yarrow yelled above the roar of the flamethrower.

"Amen, brother." Bullets that had been whizzing by us or into the sand and trees around us subsided as we quickly reduced their numbers. I stood to get a better view over the flames. I felt a sudden numbness in my side as I found myself wavering a little trying to finish off the last few enemies that had evaded the heat of the thrower.

"Let's make sure they are cooked to perfection." I said to Yarrow and the flames died down on the thrower."

"You caught one." Yarrow said quietly to me. He nodded to my side where there was blood seeping through my shirt.

"Damn, and I was just beginning to like this Jap rifle." I said. "We need to look for medical supplies anyway. Maybe we can pilfer some if you didn't over cook them." My arm strayed over the field of burnt Japanese soldiers.

I walked over to Ned's body. He had taken about ten hits in the back. When I rolled him over his eyes were wide open with a look of sheer fear on his face. I pulled his revolver from his web-belt and check the clip and chamber then went through the enemy. Any that were looking like they might be alive, I put a bullet in their head just to be sure. I spent the six remaining shells in the pistol and two more from my latest rifle.

I looked over the field of death that Yarrow and I had created and leaned over and barfed up every last bit of bile that my innards could find. I dropped my weapons and put my hands on my hips as I continued with the dry heaves until there was nothing left in me. I began to spit to clean the vile taste from my mouth and tried to wipe away the phlegm from my mouth. I felt Yarrow's hand on my back.

I heard Yarrow's voice kind of a far way off, "Clean up, hotshot. We got a long ways to go before this is over." And was he right!

Finally I gathered myself together and turned to my comrade, "I'm starved, let's go see what's for breakfast." I tried smiling before adding, "I never did find that medic's kit."

I felt like a survivor, hurting but surviving, as I reached for my side, but the pain was creeping throughout my body. I was once again hunched over in pain. I worked to looked up into Yarrow's black face and say something. Instead, I passed out.

WEDNESDAY

I woke to a rainy morning, or maybe it never stopped raining from when I arrived. Hell, it was all a mystery to me. I was sore from the activity the day before and the day before that, and I had been sleeping on the wooden floor of my new office. I hadn't asked Maxie what the rent was, or how I might find furniture, or who owned the place. I had no idea what time it was. It was daylight. That much I knew, in an overcast sky with rain falling and a slight rumble of thunder in the background. Ahh, DeNato's Rolex. It was seven-fifty. AM?

There was a sound, like footfalls across the floor. Gentle, repetitious.

Coffee, I needed coffee. I struggled to grab a chair to steady myself and rose painfully, slowly. Bathroom would be a good idea, but I doubted there was one in the office, let alone on the floor or building.

There it was again, banging. I think the banging is what woke me from my dream. That damn dream again. This time, the banging had a voice. At first, it seemed way off in the distance, but as I hoisted myself up to one knee, the voice became clearer. A muffled, but familiar voice. At least it gave me motivation to start moving again.

"Yeah, yeah, yeah. I'm comin," I muttered to no one in particular. My feet made scraping sounds as I dragged them across the papers on the floor. Christ, I only had five or six beers before Maxie threw me out, or did I leave willingly?

Finally, at the office door, I paused, leaning on the doorframe to catch my breath. I felt like a sprinter who'd just run the hundred for the first time. I had no idea where I finished. I was just glad it was over.

"If you don't have coffee, go away," I said to the door.

"I have it, and it's hot. How 'bout lettin ole Clay in?"

I shook my head and opened the door. Clay Morgan had two cups of coffee and a bag of something being squished under his arm.

"Bless you, son. You may enter if you give me a cup." I raised my hand to receive the nectar of the local barista as Clay shuffled into the office. I walked into the hall looking for a bathroom with cup in hand. It wasn't a natural walk—more like a moan, step, moan, limp, pause to catch my breath, step, moan, limp. You get the idea.

The door to my office closed behind me, locking itself with me on the outside. Lucky for me, there was a bathroom down the hall; it, too, needed maid service. I would have to speak to the landlord about that, whoever he was. I guess Maxie would know. At least there was water in the sink, which I used liberally to wake up a bit and wash off my most recent bloodstains.

Still nursing my coffee, I returned to my office. The door had been propped open with a few of the papers. So much for the self-locking door.

"Nice digs, James," Clay said.

"It's Jamie, not James. Come on, will ya?" I said with exasperation. "Step into my new office." I led Clay into the inner office and held out a chair for him. I sat where I'd hung my coat the night before. "Man, you must have had a good night's sleep. You look how I would want to if I didn't feel this bad."

"Showers do wonders." Clay sniffed the air. "You could really use one or two. Maybe steam clean that outfit, as well."

"How'd you find me?" I asked, ignoring his comments.

"Maxie said he gave you this space so you wouldn't scare

off any more customers. He told me he'd throw in a desk and a real chair if you'd sign a lease and come to the tavern only when you want food or drink. He also hinted about you doing the odd job now and again, if he should ever have the need, whatever that means." Clay paused. "Sounds pretty sweet to me."

I looked at Clay again. He really was washed, combed, and dressed in what looked like a new suit. His navy blue tie, set against his gray suit and white shirt, had him looking more like a corporate vice president than an out-of-work reporter. Except for his shoes. What's wrong with shining one's shoes?

"Yeah, just as my potential clientele was getting used to my old office, it up and changes, but I think it'll work. I'm kind of fuzzy on who the landlord is, though. Maxie was vague on that point last night."

Clay shook his head. "It's Maxie, you dolt."

"Oh." I knew I was still a little foggy, but it was a big day yesterday.

Morgan looked at me and began to laugh. It was infectious and made me chuckle until we were practically rolling on the floor. As we finally managed to contain ourselves, in walked Delores Young.

"Hello? Anyone here?" I heard the door close and latch from my perch in the inner office.

I responded, "Yeah, we're in the next office."

Clay made like he was going to leave, but I put a hand on his shoulder. "Why not stick around? Things are about to get interesting," I said softly.

"Oh?" he said.

I turned to Delores, who stood at the door. "Delores, how in the world did you find me?"

"I went back to that tavern where we met the first time

and was directed here. The owner was just beginning to open up the bar. He and a couple of other fellas were unlocking the doors."

"I didn't know Maxie had taken on any partners," I said.

"Maybe they are friends of his," Clay said. "Every once in a while, a guy needs a helping hand." He looked at me with a big smile.

"Maxie's friends don't open up the joint at this hour." I was concerned. Hopefully it wasn't some muscle from another party out to slow down our investigation.

"Did he have friends when you saw him this morning, Morgan?" I asked.

"Naw, I didn't go to the bar. I called him, and he told me you had these new digs."

"You look like you've had a hard night. Maybe I should come back another time," Delores said.

"No, no. Don't leave. I have a question or two for you," I said. I reached into my pocket and pulled out a crumpled piece of paper. Trying to smooth it out, I asked, "Do you know what this might be? I have suspicions, but I'd like your opinion, since I think you might be closer to the answer than me." I handed her the paper.

"Yeah. I've seen something like this before. It looks like a calculaton for rents from various buildings. Assuming the buildings have rental or lease space, this could be the start of an estimate of rents across various properties." Clay wandered over to look at it over her shoulder.

"RC? Rent collections?" I asked.

"Yes, something like that," Delores said. "Usually we use graph paper to show these numbers, but it is the same thing, see here…" Delores put her finger on the top line, where the initial ran across the page.

Estimated RC

BB TP AB CT T
1. (215) 100 125 50 35
2. (125)
3. (100)
4. (75) find the breakeven point
5. (15) and trending
6. 25
7. 50
8. 75
9. 127
10. 225
11. 280
12 300+ 652

"So BB could be the Baker Building," Clay said.

"If that's true, Delores, what would the other buildings be?" I asked.

"Let's see. TP is probably Talmage Place, and AB is most likely Albany Building, and if those two assumptions are correct, CT has to be City Towers."

Clay produced a pen, and I made notations on each of the four initials reflecting Delores's answer. "How did you know the buildings?"

"Mr. Clienfelter has worked on each of them. The first is, of course, owned by the Rumsfelds, and the other three by Mr. Montfort."

I sipped on my coffee then recollected what I'd dug up the previous night in the library. I looked over at Clay, who was staring into space. "Did you know that Judith Montfort and Vernon Rumsfeld were related?" I asked.

"Yes, sir. Emily covered the last Montfort wedding when she was doing a social beat for the PM paper. She told me last night, when we were sippin' grapes at her place. Said she was there. It was a real blow out. I think she said they were brother and sister, or half-brother and sis—" Clay's voice trailed off and his smile faded as he grasped the implications. "Apparently," Clay went on, "they had a falling out when Vernon married Eloise while Judith was fixin' to tie the knot with Clive. They share the same mother, you know, Vernon and Judith. Emily—"

"Emily did the research for her article, which I read in the library last night before going to Maxie's." I held my head in my hands. "Where have you been?"

Just as Clay was about to answer, another knock sounded at the door.

"May I?" Clay asked. I waved my arm and went back to holding my head and sipping my coffee. Delores had already gotten up and opened up the door. A moment later, in walked Matt Dingle.

"I see you've come up in the world, Dugan. I hope you're not paying for this with stolen cash." Dingle looked around the offices, although there was nothing to see. He sat in the remaining chair, leaving Clay and Delores to stand.

"Ah, Lieutenant," I said. "Do ya think you could let Miss Young have her chair back? We are not so well-heeled that we can afford more than two uncomfortable chairs."

Dingle rose and offered it to Delores. "Sorry."

I hadn't paid attention last night, but a closet in the inner office attracted my attention. I got up from my perch and opened the door, almost expecting a body to fall out. There were three hangers, and one held a suit coat. A mystery for another day, but it jarred my memory. I closed the closet door and picked up my jacket from the back of the chair, extracted the papers from the library that I'd penned, and handed them to Dingle, then went back to the closet and hung my jacket next to the one already there.

That's a first for me, I thought. I turned to find the others staring at me like I had just swallowed a sword. "What? Haven't you ever seen a man hang up his jacket before?"

"Yeah, just not you. Didn't know you had two jackets, where'd you get that suit coat? Looks a little snug for you."

Dingle said, then he turned back to the material I had given him. "Yeah, we know about Vernon and his sister, or half sister." He put the papers on the floor next to Delores.

"Christ sake, will people start communicating around here?" I cried in anguish.

Delores picked up the papers Dingle had laid next to her and scanned the material. "Yeah, sure, that makes sense."

"What are you saying?" Dingle asked.

"My best guess is a brother and sister are co-conspirators in the murder of Eloise Rumsfeld. Clive Montfort's demise, I know, was Rachel's doing. I can't explain the hit-and-run on Judith Montfort or Vernon Rumsfeld yet, but I bet it involves DeNato's men and property, lots of property." I tried to raise my head but a wave of dizziness swept over me and all I could do was moan, just a little.

Finally, I looked up and studied the faces of Clay, Matt and Delores, trying to read their expressions. Delores was having trouble digesting Clive Montfort's death. Clay, on the other hand, was nodding, especially with the latest information.

"What other evidence are you keeping from me?" Dingle asked.

I pulled out the piece of paper with the rent calculations on it, passed it over to Dingle, and explained what we thought it was.

"Where did we find this?" Dingle's gaze went right to me.

"It was in the Rumsfeld house. I found it the night of the murder when you let me rummage through the house with O'Malley. It was on Vernon's desk, and since he is the property owner, it stands to reason he's the one making the calculations. That line for BB, or Baker Building, is filled in. The other properties belong, for the most part, to Montfort, Delores verified that much. We've added the names of the other buildings next to the initials." Smugly, I leaned back in my chair and looked at Dingle, whose expression was stormy.

"You absconded with evidence and didn't tell me? I can't believe it."

"Believe it," Clay said.

"Oh, you're a big help," I said.

"Listen, Lieutenant," Morgan said. "Dugan and I dug up the evidence that you and your staff overlooked. It all leads back to two people. One is in the hospital and the other is probably on the way to kill her." Dingle gave Morgan a surprised look.

"We agree with you on the murder of Mrs. Rumsfeld," Dingle said. "But McFarland thinks there might be other parties at work here trying to take out Mrs. Montfort. He seems convinced that we didn't get all DeNato's thugs when they shot up Anthony's. How do you explain DeNato's shooting at Anthony's?"

We were silent for a second. Delores was not enjoying the gory details of this case. She'd paled and was looking around, like she wanted to bolt.

"Ah, Matt. We have more information to share that might help explain how the pieces fit together," I said. "Miss Young here was Clienfelter's secretary. She did some research that we think you will find interesting."

With a little coaxing, Clay and I got Delores to tell her tale. She was still reluctant to provide all the details; she specifically covered up evidence that should have gone to the police when they showed up the day Clienfelter died. She also failed to mention the dirty cop theory.

Once she finished, Dingle looked at me with amazement. "Holy shit. Oh, sorry, ma'am."

"We know Montfort fired DeNato," I said, "and I figure Rumsfeld then hired him. So Rumsfeld and DeNato were up to their eyeballs in this, and one or both offed the missus. Rumsfeld got word that DeNato had been absconded with, and he sent his boys to get all three of us. After all, Vernon doesn't want DeNato to spill the beans or to be blackmailed, and he sure doesn't want loose ends. It was his chance to close the loop, so to speak.

"He then heard that Rachel had offed her dad, so the Montfort money went to sis. He figured that as the closest relative, if anything happened to sis, what was hers became his, since Judith didn't have kids. He got one of his bodyguards, probably one of DeNato's ole boys, to rig the hit-and-run using Anthony's truck. Of course, that meant that Vernon set up the truck in the first place and had access to a New York cab." I stared into space. There it was again, the foggy place where all trails continued to lead, a big hole where some third party sat.

Clay and Matt looked at each other, silent like.

"So instead of killing for a single building, which was his in the first place, Vernon went for the whole enchilada and moved from Chelsea to uptown Manhattan in one little killing. It would be easy for someone who killed off his partners in the first place."

"So you figure Eloise wasn't going to give the building back to Vernon?" Matt asked.

257

"Over her dead body, literally. Vernon would get the Baker Building only if his wife died by questionable means. Rumsfeld tried to frame Clay for the crime. Eloise Rumsfeld must have suspected that something was up and hired me to put a tag on him under the pretense that he was running around on her. Only thing was, he was."

"When he created his frame, he chose the wrong guy," Clay said with a smile.

Matt and I shook our heads.

I continued, "My guess is DeNato was working for Rumsfeld for quite a while, even before Montfort fired him. He had to be in cahoots with Rumsfeld in order to set up the meeting with Mary Jane. Montfort didn't care if Vernon slept with Mary Jane, and he even admitted it when Rachel confronted him. Hell, he didn't even want the property back. He just didn't want Vernon to get it. He made that pretty clear." I thought about a number of other items in our theory.

"You know, everything was probably moving along really swell until Eloise's daughter showed up, but Eloise was so thrilled to meet her daughter again that she was willing to change the will, I suspect she wanted to leave the Baker Building to Rachel instead of Vernon, and Vernon found out. That would explain the inkwell on her table in her bedroom."

Clay jumped in. "So that sped up the time table for the murder." I nodded. Clay turned to Dingle. "How's Miss Somers doing, by the way? Is she recovering?"

"Yeah, she'll pull through, but it will be a long recovery. I doubt Mary Jane will return to her old profession. She is pretty well scared."

"Maybe I can offer some adjustment counseling," Clay said.

Matt and I smiled at the thought of Clay nursing a

prostitute back to health. There was a certain irony in that. I should have explained it to Delores, but the less she knew about Morgan right now, the better.

"Did you ever find out what Mary Jane did from the time she left the apartment until we ran into her at Montfort's house?" I asked.

"Yeah. According to her, she wandered the streets trying to piece her puzzle together before confronting Montfort," Dingle said. "It took a lot of courage to face him and say what she said."

"Even though she was wrong," I said. Clay had a faraway look on his face.

"Hey, how about you and Emily Ross?" I asked, oddly protective of her relationship with Clay.

"We're just good friends, James. Well, maybe with a few benefits, like a warm bed and a glass of wine. But anyway, how many times do I have to tell you that? She's all yours, if you're man enough to make the advances." I was filled with doubt about that statement, but maybe. Someday.

"I can guess why Clienfelter was killed," said Matt.

"Yeah," I said. "He had all the evidence. He had the will and the promissory note that Montfort and Eloise signed. In addition, he was trying to blackmail someone. My guess is Vernon. If that came to light, Montfort would not be such a promising suspect, and you and Sergeant O'Malley would be looking over Rumsfeld's alibi more closely. And with what Miss Young just went over, he was itching to plug the blackmail leak."

"It's all about deception. Rumsfeld wanted the cops to chase the wrong guys."

Clay slid down the wall to the floor with a grimace. I guess a night's rest and shower only last so long. "Tell Matt how you did at the track," he said.

"I'm not sure he's ready for that story." I looked at Matt's grim face.

"What? Did you hit the trifecta on your fifth at Aqueduct?" Dingle looked at me with a smile.

Clay laughed. "No, but he made the bet."

"Yes, I made the bet on a tip from a new acquaintance. But the tip became more than horses. When the favorite was pulled for some trumped up reason, I made some inquiries and found that a reliable source had more information. So after the race, I met with my tipster and track source and found that the horse got pulled for money, lots of money." I looked at Matt. "They tell me someone is pulling strings, strings that go as deep as the NYPD."

The color drained from Matt's face and then red began to rise from his throat. I stood, prepared to lean against the wall for a while, hoping my pain would subside. I offered the chair to Dingle, who shook his head. Clay gestured to me to help him up then walked over to the chair, watching Dingle and me in case an altercation broke out.

"You're telling me there is a criminal on the police force, here, in my city?" Dingle said. He spit the words as he stared into my eyes. "A dirty cop in my precinct?"

"Yup," I said, maintaining my position.

"You're lying!"

"I was told by folks that are closer to the facts than I am. To tell you the truth, I'm beginning to believe them."

"If I didn't think you were being honest, I'd punch you in the nose right here and now. Nobody says that about the NYPD to me."

Matt glared at me, steam coming out of his ears. Matt and I had been friends a long time, and if anyone was going to tell him there was a crooked copper on his force, it was better coming from me. I hoped he got through all of his emotions before he knocked my lights out.

"Calm down, big fella," said Clay, the voice of reason. The tension in the room was so thick I could have cut it with a knife.

I heard Delores's voice in the background. "I think I'll look around and see what's what." She left the room. I hoped she was looking for a bottle of bourbon.

"How do you prove such an accusation, Dugan?" Dingle said, moving to the vacated chair.

"I think we solve one thing at a time, like Eloise's murder. Then we pick up the threads and see where they lead, but you're the cop," I answered. "Can't you figure that out?" I leaned against the wall again. A swirl of pain raced up my side causing a throbbing sensation in my rib cage and echoed in my head as a headache began to take shape. I felt leery about what this day was going to bring.

"Okay," Matt said. "Let the cops find the mole and whoever is pulling his or her strings. I'll even overlook the legal infractions. But the kidnapping, that's another thing. A man lost his life. You two have gotten us into this. I think it best if the three of us come up with a plan to put this killer out of business. It would also make me feel better if I was involved to keep us all out of trouble and doing things a tad more by the book."

"Wait a minute," Clay said. "I had nothing to do with the mole theory. It's his fault." He pointed in my direction.

"Let's shelve the mole for a while," I said. "It will only bog down our investigation. Let's stop Rumsfeld, then we can get back to the mole and the next folks up the ladder, agreed?" Clay nodded, but Matt was still having trouble. He was more comfortable having the police solve internal affairs instead of an outsider and a reporter. Go figure.

"We put down the killer and then you offer up all of your theories about the mole. I'm serious. Promise me you'll hold back nothing, and you have a deal."

I nodded. "Well," I said, "let's start with sis. She's in the hospital, right? Knowing you, there are probably armed guards to protect her from further attempts on her life, right? Especially after what Clay said. Ole Vern is probably out to silence her now."

"Shit!" Matt's face turned red again. "Where's your phone?"

"Sorry, no phone yet. You might try another office down the hall."

Dingle ran out of the office.

"I have a feeling this call is important to our case," I said to a surprised Clay.

Delores poked her head in the doorway right after Matt flew by her. I turned to Delores and asked. "You doing anything for the next few hours?"

"No. Why do you ask?"

"We are going to sprint, well, shuffle out of here in a few minutes, and it would be nice to have someone around while we are gone to kinda watch over the place."

"Yeah," Clay said. "Maybe get a phone for the joint and maybe a chair. A real chair."

We heard Matt beating on an office door down the hall. I could see him waving his badge, shouting "police business," just like the good old days.

I staggered over to Clay like a seventy year old and tried to help him up. It must have sounded pitiful hearing two grown men moaning just trying to stand.

"I've got to get a sofa. A big, comfy sofa," I said to Clay.

"And a coffee maker. I need a coffee maker and a sofa."

Delores looked at us, hands on her hips. "If you think I'm going to help you get killed, you're crazy. You oughta go home and get some rest." She had not moved from the door way into the inner office.

"Thanks, Mom," I said.

"Yeah. Come on, pal, we gotta go." Clay pulled me out of the office as I dragged my coat behind me. He was moving pretty good for a fella who just yesterday was being held together with a hankie, white socks, and shoelaces. *Medicine has sure come a long way.*

About the time Clay and I made it to the stairwell, Matt came out of the office where he'd made his call. "We gotta move," he said. "The police failed to post any guards in front of Montfort's room. They are dispatching officers now, and I got McFarland to find O'Malley and head to the hospital, but I fear it's too late. Let's hustle."

Matt passed Clay and me and yelled, "I'll bring the car around front." Then he was gone.

Clay was still limping, and I felt miserable all over. We were a fine pair trying to haul ass down the stairs, limping on each step.

"I thought cops got to park anywhere they wanted," Clay said.

"He's not the kind to wait once he gets going. We better improve our speed," I said as we rounded the landing on the second floor. In the background, I heard a car horn. "That will be Dingle, trying to inspire us to move faster."

Clay and I leaned on each other for the final flight of stairs and raced like my horses at Aqueduct, in last place. Matt sat in the police car, both passenger-side doors open for us. I pushed Clay into the back seat while I climbed into the front next to

Matt. Before I closed the door, Matt put the car in gear and we sped toward the hospital, sirens blazing.

"JESUS, MARY, AND JOSEPH! YOU GUYS MOVE LIKE TWO LITTLE old women. A woman's life hangs in the balance and you need an elevator to get down three flights of stairs," griped Matt.

"Yeah, true, but she's involved in a murder, too, probably," Clay said from the back seat.

"But she is also the last living witness to all that could hang brother Vernon," I reminded Clay.

"Step on it, Lieutenant," Clay urged. Matt shot him an ugly look through the rearview mirror. That seemed to put a cap on our in-car conversation.

We sped, fighting early morning, rush-hour traffic, and it was not letting up. Even with the siren, we moved slowly, which infuriated Matt. It took us ten minutes to get to the front desk, and that was with Matt leaving his car in front of the entrance with the engine idling.

"Mrs. Judith Montfort. What room is she in?" Matt demanded at the front desk. He flipped open his badge for the receptionist.

Clay and I arrived a full thirty seconds behind him.

"Room 909," the receptionist said. "Somebody else just asked for that same room."

"Was he a cop?" Matt asked.

The receptionist shook her head. "Brother." She said something else, but I didn't hear what with all of Clay's moaning and groaning. As we approached the receptionist's desk, the lady sitting there talking to Matt looked at Clay and me, evaluating our injuries for admission. She began to raise a finger pointing in the direction of emergency admittance with her mouth open about to speak when. Matt pulled me toward a bank of elevators. I grabbed Clay, tugging him toward the same bank.

"The receptionist said that there's a nurse shift change going on about now," Matt said. "Damn!" followed under his breath.

"Perfect time for a Pearl Harbor," Clay said.

"A sneak attack. Really, Clay?" I said.

We boarded the next elevator seconds later. Matt mashed the 9 on the floor listing. It did not respond instantly, so he kept on pushing the same floor number until the doors closed.

The elevator dinged, and the doors opened. We jumped out, but it was only the fifth floor. Matt pulled us back into the car as a doctor and nurse joined us. They looked us over, nodded, and smiled.

Matt showed his badge to the doctor and nurse. "When does the duty shift take place?" he asked. I guess he needed confirmation, typical.

"Now," the nurse said. "We are on our way to the station on the seventh floor. Why do you ask?"

Matt ignored her question. "On the ninth floor, is room 909 left or right from the elevator?"

The doctor thought a second and raised his left hand. "Left."

"Maybe we should change hospital plans," I whispered to Clay

"Is there a stairwell that comes up near the room?" I asked. I thought I knew how Rumsfeld might approach the room.

The doctor and nurse eventually got off on the seventh floor, as did I. Of course, that meant having to walk up two flights of stairs in hopes of cutting off Rumsfeld's retreat.

As I trotted down the hall, pain shot up my back, and the muscles in my stomach complained. The rest of my body wasn't doing well, either, but I did have my eyesight and hearing. I wondered why I hadn't waited until the eighth floor to go to the stairwell. I eased open the stairwell door and heard a faint shuffling of footsteps above me. *There was still time,* I told myself.

Slowly, as quietly as I could, I mounted the stairs. It was all I could do to suppress the occasional grunt or moan. The distance between the eighth and ninth floor was covered by three flights of stairs with a landing after each. This allowed me to keep some distance behind whoever was in the stairwell. I hoped it was Rumsfeld; I would sure look foolish if it wasn't. I could just see the headlines: "Nurse stalked in hospital stairwell by PI."

I tried to match the stranger's pace, which helped mask my footsteps. I didn't want to be exposed in there. The echo effect was frightening and made it very hard not to be discovered. Half way to the eighth floor, I removed my shoes and left them on the landing, which meant I had to put down the jacket I was carrying and pick it back up again in order to get those shoes off. I couldn't leave my coat on the stairs, too, now could I? I could just imagine people seeing my shoes then jacket. God knows what they would expect to find next.

When the person ahead of me passed the eighth floor and moved toward the ninth, I was certain I was on the trail of the killer. The pace was slow and deliberate. He was stalking his prey.

He stopped, and so did I. I heard the door to the ninth floor open. Its hinges creaked. I edged up to the next landing and got a look as a figure in a doctor's coat disappeared into the hallway. I raced up the rest of the steps as best I could and slowly opened the door to see Vernon Rumsfeld standing in front of Room 909, his hand on the doorknob. The room was about two doors down on the other side of the hallway. In the distance, an elevator dinged, but neither Morgan nor Dingle came to the rescue. I couldn't believe they weren't there yet. New headline: "Elevator hijacked with police lieutenant and reporter aboard."

Rumsfeld's white doctor coat covered a powder blue shirt. His loafers had leather heels, the kind that made a loud clicking sound when they hit linoleum. He was trying to walk on the balls of his feet. He looked like a comic villain I once saw at the movies trying to be stealthy, only deadlier. A stethoscope was draped over his shoulders. He looked down the hall toward the elevators, but all the doctors and nurses were busy turning over the floor like the changing of the guard. He tried the doorknob, but it was apparently locked.

I was deciding what to do next when I noticed a bulge in the white jacket where Rumsfeld jammed his hand. A pistol. A nurse emerged from the next room, and Vernon asked her why the door was locked. She looked puzzled.

"We don't lock room doors. I didn't think they could be locked. I'll get someone on this right now, Doctor."

The nurse flagged down an orderly who arrived with keys while I watched, the stairwell door slightly ajar. While the three were distracted by the locked door, Clay walked down the hall.

Rumsfeld spotted Clay, took his pistol out of his pocket, and raised it to shoot. It was like slow motion.

I eased out of the stairwell as the orderly realized there were no locks on the door. Something was blocking it from inside. The orderly tried to use force to open the door, and when he pulled back to get some distance, he bumped Rumsfeld's shoulder. It was pure luck. The gun went off, and the bullet sailed into the ceiling above Morgan's head. Clay jumped back around the corner.

I thought I was home free in my ninja-like approach, but the stairwell door slammed shut behind me. *Oops.*

Rumsfeld turned and leveled his pistol at me. It was shiny and the hallway fluorescents reflected off the muzzle. He pointed the gun at my chest. He looked like he hadn't slept in some time. His pallor made him look like he'd risen from the dead, searching for a soul to take back to hell with him. It was a scary sight.

"Stop right there, Dugan," Rumsfeld said in a quiet voice.

"You're too late, Rumsfeld." I used my "big room" voice to attract attention.

The nurse and orderly backed away from the door. The orderly's eyes were twin moons over a mouth drawn taut in fright. It was a scene I'd rather see on the silver screen than in this hallway.

"Oh, no, you don't," he said. He spun the gun in their direction. "Now quietly get into the room or I'll off ya right here and now." He waved the gun toward Room 909.

"You're going to have to pull the trigger sooner or later. Why not do it in front of a few witnesses?" I said. "You're going to hang for murder, but it will be less expensive for the prosecution to get you to the gallows." I needed to stall him, but maybe this wasn't the best tactic. *Where the hell was the cavalry, hiding in the lady's locker room?*

"Get in here," Rumsfeld said.

Rumsfeld grabbed my sleeve and pushed open the door with his shoulder. I flipped the jacket in my left hand over his face while reaching for his gun, letting my momentum knock him off balance. I grabbed his wrist as he pulled the trigger. No one came out of the room to help. I half expected to see Dingle and Morgan running down the hall to the rescue, but nothing there, either. The nurse and orderly fled, leaving me and Vernon Rumsfeld fighting for dear life.

Rumsfeld let go of my shirt and threw a punch. I stepped in and wrapped my left arm around his neck while holding his wrist, trying to point the pistol anywhere but at me. I had no shoes on and my socks were slipping on the recently polished linoleum. I got a momentary rush of adrenaline and although I was fairly beat up, I was still in better shape and a tad taller and stronger than he was. I wanted to get behind Rumsfeld and put him on the ground to separate him from his pistol. A second shot sounded, ricocheting off the cinder block wall. Rumsfeld moaned and began to collapse.

I knocked the pistol from his hand and got him in a prone position so I could see if he had been hit and how badly. He lay on the floor, holding his abdomen, while I called for a doctor. The door to Judith's room opened and there stood O'Malley, his police pistol drawn. A doctor ran up the hall with Dingle in hot pursuit.

"Thanks for the backup, Sergeant," I said to O'Malley.

Dingle came to a halt as the doctor bent to inspect Rumsfeld's wound. "Is he okay, Doc?" Dingle asked.

"Yup, I'm okay here," I said.

"Hush," said Dingle.

"Where were you? I thought the plan was for you two to stop him, not hide in the closet, or play nurse," I said. "Where's Morgan, anyway? Is he okay?"

"Well, with all the running around, his wound opened

up and he started bleedin' again. He had every intent to help out until Rumsfeld fired at him. Morgan jumped from the elevator to the nurse's station. From there one of the doctors and a nurse grabbed him thinking he was about to be shot at again and...."

I looked at Matt opening my mouth about to ask another question when he cut me short. "Now, hush. Let the doctor do his work." Matt demanded.

"Work? How about me? Shouldn't he look over the good guy first?"

Exasperated, Dingle snapped, "You're fine. The good doctor will get to you in time."

"Hospitals. You know how I hate them, especially the emergency treatment, or lack thereof." A moan of desperation escaped my lips. "While I'm waitin', how about taking my mind off things and telling me where you guys really were."

"Well," Matt started. "We left you off on the seventh floor and then two more doctors and a patient got on just as the doors were about to close. We stopped for them on the eight floor and that took some time. We had a couple get in and push the down button and took us some time to get them off the elevator. Are you enjoying this?" Matt asked.

"Un-hun," I mumbled, "It's a swell story."

"Well, the rest you know. The elevator finally opened on the ninth floor and Clay jumped out and that's when Rumsfeld fired at him." Matt stood there with arms crossed looking down at me with a stone-face.

"And you, what did you do?" I guess you can tell I was pretty sore and the story just got me more aggravated.

"Well, I had to protect the hospital staff. Besides you had ole Vernon in the grasp." He said as a broad grin appeared. "I knew you were alright."

"You couldn't wait and get Morgan patched up after we caught this guy?" I asked.

"I don't think he'll live," the doctor said. "It looks like the bullet went through his abdomen by way of his chest. It looks like a downward angle. I won't be able to tell which organs have been affected and whether any vital organs are involved until I get him on the operating table." The doctor turned to a nurse who had arrived at the scene and said, "He's going into shock. We need to roll him into OR now." The doctor yelled down the hall, "Someone bring me a gurney. We'll also need an IV and prep for the OR."

I sat on the floor, my back against the wall. "Oh, goodie. More taxpayer monies down the drain." I looked at Matt. "Can't you just shoot him and save the city money and time?" I handed Matt Rumsfeld's pistol.

"And have all that paper work to fill out? Not worth it. If he lives, we'll let the courts handle it. If he doesn't, you come to my office and do the paperwork so I don't have to." Dingle was a stickler for paperwork.

"Where the devil are your shoes, Dugan?" O'Malley asked.

"I left them on the stairwell. Would you be a dear and retrieve them for me, Sergeant?"

Dingle looked at the doctor and pointed at me. "Can you check him out, too? Make sure there are no bullet holes in his head. Maybe even keep him here for a few days under medical surveillance." Turning to me, Dingle asked, "When was your last colonoscopy?"

"What? I—"

"Sure. How many days would you like me to keep him?" the doctor asked, giving me a quick once over.

"Really funny, guys," I said. I held up my suit coat and

saw a bullet hole in the fabric. "Think you can repair this, Doc? I'm down to my last one." I was still waiting for a hand up, but it looked like no one was interested in helping a poor, shoeless hero.

POST SCRIPT

"You going to fix this door or what?" The shouting came from the hallway through my office door. It was still locked.

"I thought you unlocked that door, Morgan."

Clay sat across from my desk on my new, comfortable sofa. He looked up from his newspaper long enough to say, "Huh?"

"Some partner you turned out to be. I see why Amanda tossed you out of the apartment," I said to Morgan.

I got up from my desk and made my way into the outer office with some difficulty. I was officially recuperating from two cracked ribs, a chipped tooth and a really sore head, but there was no detectable damage to my kidneys, thank God. Opening the door, I was surprised to see Delores standing there chewing her gum and giving me a disapproving smirk holding on to a large box of something I couldn't begin to think what it would be.

"I thought after your last visit, you'd be glad to get rid of us," I said. "Something about not wanting to help us get killed?"

"I heard you needed a secretary, and I felt sorry for you. And I know you need a researcher and legal advisor, so here I am." Delores walked into the outer office and put her box down on the desk. "We're going to have to move it," she said, pointing at the desk. She had a twinkle in her eye and a smug look on her puss like she knew I really needed her.

"Clay, it's for you." I went back to my desk with a grin on my face.

About twenty minutes later, there was a knock at the

office door. "It's open. Come on in," Delores shouted in her Brooklyn accent.

This was great, I thought. Afraid to open my mouth and have all go away.

I looked up from the afternoon paper as Lieutenant Dingle strode in smiling, hat pushed onto the back of his head, hands in his pants pockets. He had on a clean and pressed white shirt with a striped blue and white tie. His blue sport coat was unbuttoned; the relaxed look. This was a nice contrast to the dark and rumpled suit and shirt he normally wears.

"You two deserve each other. If it weren't for your new secretary, I doubt you could even find this place."

"I just hired her, but he," I jammed a thumb in Morgan's direction, "was just leaving. New place of work, don't you know."

"Yeah, sure," Clay muttered behind his newspaper.

"Jamie, we have some unfinished business, you and me." Dingle's smile turned into grim determination as he eased into a chair at the side of my desk. "We need to discuss this mole and ferret out if it is a valid accusation. If it is true, I would prefer to deal with it now rather than later."

I put down the paper. Clay slowly lowered his paper and turned to the lieutenant as well.

"Do y'all mind if I stay and listen? I might have something to add and I need to finish an article for the morning paper. This sounds like it could be juicy." He looked sheepish when we glared at him. "Okay, then, I'll just keep readin'. Yes, sir, just sit here and mind my own business. Nope, you won't hear a peep out of me. No, siree-bob. Just as quiet as a little mouse—"

"Tell me about your sources, Dugan. Are they reliable?"

"With the circles we've been running in lately, maybe not,

but they are fine, upstanding men. I didn't believe them at first, much like you, but over time I have seen the light and think I see how the dots are connected. Much like the great detectives of our time…"

"Cut the crap, Dugan. Let's hear the theory." There was a trace of a smile on Dingle's lips as he settled back in his chair and waited for me to tell the story. I would have to fill in the blanks as I went. Nothing new there.

"Like you, I never gave a second thought to how the investigation was going or how certain people kept poppin' up earlier than they should until a friend put me on to a downtown snitch close to the Street. He hears things from his clients, and he is no dummy. He puts them together just like you and I do. A regular Philo Vance.

"Well, 'Philo,'" and I used air quotes—after all, if you have a source as valuable as Norman, you need to protect him—"Philo informs me that I'm dealing with a straight crime of passion or greed, but one with multiple layers."

"Like a German forest cake?" Clay said, not looking up from his story.

"Yeah, like a whatever," I continued. "I tried pressing him, but all he would say was that there was a dirty cop involved and I should take care not get caught in the crossfire."

"Whose crossfire?" Dingle asked.

"He didn't say, but he did say that the connection was down on Wall Street. He didn't know who or where in the district, just that it was down there."

"Fine. What about the dirty cop?"

"Bear with me a second. Did you ever notice how some people were where you did not expect them to be? For instance, it worried me that O'Malley was at Montfort's before we had a chance to call the cops. We didn't leave a trail

275

he could follow. After all, we had just come via the subway from a cab ride bound for Harlem or wherever our last resting place was supposed to be. How did he know to be there?"

I waited for a response, any response. There was a quiet in the office. Then Matt said, "You two were in that cab that smashed into the furniture store. That was the start of some trail, probably had quite a bit of blood leading down to the subway platform. From there it was just pure deduction as to where you were headed."

"And maybe O'Malley had the Montfort house staked out and saw us enter, choosing not to take action, but wait and see," said Clay, playing devil's advocate.

"Okay, how about the hospital? How did O'Malley get to the room before any of us and then try to keep Rumsfeld out rather than come to my aid?"

"He must have been in the area when McFarland asked for police assistance at the hospital," Dingle answered. "Who knows why he didn't come to your rescue. Maybe he hates you."

"Oh, c'mon, you guys. There was no cop car at Montfort's house when we broke in—I mean, gained access. Even if he was close to the hospital and beat us there, why not try to apprehend a potential killer, unless…" I left it hang. "Another thing always bothered me. Why does he have it in for me? Why have the police goon squad not only tear up my car but push me around?" Matt shrugged. "In the Clienfelter murder, he was pretty relaxed and suspiciously ineffective. I found the clues, as if O'Malley put them there and let me discover them. He didn't take me in for a statement. It was almost as if he was relieved. His real concern was the secretary and what she might know. You should have seen him at Clienfelter's office," I said.

"You're saying that O'Malley is the mole." It was a statement, not a question, and Dingle smiled, dismissing the accusation.

"Don't do this, Matt," I said.

"Do what?"

"Dismiss it. I've seen you do this before, and it will bite you in the butt. You have to take this seriously, and if I'm wrong, then I'm wrong. But if my theory is correct, you have a tough job to do, and I would watch your back every minute."

"One thing's for sure, O'Malley doesn't have the smarts to be the head bad guy." Clay said, having laid his newspaper across his lap. "If brains were dynamite..."

"All right, that's enough. I will take it into consideration. I will even do my own investigation, okay?"

"I got a question for you lieutenant," Morgan said. "How did my clothes and cologne get from Amanda's apartment into the Rumsfeld's home?"

I nodded.

That stopped our progress dead in its tracks although it was a question I knew that Clay would have to have answered.

"That's a good question, Morgan. You got a good answer to that, Mr. PI?" Matt looked over in my direction.

I rolled my body forward in my chair and said," Not really. But let's look at the situation. Someone had to have a key to get into the place and lift your stuff. The best people we could finger all have air tight alibis. So in my mind that leaves the super." With that eyebrows went up. "He had the means and money is a real motivator for that guy. Let's just say I know that and leave it at that." It was kind of off handed answer but after it was out, I have to admit it sounded pretty good. At least to me it did.

Clay murmured and nodded. Matt sat there looking at

me lost in thought. I thought it might be nap time when all of a sudden Matt came back to life.

"I don't want to get all mushy on you, but I did want to see how you're doing and express my appreciation for your help in closing the Rumsfeld case. I also wanted to warn you that if you ever pull half of that stuff again, you'll find yourself in the city jail."

"I believe I already did that," Clay said as he looked back down at his newspaper.

"Oh, yeah. I also have a surprise for you," Dingle said. He looked around. "Don't you guys have any coffee in this office yet?"

"You'll have to go to Maxie's for a cup until we can get our own brewer installed somewhere on the floor."

Dingle smiled. "There's a silver lining to all this. Apparently, there was a sizable reward for bringing in DeNato. Even some of his gang had a reward on their heads. As you probably know, cops can't collect the reward. So I put in a good word for ya, in recognition of your minor involvement. So here is your reward." Matt handed Clay and me each an envelope with a check inside.

I took a quick gander at my check. "Some reward. He's worth more than a grand. What did you get, Clay?"

Clay looked at me, then down at his check, and then back at me. "Five hundred? A measly five hundred dollars. What gives, Dingle?"

Matt looked at us and smiled. "Most of the reward went to Anthony. We figured he needed it the most and you know, Jamie, it will probably save your life. Anthony is still plenty sore over the torching of his shop and the loss of his truck."

"You know what I can't figure, James?" asked Clay.

"What's that?" I kind of knew what coming.

278

"Who fixed the pickup truck?"

Matt smiled. "The truck had been tampered with. Some of the leads to the distributor cap had been pulled. After you abandoned it for the cab, it was a quick fix. For all I know, the would-be killers gave it a tune up."

"So it was a trick to get us to take a cab ride with one of their own? DeNato thugs working for Ole Vern." Clay shook his head. "I shoulda figured." He looked at me. "I guess you were right about that much of the case, Lieutenant."

I nodded. "That gave the bad guys a truck for the hit-and-run on Judith. Nice thinking. Who was the mastermind behind all of that? Rumsfeld, ya think?"

"Yeah, it was Vernon all right. It turns out he is quite the schemer." Dingle smiled and donned his fedora as he headed for the door. "You know, I wouldn't have caught the connection between Rumsfeld and Montfort without Miss Young bringing it to our attention. That solved a lot of crimes at once."

"Did you bring a reward for her participation?" I asked.

Dingle smiled. "I should have given her yours."

He stopped before going into our reception area. "Liked your article, Clay. You getting your sister to make a Superman cape for Dugan, here?"

Clay looked at me and laughed. "He's a dangerous friend to have, just trying to stay on his good side."

"Hey, Matt," I said. "There's something that's been bothering me."

"Yeah?"

"Rumsfeld hires DeNato, who was working for Montfort before switching sides, which I totally don't believe. But I still feel like we missed somebody in all this. Like who did Judith Montfort have lending support to her cause? And it seemed like someone out there knew a lot about me and my habits, someone we didn't uncover." I left that hanging for a few seconds to see if anyone could wrap his mind around the idea. "Remember the mole in the police department. I am convinced it is connected and that this case is not fully solved." I pointed at Dingle.

"Yeah, I'll remember. Like you, I've been giving it a lot of thought." Matt turned and walked back into the office. Clay put down his paper again. "I shouldn't tell you this, but I met with the captain of our precinct and discussed what I knew. He agreed to establish a task force and see if there is a culprit to be rooted out."

"Seems like too easy a fix," Clay said. "Are you part of the task force?"

"No. At least, not yet," Dingle said.

"I have to agree with Mr. Reporter here. You never know how high the disease might travel up and down the chain of command." I shook my head, not liking where this might end up.

"Relax, fellas. We do this by the book, and we'll find the mole and be right as rain, even if it is just O'Malley as you suspect. That is, if there really is one." A big smile appeared on my friend's face, but I remembered how by the book the lieutenant was and hoped it didn't end up killing him.

"This case might be marked closed for the administration, and you might think the corruption goes no deeper than O'Malley, but I don't think it's over and O'Malley is just at the tip of the iceberg." I put my paper in front of my face, looking at the afternoon nags running at the Duct.

"So we got the killer, but not the right guy?" Clay asked.

"I don't know," Dingle responded. "But if somethin'

ain't right, the police will find out if there is a problem, even without Jamie Dugan."

"Something ain't right," I echoed.

Dingle left and I found the horses running in the fifth. There was my surefire winner, Mystery Rider, going off at 20-1. I dialed my bookie for the bet, but I didn't put the whole thousand up, just half. I needed to start saving for a new Jag.

Clay went back to reading. He apparently found something he liked, because he began to read aloud.

"The era where the most money was spent, the era where the most parties were given, the era where the most mansions were built, and finally, the era where the most liquor was consumed."

"What a day for a party!" Clay said. "I hope you don't mind if I stay here for a while. I need to find a new office. Maybe Maxie has another he'll let me rent or we could share this one?"

Now wouldn't that be the icing on the cake?

It took Judith Montfort two weeks to recover enough from her wounds to get up and move around. She was released from the hospital after one week and moved back into the house she and Clive had shared. After an additional week of rehab, she was ready to resume her life albeit with a cane for a companion.

She made two calls. The first was to a benefactor and the second was to a cab company. Two hours later, she entered the lobby of a large building in the financial district. She stumped her way across the floor toward the one elevator that went to the twenty-eighth floor. She remembered the first time she'd come here. It had a grand view of the Hudson River over to New Jersey. She was intrigued with all the shipping activity in the harbor, and if it wasn't for the business at hand, she could have watched it all day.

On the twenty-eighth floor was a glass-enclosed anteroom with two men to greet her benefactor's guests. They searched her purse and gave her a gentle pat down before she proceeded to the office space at the end of the corridor. She let herself in and passed the receptionist desk into the large office, where she was greeted warmly.

He wore a white collared shirt under a black cassock with fuchsia piping. The cassock stretched to his ankles. Black pants extended beyond the cassock's hem. He wore black shoes and socks, too. He offered her a seat on a settee to the side of the desk, which provided her the view she loved. Coffee was served.

Judith sat, knees tightly held together as she smoothed her dark blue suit skirt over her thighs and reached for her coffee cup.

"I hope everything worked out satisfactorily, Mrs. Montfort." He said.

"It did. Thank you," she responded. "I have the rest of your payment here." She pulled out an envelope and passed it over. "I thought about your offer to manage some of my properties, and I think it would be a good idea if we did a trial run, to see how things work before we launch into a more formal agreement. You understand, I'm sure." She sipped her coffee.

Disappointment flashed across her companion's face. "Certainly, I understand. Which property did you have in mind?"

"The Baker Building," she said, a slight smile on her lips.

"Ahh, good choice. I will have that taken care of this afternoon. What time would you like to meet with my candidate?"

"How about three o'clock?" she responded.

"There is one more thing, Mrs. Montfort. I may need assistance from you in the future. If you remember, this was also part of our agreement."

"Yes, certainly," she said with distaste.

"We will probably not meet again, but I will have Erskin work with you as a contact, or conduit, if you will."

"Erskin?" she said.

From the far side of the room, a figure emerged. He had a full head of salt-and-pepper hair with eyebrows that seemed to merge over the bridge of his nose. Erskin was a handsome man with sparkling blue eyes and a bushy mustache. He wore a white shirt with a plaid bow tie and plain black jacket and pants. He nodded toward Mrs. Montfort and said with a Scottish accent, "It's a pleasure to meet you, Mum."

Made in the USA
Lexington, KY
12 May 2017